'*Good Morning, Midnight* is a remarkable and gifted debut novel. Lily Brooks-Dalton is an uncanny chronicler of desolate spaces, whether it's the cold expanse of the universe or the deepest recesses of the human heart'

Colson Whitehead, author of *The Underground Railroad*

'With imagination, empathy, and insight into unchanged and unchangeable human nature, Lily Brooks-Dalton takes us on an emotional journey in this beautiful debut'

Yiyun Li, author of *The Vagrants*

'A truly original novel, otherworldly and profoundly human . . . a fascinating story, surprising and inspiring at every turn'

Keith Scribner, author of *The Oregon Experiment*

'A beautifully written, sparse post-apocalyptic novel that explores memory, loss and identity . . . Fans of Emily St. John Mandel's *Station Eleven* and Kim Stanley Robinson's *Aurora* will appreciate Brooks-Dalton's exquisite exploration of relationships in extreme environments'   *Washington Post*

'Intimate and beautiful'   *Chicago Review of Books*

'Stunningly gorgeous . . . The book contemplates the biggest questions – What is left at the end of the world? What is the impact of a life's work?'   *Portland Mercury*

'Ambitious . . . Brooks-Dalton's prose lights up the page in great swathes, her dialogue sharp and insightful, and the high-concept plot drives a story of place, elusive love, and the inexorable yearning for human contact'   *Publishers Weekly*

'Beautiful descriptions create a sense of wonder and evoke feelings of desolation . . . Brooks-Dalton's heartfelt debut novel unfolds at a perfect pace as it asks readers what will be left when everything in the world is gone'   *Booklist*

Lily Brooks-Dalton was born and raised in southern Vermont. She is also the author of the memoir, *Motorcycles I've Loved*. She Lives in Portland, Oregon.

lilybrooksdalton.com
Facebook.com/lilybrooksdalton
Instagram.com/lilybrooksdalton

GOOD MORNING, MIDNIGHT

LILY BROOKS-DALTON

Waterford City and County
Libraries

WEIDENFELD & NICOLSON

A W&N PAPERBACK

First published in Great Britain in 2016
by Weidenfeld & Nicolson
This paperback edition published in 2017
by Weidenfeld & Nicolson
an imprint of the Orion Publishing Group Ltd
Carmelite House, 50 Victoria Embankment
London EC4Y 0DZ

An Hachette UK Company

1 3 5 7 9 10 8 6 4 2

A CIP catalogue record for this book is
available from the British Library.

ISBN (Mass Market Paperback) 978 1 4746 0060 6
ISBN (eBook) 978 1 4746 0061 3

Book design by Simon M. Sullivan
Printed in Great Britain by Clays Ltd, St Ives plc

www.orionbooks.co.uk

For Gordon Brooks

I heave myself out of the darkness slowly, painfully.
And there I am, and there he is . . .

—JEAN RHYS

GOOD MORNING, MIDNIGHT

ONE

When the sun finally returned to the Arctic Circle and stained the gray sky with blazing streaks of pink, Augustine was outside, waiting. He hadn't felt natural light on his face in months. The rosy glow spilled over the horizon and seeped into the icy blue of the tundra, casting indigo shadows across the snow. The dawn climbed like a wall of hungry fire, delicate pink deepening to orange, then crimson, consuming the thick layers of cloud one at a time until the entire sky was burning. He basked in its muted glow, his skin tingling.

The overcast sky was unusual for the spring season. The observatory's site had been chosen for its clear weather, the thin polar atmosphere, and the elevation of the Cordillera Mountains. Augie left the concrete steps of the observatory and followed the path carved into the steep slope of the mountain—down to the cluster of outbuildings nestled against the mountain's incline, then beyond them. By the time he'd passed the last outbuilding the sun had already begun to sink, the color to fade. The day had come and gone in ten minutes—less, perhaps. Snow-covered peaks rolled all the way to the northern horizon. To the south, the low, smooth expanse of the tundra flowed into the distance. On his best days the blank canvas of the landscape set him at ease; on his worst he contemplated madness. The land did not care for him and there was nowhere else to go. He wasn't sure yet which sort of day today was.

In a different life he used to pack his soft leather suitcase whenever his environment rejected him, as it often did, and find another place to go. It wasn't even a very large suitcase, but it contained the essentials of his existence neatly, with a little room to spare. There was never a need for moving trucks, or bubble wrap, or farewell parties. When he decided to go, he was gone within the week. From a postgraduate fellowship in the Atacama Desert of northern Chile where he cut his teeth on dying stars, to South Africa, Puerto Rico, Hawaii, New Mexico, Australia—following the most advanced telescopes, the biggest satellite arrays, like bread crumbs scattered across the globe. The less earthly interference there was, the better. It had always been this way for Augustine.

Continents and countries meant nothing to him; it was only the sky that moved him, the happenings on the other side of the atmospheric window. His work ethic was strong, his ego engorged, his results groundbreaking, but he wasn't satisfied. He had never been satisfied and never would be. It wasn't success he craved, or even fame, it was history: he wanted to crack the universe open like a ripe watermelon, to arrange the mess of pulpy seeds before his dumbfounded colleagues. He wanted to take the dripping red fruit in his hands and quantify the guts of infinity, to look back into the dawn of time and glimpse the very beginning. He wanted to be remembered.

Yet here he was, seventy-eight years old, at the top of the Arctic archipelago, on the rind of civilization—and, having come to the terminus of his life's work, all he could do was stare into the bleak face of his own ignorance.

⌇⌇⌇

THE BARBEAU OBSERVATORY was built as an extension of the mountain. The blunt fist of the telescope's dome rose defiantly higher than anything else for miles, surveying the rest of the mountain range like a warden. There was an airstrip and a hangar about a kilometer south, where the tundra had been packed and smoothed by a bulldozer airlifted from Greenland, marked with reflective orange flags and lined with lights that didn't work anymore. The hangar was empty, the strip neglected. The last planes to use them had come to collect the researchers from the outpost, and the last news from civilization, over a year ago, had been of war.

The outpost was stocked to last a dozen researchers for nine months: barrels of fuel, nonperishable food, purified water, medical supplies, guns and fishing gear, cross-country skis and crampons and climbing ropes. There was more research equipment than Augie could use, more incoming data than he could process in a dozen lifetimes. He was more or less content with the way things were. The observatory was the focal point of the outpost, in the center of the scattered dorms, storage units, and rec buildings. Its structure was the most permanent thing about the base—after all, the massive telescope it housed was the reason everything else was there. The outbuildings that surrounded the observatory were hardly buildings at all, more like weatherproof tents for eating, drinking, sleeping, and storage. Barbeau's standard research fellowship lasted between six and nine months, but Augustine had stayed for almost two years before the evacuation. Now it was nearly three years that he'd been here. The program drew a collection of young, bold men, often fresh out of their PhD programs, impatient to shrug off the close quarters of academia, at least for a while, before they let it encircle them for good. Augustine had despised these bookbound researchers, all theory and little or no practical skill. Then again, he would have been hard-pressed to name someone he didn't despise.

Squinting at the horizon, he could just make out the sinking orb of the sun through the thick cloud cover, sliced in half by the jagged outline of the Cordillera Mountains. It was a little past noon, in late March. Polar night had finally passed over this desolate patch of earth, and now the day would gradually return. It would begin slowly, a few hours of light at a time, peeking over the skyline. But soon enough the midnight sun would rise and the stars would fade. By the end of summer's brightness he would welcome the twilit days of autumn, then the blue-black of winter, but for now he couldn't imagine a more comforting view than the melted outline of the sun, roosting close to the horizon, its light spilling down onto the low-lying tundra.

In Michigan, where Augustine had grown up, winter came softly: the powder of the first snow, the pillowy drifts, icicles that grew long and sharp, then began to *drip drip pour* into a gush of spring. Here, everything was hard. Bleak. As unforgiving as the edge of a diamond, with great shelves of ice that never melted and the ground that never thawed. As the remaining light faded from the noon sky, he watched a polar bear lope across one of the mountain ridges, heading toward the sea to hunt. Augie wished he could climb into its thick skin and sew it shut behind him. He imagined what it would feel like: looking down a long snout at paws the size of serving platters, rolling onto his back and feeling a thousand pounds of muscle and fat and fur press into the frozen ground. Pulling a ringed seal from its breathing hole and killing it with one powerful swipe, burying his teeth in its flesh, ripping away steaming chunks of blubber and then falling asleep in a clean, white snowdrift: sated. No thoughts—just instincts. Just hunger and sleepiness. And desire, if it was the right time of year, but never love, never guilt, never hope. An animal built for survival, not reflection. The idea almost made him smile, but Augustine was not in the habit of bending his mouth in that direction.

He didn't understand love any better than the bear did. He never had. In the past, he'd felt the nibble of a lesser emotion—shame or regret or resentment or envy—but whenever that happened, he would turn his gaze to the sky and let awe wash it away. Only the cosmos inspired great feeling in him. Perhaps what he felt was love, but he'd never consciously named it. His was an all-consuming one-directional romance with the emptiness and the fullness of the entire universe. There was no room to spare, no time to waste on a lesser lover. He preferred it that way.

The closest he'd ever come to letting his adoration rest on human shoulders was a long time ago. He was in his thirties when he impregnated a beautiful woman with a razor-sharp mind at the research facility in Socorro, New Mexico. She was another scientist, a PhD candidate finishing her dissertation, and the first time he met her, Augustine thought she was extraordinary. He'd felt a warm spark for the idea of their baby when she told him the news, like the flicker of a newborn star six billion light-years away. Tangible, beautiful, but already dying by the time it reached him, an afterglow. It wasn't enough. He tried to persuade the woman to have an abortion, and he left the hemisphere when she refused. He kept to the other side of the equator for years, unable to bear the proximity of a child he didn't have the capacity to love. Time passed, and he eventually troubled himself to learn the child's name, her birthday. He sent an expensive amateur telescope when she turned five, a celestial sphere when she turned six, a signed first edition of *Cosmos* by Carl Sagan when she turned seven. He forgot her birthday the next year, but sent more books, advanced tomes on practical astronomy, for her ninth and tenth. Then he lost track of her—of them both. The chunk of moon rock intended for her next birthday, which he'd finagled from the geology department at one of his many research posts, was returned to him labeled *Invalid Address*. He shrugged it off and decided not to go looking again. This game with the gifts had been unwise, a sentimental stutter in an otherwise logical life. After that, he thought of the extraordinary woman and her child rarely, and eventually he forgot them altogether.

The polar bear ambled down the other side of the mountain and was lost to view, swallowed by the snow. Augie slouched deeper into the hood of his parka, cinching the drawstrings tighter around his neck. A frigid wind blasted through him. He closed his eyes, felt the crisp frost in his nostrils, the numb shuffle of his toes deep inside wool socks and heavy boots. His hair and beard had turned white thirty years ago, but a sprinkling of black hairs across his chin and neck persisted, as if he'd left the job of aging half-finished and moved on to another project. He had been old for years now, closer to death than to birth, unable to walk as far or stand as long as he used to, but that winter in particular he'd begun to feel very old. Ancient. As though he was beginning to shrink, his spine slowly curling in on itself, his bones huddling closer together. He began to lose track of time, which wasn't unusual in the endless dark of winter, but also of his own thoughts. He would come to, as though from a dream, uncertain what he'd been thinking a moment ago, where he'd been walking, what he'd been doing. He tried to imagine what would become of Iris when he was gone. Then he stopped himself. Instead, he tried not to care.

WHEN HE RETURNED to the control tower the color in the sky had faded to a deep twilit blue. He shouldered open the heavy steel door with enormous effort. It was more difficult than it had been last year. With each season that passed, his body seemed more breakable. The wind slammed the door behind him. To save fuel he heated only the top floor of the observatory: one long room, where he kept all of his most prized instruments, and where he and Iris slept. A few comforts from the lower floors and the outbuildings had been relocated there: two induction hot plates, a nest made of sleeping bags and lumpy single mattresses, a scant assortment of dishes and pans and cutlery, an electric kettle. Augie had to rest on each step as he climbed. When he reached the third floor, he shut the stairwell door behind him to keep in the warmth. He shed his winter layers slowly, hanging every piece from a long row of hooks on the wall. Too many hooks for one man. He gave each mitten its own peg, unwrapped his scarf and hung that too, spreading his clothes along the coat rack. Perhaps this was to make the room seem less empty—filling the space around him with traces of himself so that the howling loneliness wasn't quite so obvious. A few flannels hung at the other end, a pair of long johns, some thick sweaters. He struggled with the toggles on his parka, then with the zipper. Hung that up too.

Iris was nowhere in sight. She spoke rarely, though she hummed quietly on occasion, melodies of her own composition that seemed to rise and fall with the sound of the wind against the dome above them: the environmental orchestra. He paused and listened for her, but there was nothing. More often than not, Augustine didn't see her because she wasn't moving, and so he scanned the room carefully, watching for the subtle blink of an eye, listening for the slight sound of her breath. It was just the two of them at the observatory, and the telescope, and the tundra. The last of the civilian researchers had been flown back to the nearest military base almost a year ago, and from there had returned to wherever they belonged so that they might rejoin their families. Something catastrophic was happening in the outside world, but that was all anyone would say. The other researchers didn't question their rescuers—they packed in a hurry and did what the evac team told them to do, but Augustine didn't want to leave.

The Air Force unit that had arrived to transport the scientists home gathered everyone in the director's office before they started packing up the base. The captain read out the names of all the researchers and gave them instructions on when and how to board the Herc waiting on the runway.

"I won't be going," Augustine said when his name was called. One of the military personnel laughed. There were a few sighs from the scientists. No one took him seriously at first. But Augustine had no intention of budging. He wasn't going to be herded onto the plane like livestock—his work was here. His life was here. He would manage just fine without the others, and he would leave when he was good and ready.

"There won't be a return trip, sir," the captain said, already impatient. "Anyone left on this base will be marooned. You either come with us now, or you don't come at all."

"I understand," Augustine said. "And I'm not going."

The captain searched Augustine's face and saw only a crazy old man, crazy enough to mean what he was saying. He had the look of a wild animal: bared teeth, bristling facial hair, and an unblinking stare. The captain had too much to do as it was and no time for reasoning with the unreasonable. Too many other people to worry about, too much equipment to transport, not enough time. He ignored Augustine and finished the meeting, but as the other researchers disbanded, hurrying off to pack their things, the captain pulled him aside.

"Mr. Lofthouse," he said, his voice level but unmistakably hostile. "This is a mistake. I'm not going to force an old man onto an airplane, but believe you me, no one is kidding around about the consequences. There is no return trip."

"Captain," Augustine said, brushing the man's hand away from where it rested on his arm, "I understand. Now back the fuck off."

The captain shook his head and watched as Augustine stalked away, slamming the door to the director's office. Augie retreated to the top floor of the observatory and stood at the south-facing windows. Below, the other scientists scurried between tents and outbuildings, hauling packs and suitcases, their arms full of books and equipment and keepsakes. A few heavily loaded snowmobiles sped up and down the mountain to the hangar, and as Augie watched, the scientists began to trickle down to the runway until he was alone.

The plane rose from between the folds of the tundra where the hangar was nestled, just out of sight, and Augustine watched it disappear into the pale sky, the rumble of its engine fading into the moaning wind. He kept his post at the window for a long time, letting the loneliness of his situation settle into his consciousness. Eventually he turned his back on the window and surveyed the control room. He began pushing the remains of his colleagues' work to the side, readjusting the space to accommodate him and only him. The captain's words, "There will be no return trip," echoed in the sudden quiet. He tried to swallow the reality of that, to understand what it really meant, but the idea was a little too final, a little too drastic, to sit with for very long. The truth was that Augustine had no one to return to. At least here he didn't need to be reminded of it.

It was a day or two later that he found Iris—hiding out in one of the empty dormitories, curled up on a bare bottom-bunk mattress, left behind like a forgotten piece of luggage. He squinted at her for a while, unsure of his own eyes. She was small, maybe eight years old—Augie wasn't sure—with dark, almost black hair that fell to her narrow shoulders in a tangled mass. She had round hazel eyes that seemed to be looking everywhere at once, and there was an alert stillness about her, like a wary animal. She was so still, in fact, he could almost imagine that she was a trick of the light, but then she moved and the metal frame of the bunk groaned beneath her. Augustine massaged his temples.

"You've got to be kidding," he said to no one. "Come on, then." He turned to go and beckoned her with a flick of his hand. She didn't speak, just followed him back to the control room. He tossed her a bag of dried fruit and nuts while he heated a pot of water, and she ate the whole thing. He made her a packet of instant oatmeal and she ate that too.

"This is ridiculous," he said to no one. Still she was silent. He handed her a book and she flipped through the pages—whether she was reading it, he couldn't tell. Augustine busied himself with his work and tried to ignore the inexplicable, inconvenient presence of a little girl he couldn't remember ever seeing before.

She would be missed, of course—someone would be back to collect her any minute. Surely it was only the commotion of the exodus, a crossing of wires, that had resulted in her being left behind: "I thought she was with you," "Well, I thought she was with *you*." But evening fell and no one returned. The following day, he radioed the Alert military base, the northernmost year-round settlement on Ellesmere Island. There was no answer. He scanned the other frequencies—all of them—and as he flipped through the bands a surge of dread washed over him. The amateur waves were silent; the emergency communication satellites hummed an empty tune; even the military aviation channels were mute. It was as if there were no radio transmitters left in the world, or perhaps no souls to use them. He kept scanning. There was nothing. Only static. He told himself it was a glitch. A storm. He would try again tomorrow.

But the girl—he didn't know what to do with her. When he asked her questions she stared at him with detached curiosity, as if she were on the other side of a soundproof window. As if she were empty: a hollow girl with wild hair and solemn eyes and no voice. He treated her like a pet because he didn't know what else to do—with clumsy kindness, but as a specimen of a different species. He fed her when he fed himself. Talked to her when he felt like talking. Took her for walks. Gave her things to play with or look at: a walkie-talkie, a constellation map, a musty sachet of potpourri he'd found in an empty drawer, an Arctic field guide. He did his best, which he knew wasn't very good, but—she didn't belong to him and he wasn't the sort of man who adopted strays.

That dark afternoon, just after the sun had risen and then sunk once more, Augustine looked for her in all the usual places: buried beneath the sleeping bags like a lazy cat; twirling in one of the wheeled chairs; sitting at the table, prodding the insides of a broken DVD player with a screwdriver; gazing out the thick, dirty pane of glass at the never-ending Cordillera Mountains. She was nowhere to be seen, but Augustine wasn't worried. Sometimes she hid, but she never wandered far without him and she always revealed herself before too long. He let her keep her hiding places, her secrets. There were no dolls, no picture books, no swing sets, nothing she could call her own. It was only fair. And besides, he reminded himself, he didn't really care.

⌁⌁⌁

DURING THE LONG polar night, after several weeks of total darkness and nearly two months after the evacuation, Iris broke her silence to ask Augustine a question.

"How long till morning?" she said.

It was the first time he'd heard her make a sound, other than the eerie humming he'd grown accustomed to—that aria of long, trembling notes deep in her throat as she looked out the control tower windows, as if she were narrating the subtle movements of their barren landscape in another tongue. When she finally did speak that day, her voice came out in a throaty whisper. It was deeper than he expected, and more confident. He had begun to wonder if she was capable of speech, or if perhaps she spoke another language, but those first words fell easily from her mouth, enunciated in an American, or perhaps a Canadian, accent.

"We're about halfway there," he told her, with no indication that she'd done anything unusual, and she nodded, similarly unsurprised. She continued to chew the jerky they were eating for dinner, holding the strip of meat with both hands and ripping away a mouthful like a baby carnivore just learning to use her teeth. He passed her a bottle of water and began thinking of all the questions he had for her, only to realize he actually had very few. He asked her name.

"Iris," she said, without turning away from the darkened window.

"That's pretty," he remarked, and she frowned at her reflection on the glass. Wasn't that something he used to say to lovely young women? Didn't they usually like hearing it?

"Who are your parents?" he ventured after a moment, a question he had of course already asked and couldn't help asking again. Maybe he would finally solve the mystery of her presence here and figure out which of the other researchers she belonged to. She kept her gaze on the window, chewing. She didn't speak any more that day, or the next.

As time wore on, Augustine began to appreciate her silence. She was an intelligent creature, and he valued intelligence above everything else. He thought of his morbid rants in the beginning, just after he'd found her, when he was still scanning the RF bands and hoping someone would return for her, would emerge from the desolate silence to scoop her up and leave him in peace. Even then, while he'd been spinning through the hows and whys—the bands were empty, she was here, etc.—she had simply accepted the reality at hand and begun to acclimate. His irritation with her presence and then with her silence faded. A kernel of admiration took root and he let his unanswered questions go. While the long night blanketed their mountaintop, the only question that mattered was the one she'd asked: how long would this darkness last.

~vvvv~

"WHAT WOULD YOU think if I told you that star was actually a planet?" his mother had asked him once, pointing up at the sky. "Would you believe me?" He'd answered eagerly, yes, yes he'd believe her, and she told him he was a good boy, a smart boy, because that burning white dot, just above the rooftops, was Jupiter.

Augustine had adored her when he was young, before he began to understand that she wasn't like the other mothers on his street. He was caught up with her excitement and brought down by her sadness—following her moods with fervent loyalty, like an eager dog. He closed his eyes and saw her frizzy brown hair shot with strands of gray, the sloppy line of her burgundy lipstick, applied without a mirror, the awestruck glow in her eyes as she pointed toward the brightest star, hovering above their Michigan neighborhood.

If that good, smart boy had found himself in this inhospitable place, alone except for an ancient, unfamiliar caretaker, he might have cried or screamed or stamped his feet. Augustine had never been a particularly brave child. He might have made a halfhearted attempt to run away—gathered some supplies and marched off into the desolate distance, headed for home, only to return in a few hours. And if little Augie had been told there was no home for him to return to, no mother to soothe his tantrum, no one else in the world left for him, what would he have done then?

Augustine considered his young companion carefully. Now, in his old age, he was trapped in memories. He never used to think of the past, but somehow the tundra brought it all back to him—experiences he thought he'd left behind long ago. He recalled the tropical observatories he'd worked in, women he'd held in his arms, papers he'd written, speeches he'd given. There had been a time when his lectures drew hundreds of people. Afterward, there would be a cluster of admirers waiting around to ask him for his autograph—*his autograph!* His accomplishments haunted him, specters of sex and triumph and discovery, all the things that had seemed so meaningful at the time. None of it mattered anymore. The world beyond the observatory was quiet, empty. The women were probably dead, the papers burned to ash, the auditoriums and observatories in ruins. He had always imagined his discoveries being taught in universities after he was gone, written about by generations of scholars not yet born. He'd imagined that what he left behind would endure for centuries. In this way his own mortality had seemed inconsequential.

He wondered if Iris thought about her earlier life. If she missed it. If she understood that it was gone. A house somewhere, maybe a brother or a sister, maybe both. Parents. Friends. School. He wondered what she missed the most. Toward the end of the long night they walked around the perimeter of the outpost together, shuffling through a layer of new powder that swirled on top of the hard-packed snow. A low moon lit their path. They were both wrapped in their warmest clothes, bundled into the thick folds of their parkas like snails in their shells. The scarf tied across her nose and mouth hid Iris's expression. Icicles had formed on Augustine's eyebrows and eyelashes, framing his view with a glittering blur. Iris stopped in her tracks suddenly and pointed an oversized mitten up at the sky, directly above their heads, where the North Star glimmered. He followed her gaze.

"Polaris," she said, her voice muffled by the fabric.

He nodded, but she had already moved on. It wasn't a question; it was a statement. After a moment he joined her. For the first time, he was truly glad of her company.

THE WORK HAD seemed so important when Augie chose to stay behind at the observatory—keeping track of the data, logging the sequences of stars. After the exodus and the subsequent radio silence, he felt it was more vital than ever to continue observing, cataloging, cross-referencing. It was all that had stood between him and madness, a thin membrane of usefulness and importance. He struggled to keep his mind whirring in its accustomed track. The immensity of a civilization's end impressed upon his brain—a brain trained to absorb immensity—was almost too much for him. It was stranger and more colossal than anything he'd contemplated before. The demise of humanity. The erasure of his life's work. A recalibration of his own importance. He devoted himself instead to the cosmological data that continued rushing in from outer space. The world outside the observatory was silent, but the universe wasn't. In the beginning it was the technical upkeep of the telescope, the maintenance of the data archive programs, and the calm, indifferent anchor of Iris's presence that kept him from going mad. Iris seemed unaffected, easily lost in a book, a meal, the landscape. She was immune to his panic. Eventually he came to grips with the state of things and grew calmer. Accepted futility, then moved beyond it.

He paced himself—there was no deadline, no end in sight. The data was steady, unaffected. He reprogrammed the telescope's eye for his own curiosity and began to spend more time outdoors, wandering around the abandoned outpost buildings in the deep blue of the long night. He relocated everything he had use for to the top floor of the control building, one piece at a time. He dragged the mattresses through the snow, one by one, and up the stairs, one by one. Iris trailed behind him with a crate of cooking utensils. When he stopped for breath and looked back, he noticed that she carried it well. She was a strong little thing, and tough. Together they moved the essentials out of the dormitories and up to the third floor, where there were only desks, computers, and filing cabinets full of paper. They brought up stores of canned and freeze-dried food, bottled water, generator fuel, batteries. Iris pocketed a deck of playing cards. Augustine salvaged a sepia-tinted globe from one of the dorms and tucked it under his arm, the brass axis digging into his ribs through the thick down of his parka.

The third floor was plenty big for the two of them, but there was a shocking amount of clutter when they moved in: useless, anachronistic machines, outdated papers stating hypotheses that had long been disproved, dog-eared back issues of *Sky & Telescope*. Searching for an empty surface to display his new globe and finding none, Augustine set it on the floor, opened a heavy window with some difficulty, and unceremoniously shoved out an old, dusty computer monitor. Iris ran over from where she was plumping sleeping bags and regarded its remains below, a few dark pieces scattered across the bright snow, some still rolling down the mountain. She looked at him with a silent question in her eyes.

"Junk," Augie said, and set his sepia globe down in the space the monitor had occupied. It looked elegant there, a thing of beauty among the detritus of science. He would go out later, after the moon had risen, and collect the debris, but it felt good to send the monitor sailing out the window. A small release. He took the keyboard that went with it, the mouse cable coiled around it, and handed it to Iris. Without missing a beat, she threw it into the night like a Frisbee, and together they leaned their heads into the bitterly cold air and watched it disappear, spinning out into the dark.

AFTER THE SUN returned, the two of them began walking down beyond the outbuildings to watch it rise and set. In the beginning this didn't take long. The sun would well up from beneath the horizon, casting a soft orange arc to herald its arrival, flooding the tundra with fiery pink, and as soon as it cleared the snowy peaks it would begin to sink again, sending sheets of violet and rose and cool blue into the sky like a pastel layer cake. In one of the nearby valleys, Augustine and Iris observed a herd of musk oxen returning daily, nuzzling the snow-covered ground. The grass they were eating was invisible from where he and Iris sat, but Augie knew it was there, strawlike stalks pushing up out of the snow, perhaps trapped just beneath it. The musk oxen were enormous, their shaggy coats riddled with thick dreadlocks that nearly brushed the ground. Their long, curved horns pointed skyward. They looked ancient, almost prehistoric—as if they'd been grazing here long before humans had stood on two legs and would continue to graze long after the cities built by men and women crumbled back into the earth. Iris was transfixed by the herd. She persuaded Augustine to sit closer and closer as the days passed, tugging him silently forward.

After a while, when the sun had begun to linger in the sky for several hours at a time, Augustine considered the animals in a new context. He thought of the small armory at the observatory, the rack of shotguns he had never used. He thought of the taste of fresh meat after almost a year of timeless, tasteless food. He tried to picture himself butchering one of these woolly creatures, cutting away steaks and ribs, dissecting the organs and the bones from the meat, but even in his imagination he couldn't bear it. He was too squeamish, too weak to stomach the blood and the violence. But what about when their supplies waned—would he be able to bear it then?

He struggled to imagine Iris's future here, but it made him feel hopeless and useless and tired. And something else—angry. Angry that this responsibility had fallen to him, that he couldn't leave it behind or pass it off to someone else. Angry because he did care, despite his best efforts not to. The mess of survival was so distasteful. He preferred not to think about it. Instead he admired the gradual slope of the sun's path as it descended, then waited patiently as the stars emerged. A prick of silver, moving too quickly and shining too brightly to be a celestial body, rose from behind the mountains. Augie watched it climb forty degrees into the deepening blue. It took him a moment, but as it curved back down to the southwesterly skyline he realized it was the International Space Station, still orbiting, still reflecting the light of the sun down onto the darkened Earth.

TWO

SULLY'S CLOCK READ 0700 GMT—five hours ahead of Houston, four hours behind Moscow. Time means very little in deep space, but she roused herself anyway. The regimen that Mission Control had prescribed for the crew of the *Aether* spacecraft was precise, down to the minute, and although Mission Control was no longer available to enforce it, the astronauts continued to adhere for the most part. Sully touched the lone photograph pinned to the soft, upholstered wall of her sleeping compartment, a gesture of habit, and sat up. Running her fingers through her dark hair, uncut since the journey began more than a year ago, she began to braid it, savoring the dream that had just left her. Except for the persistent hum of the life support systems and the soft whir of the centrifuge, everything was quiet beyond her privacy curtain. Their ship: a vessel that had seemed so immense when she boarded it now felt like the tiniest of life rafts, lost at sea. Except it wasn't lost. They knew exactly where they were going. Jupiter was mere days behind them, and *Aether* was finally headed home.

At 0705 she heard Devi rustling in the compartment next to her. Sully slipped into the dark blue jumpsuit tangled at the foot of her bed. She zipped it halfway, tied the arms around her waist, and tucked in the gray sleeveless shirt she'd slept in. The lights were just beginning to come on, brightening slowly to simulate the unhurried daybreak of Earth: a perfectly gradated white dawn. The slow illumination of the compartment was one of the few Earth-like experiences available. Sully made sure she saw it every morning. It was a shame the engineers hadn't added a little pink, or a smudge of orange.

The dream clung to her. Her sleep had been full of Jupiter ever since the survey last week: that overwhelming, unstoppable girth; the swirling patterns of the atmosphere, dark belts and light stripes rolling in circular rivers of ammonia crystal clouds; every shade of orange in the spectrum, from soft, sand-colored regions to vivid streams of molten vermilion; the breathtaking speed of a ten-hour orbit, whipping around and around the planet like a spinning top; the opaque surface, simmering and roaring in century-old tempests. And the moons! The ancient, pockmarked skin of Callisto and the icy crust of Ganymede. The rusty cracks of

Europa's subterranean oceans. The volcanoes of Io, magma fireworks leaping up from the surface.

A wave of quiet reverence had overtaken the crew as they contemplated the four Galilean moons. A spiritual pause. The tension that had led them into deep space—the anxiety that perhaps the mission was beyond them, that they would fail and never be heard from again—evaporated. It was done. They had succeeded. Sully and her colleagues had become the first human beings to delve this deep into space, but more than that: Jupiter and her moons had changed them. Soothed them. Shown them how tiny, how exquisite, how inconsequential they really were. It was as though the six members of *Aether*'s crew had been awakened from the small, insignificant dreams that constituted life on Earth. They could no longer relate to their own history, their own memories. When they arrived at Jupiter, an unfamiliar layer of their consciousness overflowed. It was as if the light had been turned on in a dark room and revealed infinity, sitting naked and glorious beneath the swinging bulb.

Ivanov immediately began his work evaluating the moon rock samples they'd gathered on Ganymede and writing papers on the internal structures and surface processes they'd observed. He floated to and from meals or the exercise bike as if he were a man in love, his default frown softened into something almost inviting. Devi and Thebes nearly forgot their jobs of maintaining the ship, instead crowding into the cupola's strong, clear dome to look out at the depths that surrounded them, whiling away hours, even days, at a time. They took in the view in companionable silence, young Devi with her long hair in a messy knot, eyes wide beneath thick eyebrows, and Thebes, his round black face split in two by an easy, gap-toothed smile. Thebes called their stargazing "having a big picture moment" in his smooth South African accent. Tal, the pilot of the mission and their physics specialist, was filled with kinetic energy after experiencing Jovian space. He took extra time on the fitness equipment, did zero-G acrobatics for anyone who would watch, and told dirty jokes nonstop. His joy was infectious. Harper, their commander, channeled his transformation inward. He made sketches of Jupiter's stormy belts as seen from the surface of Ganymede, where he had stood just days before. He filled notebook after notebook and left faint smudges of pencil lead on everything he touched.

As for Sully, she turned her attention to the comm. pod. She let the telemetry flowing in from the probes they'd left behind on the Jovian moons consume her attention. It was all she could do to pull herself away from her work to eat or pedal through her allotted hours on the stationary bike, peevishly flipping her dark French braid over her shoulder as she checked her time, impatient to get back to the comm. pod. For the first time in years, she felt at peace with the sacrifices she had made to join the space program—the family she had left behind. The aching doubt of whether it had been worth it, whether she had made the right choices, fell away. She floated forward, unburdened, into the certainty that she was following the path she was meant to, that she was supposed to be here, that she was a tiny and intrinsic piece of a universe beyond her comprehension.

The night's dream slipped away and her mind was already jumping ahead to the comm. pod. Pulling on a pair of socks, she wondered what mysteries had traveled along the RF waves and into her machines while she slept. Then an unwelcome thought intruded, crowding in from a dark periphery. The mission had been a success, but the truth was she had no one to share her discoveries with. None of them did. Mission Control had fallen silent just before the Jovian survey began. During their weeklong survey, *Aether*'s crew waited patiently and continued their work. There had been no sign-off from Mission Control, no warning of a comm. interruption. The Deep Space Network was made up of three main sites around the globe to account for the planet's rotation. If the Goldstone facility in the Mojave Desert was offline, then Spain or Australia would pick up where they left off, but a full twenty-four hours passed and there was nothing. Then another day went by, and now almost two weeks. A break in contact could mean so many things, at first there was no sense in worrying. But as the silence lengthened, as their focus on Jupiter flagged and their anticipation of returning to Earth grew, it began to weigh more heavily on them. They were adrift in the silence. The magnitude of their experience, of the things they had learned and were continuing to uncover, demanded a wider audience. The crew of *Aether* had undertaken the journey not just for themselves, but for the entire world. The ambition that had fueled them on Earth was nothing more than flimsy vanity out here in the blackness.

For the first time since it had begun, Sully didn't push the thought of the blackout away. She, like the rest of them, had been trained to compartmentalize, to lock away the realities that threatened their work, their ability to function on this long, uncertain voyage. They'd had bigger things afoot. But now, letting the thought linger, a wave of panic crashed through her and swept away the serenity Jovian space had instilled in her. She was suddenly awake from the dreamy stupor of Jupiter. The chill of empty, inhospitable space fell over her like a shadow. The silence had gone on too long.

Devi and Thebes checked and rechecked the ship's equipment and Sully had conducted her own thorough examination of the comm. pod, only to find nothing amiss. The receivers were picking up the murmurs of space all around them, from celestial bodies millions of light-years away—it was only Earth that wasn't saying anything.

-wwv-

THE RAW DATA spilled across her computer screen while Sully scribbled notes with a stubby pencil on the clipboard she always kept with her. It was warm in the comm. pod and the radio equipment was humming, enveloping her in a familiar cocoon of white noise. She stopped and let the pencil float in front of her as she rotated her wrist and shook loose the cricks in her fingers, then plucked it from the air again. A droplet of sweat dislodged from her skin and hovered in front of her. The heat was stifling. She wondered if the temperature program was malfunctioning. She'd have to remember to mention it to Devi or Thebes—the last thing they needed was for the receivers to overheat. It felt as though her skin was melting into the air, the boundaries between body and environment blurring into one heated mass. There was a squawk of static from one of the receivers built into the pod's wall and Sully looked to see what frequency it had stuttered on. She'd set the receivers to scan all the usual communication channels after they lost contact with Mission Control, but so far there had been nothing. She knew immediately from the tone that the waves weren't from Earth. It was a signal from one of the probes they had left behind on Jupiter's moons. She continued to scan and let the signal play.

A noise storm between Jupiter and one of her moons, Io,

filled the pod—a deep hum overlaid with a sound like crashing waves, or whales, or wind passing through the trees, echoes of things they used to hear back on Earth. The storm died down after a few minutes, giving way to the underlying buzz of the interstellar medium and the sharp crackle of the sun. Everything was so much clearer in space: stars, sounds, the entire electromagnetic spectrum coming alive all around her, like seeing fireflies dance in a dark meadow for the first time. Without the interference of Earth everything seemed different. Sharper. More dangerous, more violent, and also more beautiful.

With each passing day, their separation from Earth became more acute. Now, after two weeks of silence, it was beginning to feel like an emergency. Without the tether of Mission Control rippling through the vacuum, they were truly alone. Even though they had begun the long journey home, gradually closing the yearlong gap instead of lengthening it, the crew was feeling farther from Earth than ever. All six of them were coming to terms with the silence, and with what it might mean—for them, and for those they'd left behind on the now-mute planet.

Sully watched the visual readout of the storm pulse on the screen in front of her. Io's magnetic field and the effect it had on Jupiter had been part of her dissertation. If only she'd had data like this at university, twenty years ago. She looped the audio back to the beginning of the storm while she worked and listened to it again. She couldn't help but imagine Jupiter as a mother calling to her children, pulling her many moons against her atmospheric bosom to soothe their various cries, then eventually letting them spin back out into the darkness to roll through the void free and alone. Sully was fond of Io in particular, the closest satellite but also the most stubborn, the loudest, a willful cannonball riddled with volcanoes and radiation. The cacophony demanded her attention and for a moment she forgot about her notes. The pencil floated free again. Watching the waves of energy pulsing between celestial bodies on the graph, the magnetic fields dancing across Jupiter's poles like an aurora, she jumped when Harper, floating into the pod behind her, cleared his throat.

"Sully," Harper said, and then stopped, as if he wasn't sure what to say next. Sully looked up in time to snatch her pencil back before it drifted away. She was suddenly self-conscious with Harper looking at her, aware of the sweat stains beneath her arms and the loose strands of hair that had come undone from her braid, streaming away from her head like sun rays.

Harper had a slow midwestern accent that seemed to wax and wane: in Houston it had been slight, but here, hundreds of millions of miles away from Earth, it grew more noticeable. She sometimes wondered how a man so grounded made his home in the sky. He had been in space more times than anyone else, a world record—ten spaceflights, Sully thought, or was it eleven? She could never remember. In the cockpit of the shuttle that had taken them to *Aether*, where the craft orbited the Earth, awaiting its crew, he had been perfect as their commander, blasting them straight through the atmosphere with Tal by his side. There was no one else like him. But Sully could see on his face that the post-Jovian mission tranquillity had passed for him, just as it had for her. He wandered from pod to pod, checking in with each member of the crew, struggling to keep them all connected. The Jovian honeymoon was over, while the effects of the communication blackout and the long journey home had only just begun.

"Commander Harper," she said in greeting. He shook his head, smiling. The titles became more ludicrous the more time they spent adrift.

"Mission Specialist Sullivan," he replied. Out of habit she smoothed the loose strands of hair down, pressing them against her head—a futile gesture in zero gravity. He propelled himself farther into the pod to get a closer look at the graphs of the noise storm.

"Io?" he asked.

She nodded. "It's a big one. The volcanoes don't ever seem to stop. Probe might not survive out there much longer." They watched the colors crackle, pulses of energy flitting between the two celestial bodies.

"Nothing lasts, I guess," he said with a shrug. Neither of them said anything else. There wasn't much to say.

~~~~

SULLY SPENT THE rest of her day in the comm. pod, monitoring the incoming telemetry from the probes and scanning the S, X, and Ka radio frequency bands just to be sure, all designated for deep space use. *Aether*'s assigned receiving frequency was constantly open, ready and waiting for an uplink from Earth, but that had begun to seem less and less likely. They had taken it for granted in the beginning, when communication was as easy as picking up the phone and calling a room full of engineers and astronomers. As the ship had traveled farther into space, a time lapse formed and then widened, but even so, Mission Control had been there, waiting, on the other end of the radio waves. Before, there was always someone keeping watch over them. Now there was no one.

Occasionally Sully would catch a stream of information coming from a probe born of another project. There were only a handful of them out there, but there was one in particular that she liked tracking: *Voyager 3*, the third man-made object to travel beyond the solar system and into interstellar space, launched more than thirty years ago by another generation of astronauts. It was dying by then, its signal terribly faint, but when she tuned her receiver to 2296.48 MHz she could sometimes catch a wheeze or two of information, like words gasped by a man on his deathbed. She could still remember when NASA announced that its predecessor, *Voyager 1*, had finally gone silent, leeched of its power supply and no longer able to communicate with its handlers back on Earth. She was a little girl at the time, sitting at the kitchen table in Pasadena, and her mother had read the headline to her while she ate raisin bran before school: *Humanity's First Envoy to Interstellar Space Says So Long.*

Voyager 3 followed the elder *Voyager's* path, through the theoretical Oort cloud, which was full of in utero comets and icy crystals, and eventually into another solar system. Someday it would fall into the gravitational pull of a celestial body—a planet or a sun or a black hole—but until then it would just keep drifting, solar system to solar system, wandering the Milky Way indefinitely. It was a chilling fate, and also a magical one. Sully tried to imagine how it would feel to have no destination. To just drift forever. There were other mechanical wanderers out there. Some were still active, others had gone silently into the void, but *Voyager 3* was special. It reminded Sully of the moment she'd begun to understand just how vast the universe was. Even as a little girl the emptiness had called to her, and now she was a wanderer too. Remembering how her journey had begun distracted her from the uneasy question of how it might end.

~~~

THEY CALLED IT Little Earth: the ring-shaped centrifuge that spun round and round, rotating independently of the rest of the ship and simulating gravity by way of centrifugal force. The crew's six sleeping compartments lined the ring, three roomy boxes on each side, with an aisle running down the middle. The bunks had thick curtains for privacy, shelves and drawers for clothes, and little reading lights for after the simulated sun had set. Farther along the ring a long table with two benches could be pulled out into the center of the aisle or pushed up against the wall, and beyond that there was a rudimentary kitchen. Coming full circle, there was a small fitness center with a stationary cycle, a treadmill, and a few weights beside the gaming console area, fitted with a futuristic gray couch. Between the couch and the bunk area was a small lavatory. There was another toilet in the zero-G section of the craft, but it was considerably less popular.

During their allotted recreation time Sully and Harper usually played cards. It was tiresome to feel the full weight of her body after spending all day floating in the comm. pod, but it was important to stay acclimated. The effects of gravity weren't all bad. The cards stayed on the table, her food stayed on her plate, and her pencil stayed behind her ear. Sully could almost forget about the emptiness outside, about the millions upon billions of light-years of unexplored space surrounding them. She could almost pretend she was back on Earth, steps away from dirt and trees and a blue canopy of sky. Almost.

Harper slapped the jack of clubs down in disgust. Sully picked it up, then laid down a run of face cards in a fan.

"Thought I'd have to wait forever for that jack," she said mildly, and discarded.

"Goddammit," Harper said, "stop rigging the deck, willya!"

Rummy was their new favorite. The whole crew had played poker until their first pass through the asteroid belt, six months into the journey. Gradually the others had faded away, then the card games had stopped altogether during the distraction of the Jovian moon survey. Only now, as the uneasiness of the comm. blackout swept in, did they return to the game, but by then it was only Harper and Sully who wanted to play. So now the game was Rummy 500.

"You're just making it really hard for me to lose," she said, and laid down another run, smacking her last card face-down on the table. He covered his head with his arms and sighed.

"Chalk it up, cheater," he said.

They counted their cards and Sully marked their scores down on her clipboard, beside some stray notes on Io's radiation signature. As she did some quick math in her head, Harper watched her as if he were drawing her, his eyes skimming the curves of her face, observing the flush creeping up her neck and into her cheeks. It felt good to be seen, but also a little painful, as if her skin were burning beneath his gaze. She scribbled down their new running scores.

"Another?" she asked, keeping her eyes on the tallies. He shook his head.

"I still need to put in an hour on the bike. I'll make my comeback tomorrow."

"I'm really looking forward to that," she said, sweeping up the cards and tucking them into their box. She stood up and pushed the table back against the wall. "Wear your brain next time, okay?"

"Watch that sass, Sullivan."

It was late, nighttime in *Aether*'s time zone. In her bunk, Sully planned to go over her notes from the day, but when she saw the single photo stuck to the wall of her compartment she didn't feel like working anymore. It was a picture of her daughter, taken when she was five or six years old, dressed as a firefly for Halloween. Jack had made the costume: a pair of black googly-eyes, antennae, a stuffed glow-in-the-dark abdomen, and wings made out of sheer black pantyhose and wire. Lucy would be nine by now, but when Sully was packing she hadn't been able to find a more recent photo to bring with her. Jack had always been the one to take the pictures.

-᠕᠕᠕-

IVANOV KEPT TO his lab lately, working more, sleeping less. It occurred to Sully that she hadn't seen him eat anything in days. One morning, she lingered in the greenhouse corridor and picked a handful of aeroponic cherry tomatoes for him.

"I brought you a snack," she said as she maneuvered into Ivanov's lab with her elbows, her hands cupped around the bright globes of red, yellow, and orange that floated in the space between her palms. He didn't look up from his microscope.

"Not hungry," he said, his forehead still pressed up against the eyepiece.

"Oh, come on, Ivanov, don't be a grump," she protested. "For later?" His hair became a ridiculous yellow bouffant in zero G and it made him look softer, more lighthearted than he actually was. For a moment she was fooled.

"Do I interrupt you while you're working?" he snapped, fixing her with a gaze that unsettled her. His eyes burned with grief and rage, and flecks of spit escaped his lips as he spoke. "I do not," he said, and turned back to the slide he'd been studying.

She ate the tomatoes herself in the comm. pod and fought back tears. They were all on edge; there had been no training for this. A seed of discord had sprouted among the astronauts. The harmony that the moon survey had brought to their tiny community had split open to reveal a volatile core. The regimen of Mission Control had gradually been abandoned and the crewmembers had become disconnected, not only from Earth but from one another. They'd stopped observing the schedules for sleeping and eating and relaxing and had begun to function as separate entities rather than a united team. Ivanov grew reclusive and temperamental, sequestering himself in his lab for hours at a time, but he wasn't the only one hiding out. Tal retreated into the world of video games, and although he could be found sitting on the couch in Little Earth, his mind was elsewhere.

Tal had been overjoyed with the precise challenge of setting down the landing modules on Callisto and Ganymede, then the ship's slingshot around Jupiter, but as their trajectory back to Earth evened out and the silence from Mission Control wore on, he became despondent and irritable. Without the periodic uplinks from his young family back in Houston, his mood deteriorated. He began to channel his distress into video games. The various controllers—the joysticks, gamepads, guns, steering wheels, flight simulators—took the brunt of his anguish. Games inevitably ended with some piece of plastic equipment flying across Little Earth and an unquenchable stream of curses, a mixture of Hebrew and English, echoing around the centrifuge.

After a particularly violent outburst, Sully watched him slouch in front of the gaming console like an old helium balloon. The levity that had been so charming, so magnetic, that had filled Tal with so much buoyancy, had dissipated into the recycled air. Eventually he crossed the centrifuge to collect the shattered steering wheel he had hurled against the wall. After silently gathering the pieces, he pooled them on the table, where he tried to put them back together. It was a futile project, but he worked on it for the rest of the day: gluing plastic to plastic, fiddling with wires, testing buttons. He just needed something to do. He didn't give up until Thebes laid a hand on his back.

"Leave it," Thebes said. "I need your help on the control deck."

Tal let Thebes distract him with work, but he was back in front of the gaming console the next day. Sully couldn't tell whether it was the games themselves that soothed him, the repetition of music and sound effects and graphics, or the excuse to emote so wildly at the end that kept him playing, again and again: win, lose, win, win, win, lose—the numbness of concentration followed by the quick release.

Devi, the youngest crewmember and unquestionably the most brilliant of them, struggled silently. While Tal and Ivanov seemed to take up more space than ever, their wild emotions overflowing their bodies, Devi seemed to shrink. She'd always been more engaged with the machines than with her colleagues, which was part of what made her such an exceptional engineer. But as the silence from Earth lengthened, she disengaged from both machines and humans. Nothing could hold her interest. She began to drift, untethered to the crew or to the mechanics of the ship itself.

Thebes noticed the lapses in Devi's repairs—she was missing obvious problems, didn't hear troubling sounds, passed over malfunctioning components, as if she were sleepwalking. He confided in Sully one afternoon, coming to visit her in the comm. pod while she worked through the probe data.

"Have you noticed anything amiss with Devi?" he asked.

Sully was unsurprised. She had been trying not to notice the growing shift in all her colleagues, but the changes in each of them were unmistakable. The crew was unraveling—slowly, one thread at a time.

"I've noticed," she said.

Together they tried to pull Devi back to them, back to their ship. Thebes worked alongside Devi, although it meant twice as much work for him, and he told her stories about being recruited into the South African space program, decades ago, when he was a young man and the program was barely a few years old. Sully kept her company during their off hours—she tried to make sure that Devi did the required amount of exercise, that she ate and slept regularly. She asked Devi about her family, about her childhood. They tried their best, but Thebes and Sully could do only so much. None of them was immune to the growing rift between *Aether* and Earth. The closer they got, the wider it became, and as the silence wore on it grew cacophonous.

THE FOLLOWING NIGHT, after dinner and the recreation hour, Harper called the crew together. Ivanov was the last to arrive, having skipped both dinner and recreation in favor of staying in the lab, cataloging moon rock samples. He went straight to the treadmill and began jogging in the corner, casting a glare in the direction of Tal, who was lifting weights.

"Did you want to use these?" Tal asked with mock politeness. Ivanov punched up the speed on the treadmill and ignored him.

"Now that we're all here," Harper began, "I think we should touch base about the blackout."

Thebes was at the table, reading the old Arthur C. Clarke novel *Childhood's End*. He dog-eared his page and joined Harper on the couch, folding his hands on the book in his lap. Devi got out of her bunk and went to sit next to Thebes, while Tal put down the weights and stayed where he was. Sully left her bunk and leaned against the lavatory door, facing the couch and the exercise area beyond it. Ivanov kept jogging, indifferent.

"I want to go over a few things," Harper continued. "I know we're all aware of the situation, but bear with me. At this point we've been out of contact with Mission Control for almost three weeks. And we're not sure why." He looked around at them as if for confirmation. Sully nodded. Tal began to chew on his lower lip. Thebes and Devi listened without expression. Ivanov kept jogging.

"Our comm. pod is functioning properly. Telemetry from the probes is coming in, commands to the probes are going out. Devi and Thebes are ninety-nine point nine percent certain the failure did not originate with us." He paused again and looked to the engineers on the couch for confirmation. Thebes bobbed his head.

"We do not think it is *Aether*'s error," Thebes said, enunciating each word, each syllable, so perfectly it was difficult to doubt his diligence.

"Which leaves us with some unattractive possibilities," Harper said.

From the treadmill Ivanov snorted and hit the Cancel button. The belt slowed and stopped. "Unattractive," he muttered under his breath, then added a few more words in Russian. He raked his fingers through his hair, which was still bouncy from being in zero G all day. Sully didn't have to understand Russian to get the drift of his mutterings.

Harper ignored him and continued. "In every instance I can think of, we're looking at a worldwide problem. Clearly all three of the DSN telescopes are down. The way I see it, either the equipment has failed, or the personnel has failed—or both. Other ideas?"

There was a pause. The centrifuge hummed on its axis and the life support ducts breathed. Somewhere in the zero-G section they could hear the hull of the ship groaning softly.

"It could be," Sully offered after a minute, "that there's an atmospheric problem. Some kind of RF pollution, a geomagnetic storm maybe—but to cause a blackout like this it would have to be one hell of a storm. Historically something like this would be brief, correlating with a solar event, but . . . I don't know, it could be."

Harper looked thoughtful. "Has that happened on this scale before?"

Ivanov threw up his hands in frustration. "A geomagnetic storm? Don't be ridiculous, Sullivan, it couldn't possibly last this long."

Sully continued, "I . . . don't think so. Years ago a magnetic storm upset the power grid in Canada and caused aurora borealis as far south as Texas, but Ivanov's right, nothing I've ever heard of would last this long and disrupt both hemispheres. It could be something nuclear—there've been experiments on how nukes might affect the atmosphere in the past, but I'm not sure there's been any hard data on it, mostly just supposition." Sully fiddled with her clipboard as she ticked off the possibilities, vaguely aware of the chill that settled over the centrifuge as she uttered the word *nuclear*. "I guess it could be airborne debris, which could come from either an asteroid impact or a massive detonation. But really—the instruments we have on board should have picked up on anything like that, and there's nothing unusual about Earth's energy signature. It doesn't make sense."

"Basically we're fucked and we have no idea why," Ivanov interjected. He brushed past Sully and disappeared into the lavatory, shutting the door behind him.

Tal sighed. "He's right, isn't he? Barring the point zero one possibility that it's our mistake." He rubbed his face with his hands as if he were trying to wake himself up from a bad dream. It was hard to tell whether Tal was more upset that Ivanov was right or that their planet seemed doomed. No one spoke for a long moment, listening to Ivanov opening and shutting the door to the communal medicine cabinet in the lavatory.

"I just don't *get it*," Tal continued. "If we're talking nuclear war—we would know. If we're talking asteroid—we would know. And if we're talking worldwide epidemic—well, fuck, I'm no epidemiologist, but I hardly think things would be fine one day, everyone dead the next."

Devi shivered but said nothing.

"So what now?" Thebes asked. He was looking at Harper. They were all looking at Harper, their commander, who raised his palms in defeat.

"There's no . . . precedent. They didn't cover this in the training manual. I think we have to continue as planned and hope that as we get closer to home we can initiate some kind of contact. There's not much else we can do in the interim. Unless someone has a different idea." The four other crew-members slowly shook their heads. "Okay, so I guess we can agree that the next step is to stay the course and see how the situation develops." He paused. "Ivanov!" Harper shouted. "Agreed?"

The door to the lavatory slid open and Ivanov took his toothbrush from his mouth. "If it makes you feel better pretending there is some other option, that we are actually making a choice, okay, great—agreed." Then he shut the door again.

Tal rolled his eyes and muttered *asshole* to no one in particular.

Thebes gave Devi a paternal pat on the back and she let her head rest on his shoulder, just for a second, then got up and climbed back into her bunk. She shut the curtain and the glow of her light was extinguished a moment later. The crew disbanded silently, defeated. There was nothing else to say. Thebes took his book and went to bed. Tal did one more set with the weights, then put them away. Inside her little compartment Sully let her gaze linger on the photo of her daughter. She closed her eyes and listened: there was the murmur of Devi's Hindi prayer, the shrill music of Tal's handheld videogame, the scratch of Harper's pencil on pa-per, the rustle of Thebes turning pages, and the hum of the ship beneath it all. Ivanov was cursing under his breath as he left the lavatory, but later, as she drifted off to sleep, she thought she heard his muffled sobs.

-∿∿∿-

THE NEXT MORNING, Sully opened her eyes a few minutes before the alarm buzzed at 0700. She turned it off, staring at the stiff ripples of the curtain, then she let her eyelids flutter back down. The prospect of returning to work in the comm. pod seemed like an unhappy chore. It was difficult to see the point of it now. She didn't care about the data rushing into her machines anymore, or the groundbreaking conclusions she might draw from all the brand-new information, the fresh discoveries that lay at her fingertips. She didn't want to leave the centrifuge at all. She wanted gravity to go on holding her.

Her dreams that night had taken her back to the surface of Callisto, where she had stood not so long ago, watching the fawn-colored stripes of Jupiter whirling, the Great Red Spot churning. Beyond the curtain, first light began to strengthen, but she didn't rouse herself to see it. Not today. It was as real as her dream and nowhere near as beautiful. She went back to sleep, back to Jupiter's moon, and let the artificial sunrise go unobserved.

THREE

ONE DARK AFTERNOON, after the sun had gone down but before the sky had erased all its evidence, Augustine and Iris headed out to the hangar. Iris wanted to go for a walk—a long walk, she said—and the hangar seemed like a new and interesting destination. Augie hadn't been there in a long time—not since his last flight in, the previous summer—but the eerie blue twilight, casting shadows on the snow, stirred his sense of adventure. They would be far from the observatory when the deep darkness of early evening fell, but they took a flashlight, and at the last minute Augustine swung a rifle across his back and made sure the chamber was full. The weight of the gun barrel against his shoulder blade and the thick yellow beam of light swinging across the blue snow in front of him quenched his apprehension.

He carried the flashlight in one hand and steadied himself with a ski pole in the other. Navigating the shifting snow-drifts on foot was difficult—his arthritis was getting worse. Iris skidded fearlessly down the mountain, running out in front of the flashlight's reach, turning occasionally to see what was taking him so long. He was out of breath before they were halfway there, and his knees had already begun to ache, the muscles in his thighs to burn. He should've taken the skis, but they were too big for Iris, and it didn't seem fair to make her walk while he sliced through the drifts. After almost an hour of walking, the roof of the hangar came into view, a glint of corrugated metal against the endless snow. Iris began to move even faster, wading through the soft drifts on her short but determined legs.

As they came closer, he noticed that the long sliding doors of the hangar were wide open. Snow had begun to accumulate inside. Where the floor was bare he could see dark oil stains soaked into the concrete. It was the scene of a hurried departure. A set of ratchet wrench sockets lay scattered across the concrete like hexagonal stars in an earthbound constellation, the empty case tossed nearby. Augustine closed his eyes and imagined the plane on the tarmac, researchers on board, luggage stowed, and one last military mechanic rushing to collect his things, picking up the case without latching it and watching the wrench sockets spin across the floor. Augustine had heard the Herc take off from the observatory, then watched it climb into the sky from afar.

Here, he couldn't help but fill the long, white runway with an imaginary plane. Augustine pictured the copilot hanging his head out the hatch, shouting *Come on,* while the mechanic decided to let the fallen pieces lie where they were, throwing the empty case down with them and running to board the waiting plane, climbing the rickety staircase, then kicking the stairs away and swinging the hatch shut. The plane thundering down the white runway, lifting up nose-first into the sky. Returning to a world Augustine no longer had access to.

Where the plane might have idled was the empty, derelict runway: the plastic glimmer of unlit LEDs, orange flags half-buried in the snow. The staircase was still there, knocked on its side, one loose wheel spinning in lazy circles in the wind. Augustine held one of the wrench sockets in the padded palm of his mitten, then let it fall to the ground with a hollow clatter. It reminded him of his father—the smell of stale grease, the tools and machine parts scattered around the hangar. Augustine used to watch his father sleep, feet propped up on the recliner, mouth half-open, a ragged snore erupting from deep in his throat. And the smell—that thick, oily smell that wafted off his father's clothes like an unlit fire or the underbelly of a diesel truck. The television would be flickering in the background, his mother either working in the kitchen or lying down in their bedroom, and Augie would kneel on the carpet, feeling the rough polyester fibers pressing into his shins, pretending to watch the television but watching his father instead.

Augustine brushed the snow off a large stainless steel toolbox in the hangar and forced open the top drawer. A jumble of drill bits and screwdrivers stared back at him, a tangled spool of wire, an assortment of thick bolts. He shut the drawer. Something moved in the corner of his eye and he turned toward the runway outside to see Iris climbing on the fallen staircase like a jungle gym.

"Careful," he called to her, and she raised her arms above her head in a defiant *no hands* gesture. She edged along the thin metal framework like a balance beam. He continued investigating the hangar, shining the flashlight into the dim corner and kicking snow off mysterious shapes buried beneath the drifts. A few limp, frozen piles of cardboard, more toolboxes, a stack of tires. Augustine arrived at a sizable mound covered with a stiff green tarp and fastened with bungee cords. He unhooked the cords and drew back the tarp to find a pair of snowmobiles. *Of course,* he thought. He, along with his luggage, had been shuttled to and from the runway on his various arrivals and departures from the observatory via these snowmobiles. In previous years, Augie had left the observatory during the summer months, when the precipitation from the melting snow clouded the atmosphere and thin blankets of fog rolled off the Arctic sea, up into the mountains, stretching over the sky like a scrim that prevented him from doing his work. He would go somewhere warm on his escapes from the Arctic: the Caribbean, Indonesia, Hawaii, a different world entirely. Staying at extravagant resorts, eating nothing but shrimp cocktail and raw oysters, drinking gin at noon and then passing out on the pool furniture and burning to a crackling red crisp. *What I wouldn't do for a few liters of gin right about now,* he thought.

Augustine ran his mittened hands over the sleek machines. The keys were still slotted into the ignitions. He turned the nearest one to the On position and pulled out the choke, then gave the start cord a pull. The engine made

a halfhearted groan but didn't catch. Augustine kept pulling the cord, as hard as he could, until finally the engine
turned over and the pistons started pumping on their own.
Oily smoke billowed from underneath the hood, and the
engine settled into a hesitant but steady beat. The smoke
thinned and Augie gave the machine an affectionate pat on
its shiny black haunch. There wasn't anywhere in particular
he wanted to go, but it was good to have an engine at his
command. Perhaps they would ride back to the observatory.
Augie grinned at the idea and wondered if Iris's limbs were
long enough to ride the other one, but when he saw her, he
immediately forgot about the snowmobiles. The cold engine
sputtered and died, and he barely heard it.

There was another shape on the runway. Augie squinted
to make out its silhouette against the luminous blue of the
snow in the fading light. It was on four legs, a grayish-white
color that almost disappeared into the background. If Iris
hadn't been so entranced by it, Augie might not even have
noticed. Iris moved toward the figure, scooting along the
thin metal poles of the fallen staircase and cooing, singing
that strange, guttural song he had grown accustomed to.
The figure cocked its head. It was a wolf.

Without pausing to think, Augustine swung the rifle
down from his back. The thick canvas of the strap buzzed
against the windproof material of his parka, and he froze.
The wolf swung its head toward him and growled, the scant
light bouncing off its eyes, making them shine like marbles.
The wolf took a step closer to the hangar. Augustine held
his breath and waited. Iris was creeping closer and closer
along the length of the staircase, reaching out her hand to
stroke its fur. The wolf sat down in the snow and watched
her, pawing the ground and pricking its rounded ears at the

sound of her voice. Augie slipped off his mittens and flexed his fingers in anticipation. He hadn't fired a gun since he was a teenager, hunting with his father in the woods near their house in Michigan. The two of them would wait in silence, father and son, and when the moment was right and something found its way into their crosshairs, they would aim their guns and squeeze. Augustine hated every minute of those trips.

He lifted the rifle and rested the butt of it against his shoulder. He found the wolf in the scope and trained the crosshairs on its shaggy head. Iris was still creeping closer and closer, shedding her mittens and outstretching her hands, making soft, sweet noises. Just as his finger found the trigger, the wolf moved. It threw back its head and howled, a mournful, lonely sound, then took another step closer to Iris. Augustine corrected his aim, the wolf stood up on its hind legs, raising its snout toward Iris's tiny palm, and he pulled the trigger.

〜〜〜

THE SOUND OF the shot must have echoed over the mountain range, bouncing from peak to peak, reverberating in the valleys, but Augie didn't hear it. Everything was silent as he watched the wolf's head snap back, the fine mist of red that fell on the snow as its body hung in midair, then collapsed onto the ground in a crumpled heap. When it was over, all he could hear was Iris screaming.

He loped toward her, the glowing flashlight forgotten on the seat of the stalled snowmobile. Iris had tumbled down from where she had been balancing on the stairs and landed face-first on the snowy runway. White powder clung to her hair and eyelashes, her nose and cheeks red from the cold, and she was still screaming. She threw herself on the body of the wolf, burying her tiny hands in its white fur. Augie struggled to move fast enough. He didn't have the breath to call to her, the weight of the rifle slapping the leftover air from his lungs with each awkward stride. When he finally reached her he saw that the wolf was still alive, but just barely. He had caught it in the neck. As the blood soaked into the snow, the shallow heave of its belly slowed. Augie reached out to pull Iris away from the dying creature and he saw that it was washing the tears and the snow from her face with its lolling pink tongue, as a mother might do to her cubs.

The wolf's blood was on Iris's face, in her hair, and on her hands, but she didn't seem to notice. The animal drew a few more ragged breaths, then expired, its hot tongue collapsing in its mouth, the gleam of its eyes clouding into darkness. The wind stirred the snow around them and sent the shards of ice sideways like a million tiny razors. Augie put his hand on Iris's tiny, shuddering back. She let him keep it there, but she wouldn't release the dead wolf's fur, nor would she stop her low, keening moan. She kept her fingers knotted in its warm, shaggy coat as the snow stung their exposed skin.

"I'm sorry," he said. "I thought—" but he couldn't finish. He tried again. "I thought—"

But he hadn't thought. He had identified a target before thinking anything at all. And he knew, with a sinking burn in his gut, that he would do it again. He told himself it was to protect Iris. To keep her safe from the danger that lurked all around them. And perhaps that was true—wolves are not harmless creatures, after all—but there was something else. A primal taste, sour, like fear, rising in the back of his throat, or maybe loneliness. He looked up to the stars, waiting for them to dwarf the immensity of emotion welling inside of him, as they had so many times before. But it didn't work this time. He felt everything, and the stars winked down on him: cold, bright, distant, unfeeling. He was filled with an urge to pack his suitcase and move on. But of course there was nowhere else to go. He stayed where he was, still looking up, still with his hand on Iris's back, and he felt—for the first time in so many years, he *felt:* helpless, lonely, afraid. If the tears hadn't frozen in the corners of his eyes, he might have cried.

THE FLASHLIGHT WAS lost, burned out and left in the dark hangar somewhere, so they made their way back toward the observatory in the dark, following the hulking black shadow of its dome set in relief against a starlit sky. Augustine had lost his ski pole as well, and he moved slowly without its support, his joints exploding in pain with each step. He shifted the rifle to the other shoulder. He wished he had left it on the runway. Wished he hadn't thought to bring it at all. His spine and shoulder were bruised from where the heavy barrel had been knocking against him and his chest ached from the recoil.

Iris was solemn but dry-eyed. As they walked she took up her usual song, low and desolate; Augustine was grateful for it. Anything to drown out the echo of her screams. They had covered the wolf's body with snow and packed the bulging grave down as best they could, a glowing white mound streaked pink with blood. Iris had made a plow with her mittens and pushed the powder up over the corpse with vigorous thrusts. If it weren't for the hollowed half moons beneath her eyes and the inconsolable quivering of her chin, he might have mistaken her for a child at play in her own backyard. He tried to imagine that this was the case, but there was no snowman when they were finished, only a swollen grave.

At the observatory, Iris went straight to their home on the third floor. Augustine stowed the gun in the armory cabinet in one of the outbuildings. The rifles were stored in an unheated building to keep the mechanisms from reacting to abrupt changes in temperature when they were used outside. He remembered learning when he first came to the outpost about the special Arctic lubricant used on the guns to keep the pieces fluid, and how little he cared at the time. The man who had showed him the guns had been a Marine before becoming a scientist, and the loving way he handled the firearms reminded Augustine of his father. Augie had told the man abruptly that he wouldn't be using the armory while he was there.

When he reached the observatory and pushed open the door, his legs finally failed him. He fell into a chair on the first floor and waited for his muscles to respond to his brain's commands. It took the better part of an hour for the cramps to fade. The warmth was just out of his reach, at the top of three flights of stairs. Augustine finally found the strength to haul himself up by the railing. When he burst into the heated control room, his chest heaving, he collapsed onto the nest of mattresses and sleeping bags on the floor. Piece by piece, and with great effort, he removed his boots, his parka, his hat and mittens. As he lay there he wondered why he hadn't just chased it away, why he couldn't have aimed high and let the crack of a warning shot send the wolf running back into the wilderness. A few minutes later he was asleep.

~WWV~

WHEN HE FINALLY woke, the sun was beginning to show, sending faint fingers of light in through the thick windows of the control room. The clock said it was noon. Augustine let himself lie there for a long time before he got up. The sun had already reached the zenith of its shortened day before he dragged himself to the window. He could see Iris sitting down the mountain a fair distance, past the outbuildings, watching the horizon. At first he was annoyed and wanted to tell her not to wander so far without him, but he realized he had no right to disturb her, nor to limit her movements. She understood the tundra better than he did. She was more at home here than he would ever be. And yet—it was his job to keep her safe, wasn't it? There was no one else to do it. No one to help, no one to intervene if he was doing it wrong. No Internet, even, to ask for advice. Again, he was afraid, and again he pushed the emotion away, a feeling too strange, too unpleasant to sit with for long. He stared at his own reflection in the window, his skin crinkling around his features like a sheet of notebook paper balled up and then smoothed out again. He looked even older than he remembered, and more tired.

Augustine took a granola bar from their food stores and sat at the table Iris liked best while he ate it. The field guide he had given her was open and lay facedown, its spine cracked in a dozen different places. He picked it up and found himself looking at a photo of the Arctic wolf. He read and reread the section on the white wolf's forty-two teeth and didn't let his eyes wander to the picture of their pups. *The Arctic wolf is generally unafraid of humans, as their habitat is so desolate they rarely come into contact with them.* Augie snapped the book shut. Forty-two teeth.

～WWW～

IRIS WAS STILL out there, unmoving. When the sun had sunk behind the mountains for the day, Augie abandoned the old astrophysics journal he had been trying to distract himself with. By then, he'd read and reread every journal, every magazine, every book left in the control tower. He felt strange, as if his own mind was unfamiliar to him, stricken with a deep wave of emotions he couldn't name, didn't recognize, and was unwilling to look at head-on. Augustine closed his eyes and did what he always did: he imagined the blue dome of the planet as seen from the other side of the atmosphere, and the emptiness beyond it. He pictured the rest of the solar system, planet by planet, then the Milky Way, and on and on, waiting for the awestruck relief to wash over him—but it didn't come. All he could see was his own haggard reflection in the window, the bright rim of his white hair and wiry beard, and the empty holes where his eyes should be. The dead wolf, and the little girl stretching out her bare hand to a snout bristling with teeth. Was it remorse, he wondered, or cowardice? Perhaps he was ill. He touched the back of his hand to his forehead and found it very warm. That was it. He was ill. He could feel a fever building beneath his skin, heating his blood to a simmer. A buzz filled his ears and a pressure began to throb behind his eyes, beating against the inside of his skull like timpani. Was this it, then? The end? He thought of the first aid kit, down in the director's office on the first floor. Should he get it? Was it worth it? He thought of all the medicines that weren't in it, all the anatomical knowledge he didn't possess, all the diagnostic equipment he didn't have and wouldn't know how to use anyway. Augustine went back to bed and imagined that it was his deathbed. Just before he drifted off, he thought of Iris, still out there, all alone on the tundra. Sleep overtook him slowly, like a wave rolling up the length of his body, and just before it reached his brain he wondered if this was what it would feel like. He wondered what would become of Iris if he never woke up.

FOUR

AETHER'S CREW STRUGGLED with time. There was so much
of it—the hours in each day and the hours in each night,
again and again. Weeks, then months to fill. Without knowing what was waiting for them on Earth the prescribed tasks
and routines became empty. Pointless. If they would never
feel Earth's gravity again, then why bother with all the medi-
cation and exercise to remind their bodies of its weight? If
they would never share their discoveries from the Galilean
moon survey, then why continue the research? If their planet

and everyone they had ever known was burnt or frozen or vaporized or diseased or some other equally unpleasant version of extinction, then what did it matter if they became careless and depressed? Who were they trying to make it home for? What did it matter if they overslept and overate, or underslept and underate—wasn't despair appropriate? Didn't it fit their situation?

Everything seemed to move more slowly. A tense apprehension settled over the crew: the weight of the unknown, of creeping futility. Sully found herself typing more slowly, writing more slowly, moving less, thinking less. At first the crew's collective curiosity burned brightly, as they struggled to understand what had happened, but soon it gave way to a hopeless surrender. There was no way to know, no data to study except the lack of data. Their silent Earth was still ten months away, a long journey to an uncertain home. Nostalgia crept up on her—on all of them. They missed the people, the places, the objects they'd left behind—things they were beginning to think they would never see again. Sully thought of her daughter, Lucy, exuberant and high-pitched, a little blond-haired, brown-eyed cyclone that spun through Sully's memory the same way she'd spun through their small house. She wished that she had brought more pictures, that she had had a whole thumb drive full of them—more than just the one, which was out of date even when they left. What kind of mother wouldn't have brought at least a dozen, she thought. And on a two-year trip, when her daughter was turning into a young woman? Sully hadn't received video uplinks from anyone except work colleagues the entire time she'd been on *Aether*. She would have treasured them, replayed them over and over, but there was nothing from Lucy, and definitely nothing from Jack. The estrangement of her family hadn't broken her heart until she left the atmosphere—then all of a sudden it felt like a tragedy that had just recently befallen her, even though it had been that way for years. She tried to re-create the missing photos in her mind, the Christmases and birthdays and that time Lucy and Jack and Sully went whitewater rafting in Colorado, before the divorce. The scenery was easy to fill in—a lopsided blue spruce tree hung with silver tinsel, that green plaid sofa from their old apartment, chili pepper lights in the kitchen, the row of potted plants behind the sink, the red Land Rover packed for a road trip—but it was their faces that were hard to recall.

Jack, her husband for ten years, her ex for five. She started by picturing his hair, which he always kept shorter than she liked it, and then she tried to fill in the features one by one: eyes, green and fringed with thick lashes, shadowed by dark eyebrows; nose, a little bent, broken one too many times; mouth, dimples on either side, thin lips, good teeth. She thought about the day they met, the day she married him, the day she left him, trying to account for every minute, every word. She re-created the scenery of their life together: that tiny apartment in Toronto they shared when she was pregnant for the first time, while she was finishing her dissertation and he was teaching particle physics to undergrads, and then the brick loft with big windows they moved to after the miscarriage. He'd been so disappointed when she told him that the baby they'd only just learned about was lost—it was early, only six weeks in, and Sully'd barely had time to settle into the idea. When she felt the cramping she knew it was over, and when she saw the blood soaking through her underwear she was relieved. She cleaned it up, took four ibuprofen tablets, and wondered how to tell Jack. That afternoon she cradled his head in her lap and tried to feel the sadness she could see written on his face. But she couldn't feel anything. The light had faded from the big windows in the living room, but still they sat, the curtains undrawn, the glass darkening to tall black eyes—looking in, or looking out, she couldn't tell.

Their wedding a year later, at city hall, with the gray tiled corridors and the dark polished wood benches that lined them, other couples sitting and waiting their turn. The birth of Lucy, four years after that, in a minty green hospital room. The unquenchable joy on Jack's face when he held her, the unmistakable fear in Sully's chest when he handed the baby back to her. Lucy's first steps, on the linoleum kitchen floor, first words, *Daddy, no,* when they tried to leave her with a babysitter. Sully thought of the day the space program invited her to join the new class of astronaut candidates, the day she left Jack and five-year-old Lucy behind and went to Houston. At first she remembered the milestone moments, the days that changed everything, but as time wore on she began to think more about the little things.

Lucy's hair, how it looked like spun gold when she was small, then darkened as she grew. The veins pulsing beneath her translucent skin just after she was born. Jack's broad torso, the way he left the top button undone and rolled up his sleeves, never wore a tie and rarely bothered with a jacket. The lines of his clavicle, the hint of chest hair, the inevitable smudge of blackboard chalk on his shirt. The copper saucepans that hung above the gas stove in the Vancouver house where they moved after Sully got her PhD; the color of the front door, raspberry red; the sheets Lucy liked best, midnight blue, scattered with yellow stars.

Everyone on *Aether* was lost in a private past, each bunk like a bubble of memory. The absorption with things gone by was visible on all of their faces when they weren't exchanging terse, necessary words with one another, struggling through the grim demands of the present. Sometimes Sully watched the others, imagining what they were thinking about. The crew had been training together in Houston for almost two years before the launch; they'd grown close, but the things you tell your colleagues when you're practicing simulated disasters and the things you think about when the world ends while you're far away are so very different.

-∿∿∿-

IN HOUSTON, ABOUT a year before the mission launched, Sully recognized the Ivanov family having an early dinner at an outdoor café in the city. She was parking on the other side of the street and watched them while she slotted change into the meter. She thought about crossing to say hello but stayed where she was. They were all lit up and sun-gold, five heads of white-blond hair illuminated like dandelion puffs. She saw Ivanov lean over to cut up his youngest daughter's dinner. His wife was animated, gesticulating wildly with silverware in her hands, her husband and children laughing with open, food-filled mouths.

A waiter stopped at their table with a ramekin, and when he set it down next to Ivanov's elbow a chorus of thankyous erupted from the children. Sully could hear it from across the street. Arms loaded down with half-empty plates, the waiter was beaming when he left the table. Sully's gaze rested on Ivanov's wife—now waving a salad-loaded fork while she talked. Sully wondered if she'd ever looked so joyful with her own family, or so present. Sully lingered at the meter until she felt that she was trespassing on a moment that didn't belong to her, then moved off down the street to a small greengrocer's where she bought her produce. Ivanov seemed chronically serious at work, but not tonight, not with his family. She selected peaches, and as she cupped the warm heaviness of the fruit and felt the delicate fuzz against her palm, she was reminded of the weight of her daughter's head when she was born.

-᰾᷍᰾-

SIX WEEKS INTO the communication blackout, Ivanov returned to Little Earth late, after a few of the others had eaten dinner together. He went straight to his bunk and snapped the curtain shut behind him. Thebes considered the drawn curtain for a moment and knocked on the side of his compartment.

"There is a stew if you're interested, Ivanov," he said to the gray partition.

Tal, from his usual place in front of the gaming console, snorted. "He won't come out," he said, with a taunting edge in his voice. "He's probably too busy crying himself to sleep."

Sully froze in her bunk, where she had been making notes on a telemetry readout. So she hadn't imagined it. There was a beat of silence, then Ivanov ripped his curtain back and charged across the centrifuge toward Tal. He had his fists buried in the fabric of Tal's jumpsuit and had yanked him to his feet before Tal even saw him coming. Tal snarled in Hebrew and broke Ivanov's grip with a blow to his wrists, and then Thebes was on them both, dragging Tal back toward the sofa while Ivanov spat on the floor. Ivanov's face was a vivid red, and he stalked back to the zero-G section of the ship. Harper arrived just as Tal kicked his game controller across the room. The centrifuge was suddenly quiet. Sully sat on her bunk, unsure what to do, whether to say anything.

Harper and Thebes conferred in low tones. They came to some sort of conclusion and Thebes left Little Earth, presumably to speak with Ivanov. Harper absentmindedly massaged the muscles of his jaw with the heel of his hand, then he went to Tal's bunk. Sully drew her own curtain, not wanting to eavesdrop.

In the beginning, when communication with Earth was clear and easy and uninterrupted, Tal would spend hours talking to his wife and sons. The boys were eight and eleven years old when *Aether* launched. There had been a little party at a training facility in Houston for them before the launch, their birthdays only a week apart. Tal's sons played the same video games back in Texas, and on board the spacecraft Tal kept his high scores handy for when he video-chatted with his family, so that he and the boys could compare. Later, even when the time lapse became unwieldy and they could only send one-sided messages, the competition continued. A few days ago, Sully had watched Tal beat his sons' record for one of the racing games. His triumphant fist shot into the air, but then his face crumpled, his breath became shallow, and the plastic controller fell from his hands. Sully went to sit with him, cautiously placing a hand on his back, and he pressed his face into her shoulder, something he'd never done before. It was the most vulnerable she'd ever seen him.

"I'm winning," he said into the mesh sleeve of her jumpsuit, and they sat in silence as the victory music looped over and over, shrill trumpets over a steady, hollow beat.

~~~~

As THE LAST few weeks of training in Houston had trickled away and the launch neared, the crew's excitement began to build, their camaraderie to intensify. After a long Friday full of Jovian lunar landing simulations, they all went out for drinks at a local bar. Thebes flipped through the juke-box songs with a fistful of quarters while Devi drank cran-berry juice through a straw beside him and contemplated the machine itself. At the bar, Tal, Ivanov, and Harper lined up shots of tequila, Tal insisting that they drink one for ev-ery Galilean moon—four apiece. Sully was late arriving and she scanned the scene from the doorway. The bartender was doling out wedges of lime as Thebes's first selection from the jukebox began to play. Harper called her over and ordered her a shot.

"You're playing catch-up," he said, and slid the glass in front of her. "This one's for Callisto." She tossed it back and waved away the lime he offered her.

Tal grinned wickedly. "Excellent," he said. "Another!"

Ivanov pounded the bar with his shot glass. "Hear, hear," he said, his face a luminous shade of rose. Tal was buoyant, bouncing on his bar stool as he counted down a Galilean moon for every shot the astronauts downed.

"Ganymede!" he shouted.

Sully slammed another glass back down on the table. "That sweet, sweet magnetosphere," she shouted back. Iva-nov nodded, solemn, but excited in his own way. They all were.

Over at the jukebox, Thebes and Devi took up the cry of "Ganymede," to the confusion of the other patrons. It was still early then, the bar relatively quiet, but the next time Sully took stock of their surroundings a few hours later she realized the room was full and she was drunk. Devi and Harper were dancing near the jukebox. Devi bounced her knees and swirled her arms around her head while Harper did some version of the twist, mixed with an occasional raise-the-roof gesture. Tal, Sully, Ivanov, and Thebes were crowded around the bar. Tal snorted a mouthful of beer out of his nose, laughing at one of his own jokes, and Ivanov swayed next to Sully, his forearm resting on her shoulder.

"Who's Yuri?" Ivanov was asking, looking perplexed. Sully and Thebes glanced at each other, not sure whether to laugh or to change the subject. They had heard Tal speak of Yuri before, but never in Ivanov's presence.

"You know—that bug living up your ass," Tal said, laughing so hard he could barely get the words out. "Yuri Gagarin. How's he doing?"

Ivanov swayed, his arm still on Sully for balance, a pensive frown etched in his face. There was a long pause. "He's good," Ivanov finally said, his voice booming and jovial, "but he'd be better if he didn't have to look at your ugly face every day."

Harper tapped Sully on the shoulder and she turned to see his face, shiny with sweat. Devi was a few feet behind him, beckoning to her. "Dance with us?" he said. "It's our song."

She nodded. He meant all of theirs, but for a minute, as Sully slid off her bar stool and moved toward the crush of bodies, jerking and swaying and twirling in time with "Space Oddity," she thought he meant just the two of them. Our song. David Bowie's voice filled the bar and Harper led her onto the dance floor, toward Devi, who was still waving. He reached back to make sure she was following and took her hand, pulling her forward, into the center of the crowd.

〰〰

TWO WEEKS AFTER Ivanov and Tal's fight, while they were still passing through the asteroid belt, Sully awoke to hear Devi whispering to her in the darkness.

"Are you awake?" she asked, from the other side of the privacy curtain.

Sully rubbed the sleep from her eyes and pulled back the curtain, motioning for Devi to climb in. They lay there in the dark, side by side, letting each other's body heat soothe their frayed nerves, which sparked like live wires as soon as the lights went out and there was nothing left to do but obsess over an unknown future or dwell in the past. Devi was close enough that Sully could feel the quiver of a suppressed sob. She ached to reach out, to wrap her crewmate in her arms and tell her that everything would be all right—but she couldn't lie, and she wasn't sure how to connect with a woman so disconnected. Devi had grown quieter and quieter as the weeks passed. These days, she said barely anything. Sully lay still and let her foot collapse sideways to gently brush against Devi's. Sully had almost fallen asleep again when Devi began to talk.

"I keep having this dream," she murmured. "It starts with the colors and smells of my mother's kitchen in Kolkata, just blurriness and spices. Then my brothers come into focus, sitting across from me, jabbing each other with their elbows, scooping up rice and dal with their fingers . . . and I see my parents at the head of the table, sipping chai, smiling, watching all three of us. It's always the same, over and over. We are just sitting and eating and it seems to last for hours. But then eventually it fades away. Suddenly I know that they are gone, that I am alone. And I wake up." Devi heaved a long, slow sigh. "It starts out so beautifully," she whispered, "but then I am awake and I'm here and I know I'll never see them again. How can a dream hurt so much?"

Eventually the two women drifted off to sleep, and in the night they overlapped, knotting their limbs together as if it might make them stronger. When Sully woke she saw tears running down Devi's face in silence, pooling against the side of her nose, wetting the pillow. Sully thought of what it felt like to have Lucy climb into her bed after a nightmare. The small, warm body, encased in flannel pajamas, the hot, wet face, the shuddering of her breath inside her lungs. Sully tried to remember what she used to say to Lucy, how she used to comfort her—but she couldn't. It had always been Jack who took her back to her own bed. Sully moved closer to Devi, and she wept, too.

~~~~

SULLY HAD LOVED Devi almost immediately when they met in Houston.

Devi was a quiet woman; her small stature and large, dark eyes made her seem innocent, young, even confused—at odds with the deeply analytical mind moving beneath the surface. At the beginning of their underwater training in Houston, Sully came upon Devi standing below one of the overhead cranes used to haul the astronauts in and out of the pool, staring up at the hoist with a pensive look. Tal and Thebes were finishing up an extravehicular activity simulation, an EVA, below the surface while the two women waited their turn to be hoisted into the water. Finally Devi let out an amused laugh and looked away from the crane, back to the pool.

"Fantastic," Devi murmured.

"What is?" Sully asked.

"My father has the same machine in his warehouse," she said. "The same exact one. I will have to tell him, he'll be very proud for choosing it."

The surface of the pool rippled and a cluster of bubbles

frothed near their feet. Below the water, an enormous mock-up of the *Aether* craft shimmered, illuminated by floodlights. Reflections of the flags that crowded the walls of the facility lined the edge of the water, lapping at the edge of the pool in gentle waves, the vivid colors of the different nations swirling together and then separating, over and over. Sully peered into the depths of the pool and saw one of the astronauts beginning to rise. Two divers hooked the astronaut's bulky white suit to the hoist and the crane's gears above their heads began to whir. Devi looked up at the crane once more, but Sully kept her eyes on the rising astronaut.

"Fantastic," Devi said again.

The white shell of Tal's helmet broke free of the water and Sully let out the breath she didn't know she'd been holding.

~~~

As THEY DRIFTED through the asteroid belt, still months from home, they began to lose themselves. Everyone except Thebes: he patiently guided Devi through her work, even as she slept less and her attention wandered more. He could occasionally coax Tal away from the gaming console and into the greenhouse corridor, to harvest vegetables. He visited Ivanov in the lab to see what he was working on, asked him kind and attentive questions, and set aside leftovers for him. Sully watched Thebes doing all this, curious, observant. He would sit and talk with Harper in quiet tones and afterward Harper's face seemed softer, his head held a little higher. Thebes was strong and hopeful, but he was only one out of six. He couldn't save them from themselves, could only try to make things a little easier. He understood what was happening better than the rest of them.

One morning, just after the sunrise had crept over Little

Earth, Sully drank lukewarm coffee across from Thebes at the kitchen table. He was reading—if he wasn't working, he was reading. The rest of the crew was either sleeping or working in the zero-G section of the ship. They were alone, and Little Earth was quiet, but even so, when she asked him how his family had died, she whispered. She already knew the answer, but it wasn't the gruesome details of the car accident she wanted to hear about—it was something else, something she didn't have words for. Thebes dog-eared his page in *The Left Hand of Darkness* and closed the book. Set it on the table.

"Why do you want to know?" he asked patiently.

"I'm just trying to understand," she said. She tried to swallow the shrill note of desperation that had crept into her voice, grinding her teeth together to keep her tone steady. "How you're still here. How you kept it together—why you didn't go to pieces."

Thebes considered her for a long moment. He ran his hands over his closely cropped hair, his thumbs skimming his ears. The gray in his hair was creeping up past his temples, toward the crown of his head, like ivy climbing an old brick wall. It had spread since she'd met him, now threatening to consume his scalp. But his cheeks were smooth— the other men had given up on shaving, letting themselves become scruffy and unkempt, but not Thebes. The Thebes of the present was remarkably similar to the Thebes of old— the others had changed, had become diminished and dark and more severe. But Thebes was just as he was when the journey first began. He smiled at her, showing the gap between his front teeth.

"I'm still here because I have nowhere else to go," he said. "I've had a long time to come to terms with that. Understand, I am in pieces just like you, but I keep them separate. I'm not sure how else to explain—one piece at a time. You will learn, I think."

"And if I—if we don't learn?"

"Then you don't." He shrugged. His voice was a smooth, low rumble that harmonized with the hum of the centrifuge, his South African accent round and seamless, syllables falling together in his mouth like a melody. "These things are different for everyone. But I see you learning—you are far away and then suddenly you are here again. Asking me these questions. Do you know what I do? I brush my teeth and think only of brushing my teeth. I replace the air filter and think only of replacing the air filter. I start a conversation with one of the others when I feel lonely, and it helps both of us. This moment, Sully, this is where we must live. We can't help anyone on Earth by thinking about them."

She sighed, dissatisfied.

"Not what you wanted to hear?" he asked, mouth curved in a wistful smile, sadness lurking in the shadows beneath his eyes.

"It's not that. I just—it's hard."

He nodded. "I know," he said. "But you are a scientist. You understand how this works. We study the universe in order to *know*, yet in the end the only thing we truly know is that all things end—all but death and time. It's difficult to be reminded of that"—he patted her hand where it lay on the table—"but it's harder to forget."

〰〰〰

GORDON HARPER HAD been the last crewmember to arrive at the training facility in Houston, a week after the others. He'd had his own separate orientation in Florida, isolated from the crew, conditioned for command. By the time he arrived, the bond between the others was solid. He'd been a commander before, at least half a dozen times, but this was different. Harper joined them halfway through a rigorous morning in their spacesuits in the Neutral Buoyancy Lab, taking turns getting dunked in the pool and practicing EVA repairs on the mock-up of *Aether*. Sully and Devi were underwater when he arrived, and when they surfaced he was already standing with the others, smiling at Tal's jokes, asking Ivanov about an astrogeology article he'd written, greeting his old friend Thebes.

Sully was facing the little knot of *Aether* men while they extracted her, first from the pool and then from the suit, a drawn-out process, and she watched Harper with curiosity and some apprehension. She decided she had a good feeling about him. He seemed to be listening more than he was talking, and the conversation was spread evenly across the men standing with him. All of them were smiling, except Ivanov, which didn't really indicate anything. They seemed to be enjoying themselves. She could tell that Harper was putting them all at ease.

She'd seen pictures of him before, floating on the ISS, or on the tarmac in his orange launch suit, but he was older now, his face more angular, his tan deeper. He was bigger than she'd expected, easily taller than the other three men: an inch or two over Ivanov, a few more over Thebes, with nearly a foot on Tal.

"How is the training so far?" he was asking the other men. "Smooth sailing?"

Ivanov and Thebes nodded, while Tal cracked a joke Sully couldn't quite hear. The four of them laughed and Sully strained against her suit, impatient for the tech assistant to finish unhooking her from the hoist so she could join the circle.

Harper was wearing the bright blue jumpsuit they all wore to training, with a big American flag sewn onto his left shoulder and an even bigger U.S. Air Forces patch over his heart. He had his hands in his pockets, his sleeves pushed up to his elbows. His sandy hair was short, his tan paler around the nape of his neck and his jawline, as though he'd recently had a haircut and a shave, uncovering skin that had been shaded from the sun.

When she was finally freed from her suit, Sully walked over to introduce herself. Despite her impatience to meet him, she felt suddenly shy. She held his blue-gray gaze as long as she could, but she was the first to look away—something in his eyes made her nervous, as if he were seeing beneath her skin, straight into the quickened muscle of her heart thudding inside her rib cage.

"You must be Specialist Sullivan," he said, before she'd had the chance to speak. "It's a great pleasure to serve with you. I can't wait to hear about your plans for the comm. pod."

They shook hands and she noticed the watch strapped to the inside of his wrist. It had an antique gold face and a battered leather band. His hand felt large and warm and dry, his grip firm and gentle at the same time.

"Thank you, Commander," she replied. "It's an honor. Good to meet you."

He released her hand. She'd always found the habit of clasping a watch face to the soft side of the wrist to be somehow intimate, as though by checking the time the wearer was flashing a private piece of themselves: exposing the palm, baring the pulse. After a few moments, a whistle blew and the crew was moved into one of the conference rooms, where Commander Harper was formally introduced. The crew crowded around the long, polished conference table and listened as the director of the space program, a woman named Inger Klaus, who had led the committee that selected the crew for *Aether,* spoke about Harper's qualifications. She spent at least fifteen minutes on his biography, listing honors and accomplishments until Harper was red in the face and everyone in the room longed for her to cede the podium. When she finally did, Harper stepped forward to shake her hand and address the entire crew for the first time. What was it he'd said? Sully struggled to remember. He had notecards, she recalled, and despite the easygoing chatter by the pool, he was nervous. "I'm honored to serve with you all," he declared, "as we step forward into the unknown—as a team, as a species, as individuals."

On *Aether,* even as the communication blackout continued, Harper was the ground, the tether that made his crew feel just a tiny bit closer to Earth. With Devi he requested tutorials on the mechanics of the ship, plying her with questions about life support and radiation shields and the centrifugal gravity of Little Earth, trying to draw her back to the present. He played videogames with Tal and listened diplomatically to Tal's fount of gaming advice, pretending to take the games as seriously as Tal did. Even Ivanov became civil when Harper went into his lab, showing him the work he had been doing and explaining its significance in an only slightly condescending tone. The old friendship with Thebes grew ever deeper; Sully could see him drawing strength from the older man's stoic calm, funneling it into his own body and channeling it back out to the rest of the crew. The two had been in space together before, more than once, and they had always survived. Between them, they were keeping everyone else sane.

With Sully, Harper listened to the probes in the comm. pod or played cards or sketched her profile while she went over Jovian data. He didn't have to work as hard with her; she liked his company. Looked forward to it. They spent hours sitting across from each other at the kitchen table on Little Earth. Sometimes she read to him from dense scientific papers while he exercised, and with sweat glistening on his face he would poke fun at the stilted turns of phrase. She humored him, all the while suspecting that his questions about the research were for her benefit, not his. Sometimes they talked about home, about what they missed, but home was an uncertain and dangerous variable. It was the lead weight that tugged each hopeful feeling back to the cold, dark bottom of their consciousness.

Sully found herself thinking more and more about what Thebes had told her: how to survive as a broken vessel. Tal and Ivanov and Devi had begun to spin out of sync, to exist either in memories or in projections, never fully present when she spoke to them. Sully tried to stop herself from doing the same, tried to brush her teeth and think only of brushing her teeth, to stop reconstructing the house in Vancouver, the smell of Jack's cologne, the sound of Lucy splashing in the bath down the hall while she filled her drawers with clean, poorly folded laundry. When she caught herself dwelling in another year, another place, she counted to ten and discovered herself back on *Aether*, still in the asteroid belt, still en route to the silent Earth. She would put down her notes for the day, turn off the sound on her machines, and propel herself back to the entry node of Little Earth. She would feel the strain of gravity returning to her muscles, the food in her stomach settling to the bottom, the tail of her braid slithering down her back. She would be home, the only home that mattered just then. If she was in luck, Harper would be there, at the table, shuffling a deck of cards.

"C'mere, Sully—this time, you're going down," he would say, and she would sit, and she would play.

FIVE

THE SUN CAME and went so quickly that it was hard for Augustine to tell how long he was laid out. Drifting in and out of dreams, his fever burning red hot, he would wake in the dark and struggle to sit up, thrashing in the tangle of sleeping bags like a fly caught in a web. At other times he opened his eyes to see Iris hovering above him, offering him water or a blue camping mug full of chicken broth— but he couldn't raise his arms to take it, or even command his tongue to form the words that tumbled through his hot, heavy brain: *Come closer* or *How long have I been here?* or *What time is it?* He would close his eyes, and again he would sleep.

In his fevered dreams, he was a young man again. His legs were strong, his eyesight sharp, his hands smooth and tanned, with wide palms and long, straight fingers. His hair was black, and he was clean-shaven, the prick of dark stubble always just beginning to shadow his jawline. His limbs were responsive, fluid and nimble. He was in Hawaii, in Africa, in Australia. He wore a white linen shirt barely buttoned, pressed khakis turned up to his ankles. He was wooing pretty girls in bars, classrooms, observatories, or else he was in the dark, wrapped in an olive field coat, pockets bulging with snacks and gear and pieces of rough quartz or stones with pleasing shapes and colors, looking up into the starry night sky above whichever corner of the earth he was presently passing through. There were palm fronds, eucalyptus trees, fields of sawgrass. White sand next to clear water, yellow mesas punctuated with lonely baobab trees. There were long-legged birds with multicolored wings and curved bills, little gray lizards and big green ones, African wild dogs, dingoes, a stray mutt he used to feed. In his dreams, the world was big and wild and colorful again, and he was part of it. It was a thrill just to exist. There were control rooms full of humming equipment, enormous telescopes, endless arrays. There were beautiful women, college girls and townies and visiting scholars, and he would've slept with them all if he could have.

In his dreams he was a still-young man just beginning to fall in love with himself. He was growing more and more certain that he could, should, have whatever he wanted. He was smart, and ambitious, and destined for greatness. The papers he wrote were being published in the best journals.

There were endless job offers. He was written up in *Time* magazine's "young science" issue. A wave of praise and admiration followed, which he rode into his late thirties. His work was written about with unmistakable reverence. The word *genius* was tossed around. All the observatories wanted him to do his research there, all the universities were begging him to teach. He was in high demand. For a time.

But delirium wasn't his friend. The sun began to fade, the stars to dim, and the clock ran backward: he was an awkward, spotted sixteen-year-old again, in the lobby of a mental hospital, watching two men escort his mother to the locked ward while his father signed forms at the front desk. He was alone with his father in an empty house, hunting in the woods with him, riding in the truck with him, living with his foot poised above a perpetual land mine. He was visiting his overmedicated mother at the hospital before he left for college, listening to her mumble about fixing dinner, her eyes half-closed, hands trembling in her lap. And he was at his father's grave ten years later, spitting on the freshly laid turf, kicking the tombstone until his toe broke. Augustine watched himself from afar in these scenes. He saw his own face, over and over, from behind the eyes of women he'd abused, colleagues he'd cheated, servers and bellhops and assistants and lab techs he'd neglected, slighted, always too busy and ambitious to pay attention to anyone but himself. For the first time he saw the damage he had caused, the hurt and sadness and resentment. He felt shame, and deep inside the husk of his illness he named it.

The warmth and the beauty and the vistas were tantalizing, but they slipped away when he tried to hold on to them. The other, more painful memories were a reckoning in real time. Long minutes and even longer seconds: the feeling of his hunting knife slicing into taut, living deer skin, the pulse of its lifeblood, the metallic stench of it; the sensations of guilt and regret, emotions that in the past he had mistaken for physical ailments, burning deep in his stomach or intestines or lungs; the sound of his father's fist against a wall, against his own body, against his mother's. His mother before she went to the hospital: an unmoving mound beneath her patchwork wedding quilt, day after day, week after week, then watching her rise like a phoenix and burst into the living room, fire in her eyes, ready to *do do do, go go go*. Not stopping until she had spent all she had—energy, money, time, and then collapsing back into the blankets, to remain dormant until she would rise once more, or until her husband dragged her out to test her resolve. Augie was trapped in these moments by his sickness, held captive within the walls of memories he wanted to forget.

-vvvv-

AFTER A TIME—HE couldn't tell how long—the fever passed. The nightmares finally left him, and he became aware that he was awake. Weak but conscious; hungry. Pulling himself to a sitting position, Augustine looked around the control room, rubbing the sleep from the corners of his eyes. The room was unchanged. He swiveled his head and let out a short sigh of relief when his eyes found her. Iris was sitting on the windowsill, looking out onto the twilit tundra. When she heard him getting up and kicking off the heap of sleeping bags, she turned. He realized that he had never seen her smile before. One of her bottom teeth was missing, and he could see the pink wrinkle of her gums showing through the gap. A dimple lingered on her left cheek and a flush crept across the bridge of her tiny nose.

"You look terrible," she said. "I'm glad you're awake."

It was still rare to hear her voice, and it again surprised him with its deepness, its scratchiness. He was relieved to hear it. She circled the nest of sleeping bags like a wary animal, tempering her excitement, surveying all the details before she moved closer. She produced a vacuum-packed serving of jerky, a can of green beans, and a spoon, and held them out to Augie.

"Do you want broth also?" she asked as he took the food. He peeled back the tab on the green beans and began scooping them into his mouth. She ripped open the jerky package with her teeth and set it down beside him, then went to heat the electric kettle. He was ravenous, and suddenly alive again. After the can was emptied he turned his attention to the jerky, wiping bean juice from his beard with the back of his hand.

"How long was I out?" he asked.

Iris shrugged. "Five days, maybe?"

He nodded. It seemed about right. "And you . . . you're okay?"

She looked at him strangely and turned back to the kettle without answering, unwrapping the foil from a bouillon cube and dropping it into the blue mug while she waited for the water to boil. The mug was too hot to hold, so she let it cool on the countertop and returned to her perch on the windowsill, silent once more, looking out over the darkening tundra.

～～～

AUGUSTINE BEGAN TO test his atrophied muscles on the stairs of the control tower. When he could trudge down to the first floor and back up to the third without collapsing, he decided it was time to go farther afield. Navigating the snow and ice outside tired him even faster than the stairs, but he went out every day, sometimes more than once. After a while, his endurance returned. He would walk down the narrow path cut into the mountain, through the abandoned village of outbuildings, and out onto the open, rolling mountains. He was winded and weak, but alive, and the joy of that simple fact flooded his tired old body. Both the joy of survival and the weight of regret were unfamiliar to him, but neither would let him go, as hard as he tried to sweat them out. The feelings from his fevered nightmares still remained vivid. His muscles ached from exercise, but also from the unfamiliar emotions that coursed through him, like someone else's blood running through his veins.

On these walks Iris often tagged along, either running in front of him or lagging behind. The snatches of daylight lengthened from barely an hour, to a few hours, to a whole afternoon. As the days progressed Augustine began to walk farther, always keeping the emerald green of Iris's pompom hat in his sights. She seemed different since his fever, as though there was more of her—more energy, more physicality, more words. Before, she had hung back in his peripheral vision, sitting aloof in the control room, wandering stealthily among the outbuildings, always elusive. Now, Augie couldn't seem to take his eyes off her. She was everywhere, and her smile—still rare but somehow always hinted at just beneath the curve of her cheeks—was glorious.

One day, when the sun had been hanging low in the sky for several hours before it began to sink, Augustine went farther than he had been able to go since the hangar— since the fever. Now he always went north, over the mountains. Never south, toward the tundra and the hangar and the wolf's mounded grave, marked with veins of pink blood running through the white. To the north, the Arctic Sea stretched up over the top of the globe, an icy blue cap covering Earth's cranium. The shore was miles away, a distance he could never hope to cross on foot, but he imagined that when the wind was blowing in the right direction he could smell the crisp salt air from the unfrozen sea, rolling up over the glaciers and traveling to his keen, searching nostrils. He decided that the farther he walked, the stronger the brackish smell became.

That day, they'd already been walking long enough that his muscles burned and even Iris had slowed her gait, dragging her little boots through the snow instead of lifting them with each step, but Augustine wanted to go farther. There was something ahead, he told himself, something he must see. He didn't know what. The sun slipped behind the mountains, sending shots of color into the sky like a dancer throwing silk scarves in the air. He was admiring the sunset melting into the snow when he saw it: the solid outline of an animal against the changeable northern sky. It was the polar bear he remembered from the first day of sunlight— the same bear, he was sure of it, not because he could see any distinct features but because he recognized it by the quickening of his heartbeat. It was so big it had to be a bear, with long, shaggy fur, a deep, aging yellow. Augie was at least a mile away, perhaps several, but he saw these details with telescopic clarity. This was what he'd been searching for. It was as though he were standing next to the bear, or as though he were riding high on its massive, arched back, his fingers dug deep into the matted fur, heels locked around the wide, padded rib cage. He could feel the thick fur between his knuckles, see the yellow tint of it, the pink stains on its muzzle, and smell the musky, rotten odor of old blood.

The bear stopped at the top of the peak and raised its snout. It swiveled its head one way and then the other, finally turning to look in Augie's direction. Iris was skidding down a small slope on the seat of her snow pants, green pompom bouncing as she went, unaware of what Augustine was seeing. Augie and the bear looked at each other, and across the miles of snow and jagged rock and buffeting wind that separated them Augustine felt a strange kinship travel between them. He envied the bear its immensity, its simple needs and clear purpose, but across the vista a whiff of loneliness swirled, too, a feeling of longing and doom. He felt a piercing sadness for the bear, all alone on the mountain range—a creature consumed with the mechanics of sustenance, the killing and gnawing, rolling in the snow, the necessary bouts of sleep among the drifts and in the snow caves, the long walks to and from the sea. That was all it had, all it knew, all it needed. An emotion stirred in his stomach and Augustine realized it was discontent—for the bear, but also for himself. He'd lived through his fever, but for what? He looked down the slope in front of him in time to see Iris barrel-roll to a stop and sit up, her green pompom dusted with white. She was waving up at him, smiling—a child at play. The usual pallor of her face was lit from within, a pink glow flooding her white skin. When Augie looked back to the mountain range, the bear was gone.

"Iris," he called, "time to go back." On their way home, Iris stayed close, by his side or right in front of him, looking back to check on his progress from time to time. In the last stretch, as they climbed the path up the mountain to the observatory, to their home in the control tower, she took his mittened hand in hers and held it till they were inside.

~~~~

IN THE BEGINNING, Augie had felt it fitting that his life should end so quietly, so simply: just his mind, his failing body, the brutal landscape. Even before the exodus of the other researchers, before the eerie silence and the presumed cataclysm—even before all of that, he had come here to die. In the weeks before his arrival, when he was still planning his Arctic research from a warm beach in the South Pacific, he'd considered the project to be his last. A finale, the capstone of a career, a bold conclusion for the biographer who would someday write a book about him. For Augustine, the end of his work was inextricable from the end of his life. Perhaps his heart would beat for a few more empty years after the work was done, or perhaps not; it didn't trouble him to think of it. So long as his legacy burned bright in science's archives, he was content to flicker and die alone, a few degrees shy of the North Pole. In a way, the evacuation only made it easier. But something happened to him when he looked across the Arctic mountains and saw the great yellow polar bear looking back at him. He thought of Iris. He felt gratitude for a presence instead of an absence. The feeling was so unfamiliar, so unexpected, it moved something inside him, something old and heavy and stubborn. In its wake there was an opening.

In the early days with Iris at the observatory, he had idly wondered what would become of her when he died. But following the bear sighting, as the sun hung in the sky longer and longer, he began to consider it more carefully. Augie began to think beyond his own timeline and into hers. He wanted something different for her—connection, love, community. He didn't want to go on making excuses for his inability to give her anything but the same emptiness he'd given himself.

After the other scientists had evacuated, he'd made half-hearted attempts to contact the theoretical remnants of humankind, to find out what had happened out there beyond the icy borders of his reach, but once he'd realized the satellites were silent and the commercial radio stations had gone off the air, he'd abandoned the search. He got comfortable with the idea that there was no one left to contact. That something, everything, had ended. He wasn't troubled by the physical reality of being marooned—that had always been his plan.

But things had changed since then. He was suddenly burning with determination to find another voice. The probability of survivors had always been in the back of his mind, but even if he had cared enough to search them out, the remoteness of the observatory made such contact logistically useless. Assuming he could locate a leftover pocket of humanity, there would be no way to get there. And yet—it was suddenly the connection itself that was important. He knew the odds—in all likelihood his search would yield nothing, or as good as nothing. He knew they weren't going to be rescued, or discovered. Even so, he was fueled by this new feeling, this unfamiliar sense of duty, this determination to find another voice. He abandoned the telescope and turned his attention to the radio waves.

~~~

As a boy, eleven or twelve or so, Augustine knew the radio bands better than he knew his own body. He cobbled together crystal sets out of wire and screws and semiconductor diodes and quickly tackled more-complex projects—transmitters, receivers, decoders. He built radios with vacuum tubes and with transistors, analog and digital, from kits, from scratch, from scavenged appliances. He constructed big antennas, dipoles in the backyard, delta boxes hoisted up into the trees—whatever he could forage the parts for. It took up all of his free time. Eventually Augie's interest caught the attention of his father, and this new intimacy was a surprise to them both. His father was a mechanic, not for cars but for car factories. The machinery he spent his time on during the day was enormous, bigger than houses, and so when his son began to tinker with the tiniest of mechanisms, the boy piqued his curiosity. Before he built radios, Augie had been his mother's son, stirrer of batter, peeler of potatoes, escort to the hair salon. He'd do his homework at the kitchen counter when she was well enough to cook, or in her bedroom, curled at the end of the bed like a dog, when she wasn't. He was her mascot, a little boy easily molded to fit any of her moods. Even as a child, Augustine sensed, without knowing why, that his father hated their rapport.

He felt the shift of his mother's moods keenly. He could sense the darkness descending before she did. He knew when to let her wallow in her dim bedroom and when to lift the blinds; he knew how to coax her back home when things got out of hand during one of their errands. He managed her with such subtle skill that she never suspected manipulation, never saw him as anything more than her little boy, her trusted friend, her constant companion. No one else could soothe her the way he could, especially not his father. Augie engineered his mother's moods out of necessity. Reining her in was the only way he could protect her, and as he got better and better at it he began to think he had decoded her affliction, that he had bested it—that he had fixed her.

The winter he turned eleven she went to bed and didn't get up until spring. That was the winter he realized she was a puzzle he'd never be able to solve, that despite all his efforts and skill, she was beyond his understanding. He was alone, all of a sudden, and lonely. He didn't know what to do without her. While his father berated the inanimate mound of her fetal form beneath the bedspread, Augustine retreated to the basement and found a new pleasure in the clarity of electronics: the joining of wires, the flow of current, the simple mechanisms that fit together and made something so wonderful it bordered on magic, plucking a symphony of music and voices from thin air. The basic lessons he received in school on amps and watts and waves were all it took to give him a running start. He'd always been a good student. In the dark, musty cellar, in a circular pool of yellow light, he taught himself the rest. On rare occasions, Augustine's father descended the crumbling wooden steps and sat with his son, and on even rarer occasions, Augustine enjoyed these visits. More often than not, his father came to chide him, to show him his errors, to gloat over his failures. By then it was clear to everyone in their household that Augie had no ordinary intellect, and his father was sure to punish him for it every chance he got.

Now, years later, in the cold Arctic, Augustine remembered that basement as clearly as if he were still sitting down there, alone at his work table with the spools of wire, germanium transistors, rudimentary amps, oscillators, mixers, filters laid out before him. The soldering iron at his right elbow, plugged in and already warm, the schematics for his latest endeavor to his left: a smudged pencil sketch, little arrows and clumsy symbols to remind himself of the current's flow. His father wasn't welcome in these memories, but his voice intruded from time to time:

"What kind of an idiot can't fix a transistor?"

"This looks like a two-year-old made it."

At the observatory, in the control room, Augie double-checked the satellite phones and the broadband network to be sure he hadn't overlooked something. Communication from the outpost had always been haphazard, mostly reliant on satellites, but without the satphone or broadband working, with no satellite connection to speak of, there was only ham radio. He hunted through the control tower and the outbuildings for anything that might be useful, but there wasn't much. The equipment was there only for backup. The system in place was less than ideal, barely powerful enough to talk to the military base on the northern tip of the island, mostly used for communication with planes passing over. The power supply was weak and the antenna sensitivity even weaker; a signal would have to be very close, very powerful, or riding a lucky sky-wave to register. Assuming there was anyone out there to hear it in the first place.

It reminded him of his years in the basement, turning his machines on and transmitting the first CQ of the day. Simple, straightforward, with a single purpose. He was seeking anyone, it didn't matter who. He'd collected QSL postcards—confirmations of radio communication between two ham operators—from his various contacts and filed them away. There were earnest cards with call signs scrawled over an outline of the operator's home state, silly cards with cartoon sketches of the operators hanging from their antennae like monkeys or wet laundry, dirty cards with busty, half-naked women draped over radio equipment and murmuring into a handheld microphone. Augustine would sit down at his microphone in the basement and scan the empty ham frequencies, issuing his call as he moved through the dial, and whether it took him a minute or a few hours, someone would eventually respond to him.

A voice would fill his speakers and say, "KB1ZFI, this is so-and-so responding." They would exchange locations and Augie would add up the miles on the atlas he kept nearby—the more distant the contact, the better. The QSL cards were just for fun—it was the contact itself that thrilled him most, the idea that he could send his signal out across the country, across the world, and make an immediate connection some-where, anywhere. There was always someone at the other end—someone he didn't know, someone he couldn't picture and would never meet, but a voice all the same. He didn't bother chatting over the airwaves after the initial contact. He just reached out to see if someone was there, and he was satisfied once he knew there was. After the initial con-nection had been made, he might go for two, three, half a dozen if the weather conditions were prime and the sig-nals were traveling far. When he was finished with his CQs he'd turn off his equipment, address a few QSL cards of his own—a simple globe with a signal shooting off into space, scattered stars and his own call sign in block letters at the top—and then tinker with the electronics in the quiet soli-tude of the basement. These were his happiest moments as a child. Alone, without the cruelty of the other kids at school, without the volatility of his mother, without the belittling comments of his father. Just him, his equipment, and the hum of his own mind.

In the Arctic, he fine-tuned the equipment, and when he was finally satisfied he turned it all on. Iris had been watching him work with vague curiosity but didn't say anything. She was outside wandering among the outbuildings when he began transmitting. Augie could see her from the window, her small shape dark against the snow. He picked up the handheld microphone, pressed the Transmit button, then let it go. He cleared his throat; pressed it again.

"CQ," he said, "CQ, this is KB1ZFI, kilo-bravo-one-zulu-foxtrot-india, over. CQ. Anyone?"

SIX

SULLY DRIFTED THROUGH the comm. pod from one machine to the next. She kept her knees slightly bent, her ankles tucked around each other, and used her arms to propel her, like a swimmer. Her braid floated out behind her and the empty arms of her jumpsuit, tied at her waist, hovered in front of her stomach like extra limbs. *Aether* had traveled far enough into the belt that a lag in the transfer of data from the Jovian probes had developed. The information from Jupiter's system was already old by the time it arrived in Sully's receivers, and it got older each day as they moved a little farther away from Jupiter and a little closer to Earth. Lately she'd been neglecting her probes and scanning the radio frequencies of home instead. She swept the entire communication spectrum again and again, no longer content to monitor the designated DSN bands. There should be some noise pollution: satellite chatter, errant TV signals, very high or ultra high frequency transmissions that slipped through the ionosphere and out into space. There should be *something*, she thought. The silence was an anomaly, a result that shouldn't, couldn't, be correct.

Sully kept it to herself. There wasn't much use in sharing empty sine waves with the rest of them, just confirmation of the same bad news, but at least the act of scanning helped her through the days, helped her to feel she was doing something. One way or another, the closer they got, the more she knew. It's strange, she thought, how pointless the Jovian probes seemed now. She would trade them all, every byte of data they'd collected, every single thing they'd learned, for just one voice coming into her receiver. Just one. This wasn't wistful bargaining, or hyperbole, just a fact. She had boarded *Aether* believing that nothing could be more important than the Jovian probes, and now—everything was more important. The whole purpose of their mission seemed insignificant, pointless. Day by day, there was nothing except the digital binary of mechanical wanderers and the cosmic rays from the stars and their planets.

Sully propelled herself back to Little Earth, floating through the twists and turns of the spacecraft: seemingly empty stretches padded with storage and electronics, *Aether*'s organs secreted behind her light gray tunnels. As Sully drifted headfirst down the greenhouse corridor, where the walls were lined with grow boxes for aeroponic vegetables, she untied the sleeves of her jumpsuit from her waist and shrugged into the top half. Approaching the entry node, she reached up and caught one of the rungs studding the padded walls, then flipped herself around to enter the node that connected the rest of the craft to Little Earth feetfirst. She dropped through a short tunnel, gravity gaining on her as she moved, and was deposited on the centrifuge's landing pad with a thump, right between the couch and the exercise equipment. Sully's feet were grabbed by the ground as if there were suction cups on the soles of her shoes, and she paused while her body recalibrated and found its balance. She zipped up the front of her suit and untucked her braid, which fell heavily on her shoulder like a length of rope. The centrifugal gravity made her feel instantly exhausted, as though she'd been running for hours, awake for days. As soon as she trusted her legs she walked over to the sofa and sat down next to Tal, disguising her fatigue by watching him finish a first-person shooter game. The two-year journey was taking its toll—she could feel her muscles weakening, her health waning. She'd been in the best physical shape of her life when they left, but not anymore. For a moment she wondered what it would be like reacclimating to Earth's twenty-four-hour gravity, and then she cut the thought short. No point thinking about it now. Tal tossed the controller onto the floor and turned to her.

"Wanna play something?" he asked.

She shook her head. "I don't think so," she said. "Maybe later."

He sighed and waved her off, quickly distracted again by the glow of the screen. Sully got up and walked along the slope of the ring, through the kitchen area, to where Thebes and Harper sat reading, Harper on his tablet, Thebes with another one of the paperback books he had insisted on bringing—Asimov this time—despite the initial uproar over the amount of space they would take up. It wasn't that much space, Thebes had argued, and because Thebes never argued about anything, the mission's oversight committee stepped in and overrode the naysayers. The committee wrote off the extra cargo as psychologically necessary equipment. The crew had laughed about it at the time, but now, watching Thebes turn the page, Sully wondered about that phrase. *Psychologically necessary equipment.* The human mind had never been tested quite like this. Could they have been better prepared? Trained more extensively? What tools would help them now? It seemed ridiculous, but perhaps these books, sheaves of paper made from trees that had once grown on their home planet, full of made-up stories, were what kept Thebes so much more grounded than the rest of them.

Thebes and Harper both looked up as she slid onto the bench. "How is the comm. department faring?" Thebes asked.

She shrugged. "Fine," she said. "Did you guys eat on schedule?"

They nodded. "I saved you some," Harper said. "Would've radioed over that we were starting, but I figured you were wrapped up in something."

Sully found the plate waiting for her on the range, a few strips of test tube beef, aeroponic kale, and a puddle of freeze-dried mashed potatoes. She couldn't help but smile when she saw the dinner, carefully arranged on the plate, a few notches above the usual fare. "Wow, classy," she said, bringing the plate back to the table. Thebes jerked his thumb toward Harper.

"All him," he said. "The commander's showing off tonight."

Sully scooped up a forkful of mashed potato and speared a leaf of kale. "It shows."

"Shucks." Harper pretended to be embarrassed, or maybe he actually was—she couldn't tell. He put down his tablet and raised his voice a little so Tal could hear him. "Anyone up for a round of cards?"

He was looking at Sully as he spoke—he knew she was the only one who would play. Tal declined, as did Thebes, and a muffled "No, thank you" came from inside Devi's curtained bunk. "Whaddaya say, Sullivan?" Harper persisted.

"Yes, but in a minute," she said, thinking of Devi's listless reply. Sully walked to Devi's bunk and rapped her knuckles on the side of the compartment. "Hey, can I come in?" She slipped inside without waiting for an invitation. Behind the curtain Devi lay curled around one of her pillows, holding it tightly against her chest, her nose buried in the top, her thighs locked on either side.

"Sure," Devi whispered, belatedly, but she didn't move.

"What did you do today?" Sully asked, sitting on the bed. Devi shrugged but said nothing. "Have you eaten anything?"

"Yeah," she said, without elaborating. Then, after a minute: "Tell me something."

Sully waited, but Devi was silent. That was it. *Tell me something.* Sully flopped onto her back and tucked her arms under her head, searching for something to tell. What was worth saying? After a moment she remembered passing through the greenhouse corridor that morning, and the day's thoughts came tumbling out—an edited version, without any mention of Earth.

"You know that yellow tomato plant that hasn't been yielding? I noticed a few flowers on it today, might do something yet. And Tal says we're nearly through the asteroid belt, a few more weeks maybe." Sully walked her feet up to the ceiling of Devi's bunk and looked at her toes, shod in the rubber slip-ons they'd all been issued. They seemed strange from this angle, like alien hooves. She let her legs flop back down onto the bed.

"The Jovian probes are all still transmitting, but there's so much data coming in sometimes I feel like I don't have the heart to catalog it all. It's hard to care." She paused, suddenly afraid she'd veered into dangerous territory, but Devi didn't say anything. Sully continued in a different direction, her voice low and confidential. "I ran into Ivanov coming out of the lavatory today, literally ran into him. He was a jerk about it—like it's my fault this ship is so fucking small, you know? Like he would be so much better off without us, all alone out here, taking his shitty mood out on his rock samples."

That worked. Devi turned over at least, and gave her a half smile. "He would never be angry at his rock samples," she whispered.

They both laughed quietly, but the smile that flashed across Devi's lips shriveled and died away almost immediately.

"I think he's unkind because it's easier to be angry than frightened," Devi said. She paused, then pulled the pillow tighter against her chest. "I'm really tired, okay? Thanks for saying hi, though."

Sully nodded. "Let me know if you need anything," she

said, and wriggled back out of the bunk. Harper was waiting for her at the table, shuffling a deck of cards, score sheet at hand.

"Ready?" he asked.

"Well, I'm ready to kick someone's ass," she joked. It felt hollow and forced after seeing Devi so low. "Might as well be yours." Her plate was still half-full of dinner, which had been lukewarm to start with and had now grown cold. She didn't mind, folding a leafy bite of kale into her mouth and wiping a smear of olive oil from her face. They played rummy, as always. Sully won the first hand, then the second. An hour later, Thebes wished them good night and retired to his bunk. Harper dealt a third hand, and when he laid down the deck and flipped over the ace of spades, Sully was reminded of learning to play solitaire when she was a little girl. The silver centrifuge of Little Earth melted away, and for just a second she was looking at her mother's delicate, tapered fingers snapping down cards onto her imitation wood desk deep in the Mojave Desert.

Her mother had taught her one afternoon when she was about eight years old, when Jean worked long hours at the Deep Space Network's Goldstone facility. The two of them, mother and daughter, lived in the desert. It was a boiling hot afternoon, and Jean—Sully had always called her mother by her first name—was stuck in signal processing meetings all afternoon. With no one to take care of Sully and no one to take her home, Jean borrowed a deck of cards from one of the interns. Between meetings, she took Sully into her office, barely more than a cubicle, really, sat her down and showed her how to lay the cards out. Sully fiddled with her mother's plastic nameplate, *Jean Sullivan, PhD,* and pretended to pay close attention.

"So then it goes black on red, red on black, in order, until you can get all the suits sorted onto the aces. Understand, little bear?"

Sully had, in fact, known all along how to play. She'd learned from a babysitter. But when Jean asked if she wanted to learn she'd nodded vigorously. It was, if nothing else, a chance to earn an extra five minutes of her mother's time. Sully didn't mind being stuck at her mother's office, she was used to it by now. As far as she was concerned, the closer she could be to Jean, the better. It had always been just the two of them, which was how Sully liked it. Sully didn't question the absence of a father—she had nothing to compare it to.

Harper picked up his hand and automatically she picked up hers, too, then stared at it for a few minutes before seeing the run she already had: nine, ten, jack of hearts. She laid it down in a fan, drew, then discarded, covering up the offending black ace with a three. She looked at Harper over the top of her cards and met his eyes, which were already on her. Deep lines punctuated his face, and she tried to read them like a sentence. Three crooked dashes above his eyebrows, parentheses around his mouth, half a dozen hyphens traveling outward from the corners of his eyes, like the rays of a sun. A thin white scar running through one sandy eyebrow and another on his chin, cutting through the stubble.

"What are you thinking right now?" Harper asked, and the question startled her with its intimacy. It was the kind of question a lover might ask. She felt suddenly exposed and blinked back an unexpected film of moisture from her eyes, tears she was unwilling to shed in another person's presence. She waited until her throat unclenched and she could be sure the timbre of her voice wouldn't give her away before she answered.

"I was just thinking about Goldstone," she said. "About when I lived there as a kid. My mother worked in the signal processing center."

Harper kept looking at her. His eyes were a pale, steely blue. "Like mother, like daughter," he said. It was his turn, but he didn't draw. He was waiting for her to continue.

"She taught me solitaire one summer. I already knew how to play, but I wanted the attention, so I let her teach me again." Sully arranged, then rearranged her cards. "It's funny, I would've killed for a few minutes of her attention. She was all work back then. Before she got married and had two more kids and stopped working entirely. But by then I was older and the twins were more interesting and . . . I don't know. I guess I didn't need her as much anymore, and she didn't need me, either."

Harper slowly took a card, glanced at it, and laid it back down.

"How old were you?" he asked.

"I was ten when she got married and my stepfather moved us back to Canada, where she was from. He was her high school sweetheart, before she left for grad school and ended up at Goldstone with me. I don't know, I think she just gave up at a certain point, like she expected everything to get easier, as I got older, as she found firmer ground at the DSN. Instead it got harder. She couldn't catch a break. And there was this guy, my stepdad, this perfectly nice guy waiting in the wings, still pining after all that time, calling, writing letters. Finally she just . . . gave up. Quit her job. Went north. Married him, finally. The twins showed up really fast after that; I was eleven when they were born, I think."

The dashes in Harper's forehead fluttered and drew up

toward his hairline. She stared at her cards so she didn't have to see his look of sympathy. *Stop talking*, she reprimanded herself. It all sounded so simple out loud—an ordinary childhood, marriage and babies—but Sully was still thinking of leaving Goldstone behind for the cold loneliness of Canada. Of losing her beloved, brilliant mother to two screaming infants. Of gaining a stepfather who was kind but distant, decent but uninterested—not cruel enough to be hated, not loving enough to be loved. She remembered the telescope she and Jean used to take out into the desert in the back of their rusty green El Camino, just the two of them. They would drive with the windows down and Jean's long hair would fill the cab, a dark tornado whipping against the sagging upholstery on the roof, reaching for the open window, trying to touch the cool, dry night.

They would set up the telescope, spread out a blanket, and stay there for hours. Jean would show her the planets, the constellations, clusters of stars, clouds of gas. Every once in a while, the ISS would spin into view, a bright, quick light. There and then gone, spinning over some other part of the world. The next day Sully would arrive at school tired but content. Her mother was showing her the universe, and school was so easy she could sleepwalk through her classes. In Canada, when her mother was married and pregnant and then consumed by the twins, Sully hauled the telescope outside by herself, onto the icy second-floor deck crowded by pine trees, their needled boughs swinging over the wooden platform and blocking her view of the horizon. The stars didn't seem quite as clear without her mother beside her, but still the constellations comforted her. Even in the cold loneliness of this new place, she could find the map she'd grown up learning to decipher—a different latitude, but the same points of reference. Even there she could see Polaris, burning above the feathery tips of the tall pines.

"Anyway," Sully said, but had nothing to change the subject to. Harper put down a run and discarded. "Did you—do you have brothers and sisters?" she asked, trying to fill the silence and to even the exchange of personal information, as if they were keeping score: one point for every revelation extracted.

"Yeah," he said, but slowly, as if he weren't sure. For a moment it seemed he wasn't going to say anything more. "Two brothers, one sister." Sully waited, and after a few more rounds of drawing and discarding, Harper finally went on.

"Both of my brothers are dead, but it's too weird not to count them—one of them overdosed a few years ago and the other drowned when we were teenagers. My sister lives in Missoula with her family. Cute kids, two girls. Her husband's a real shithead." He snapped a run down onto the table with a mischievous grin. "You're in trouble now, Specialist," he said, even though she was clearly winning. She shook her head at him.

"Keep dreaming, Harper," she said. She considered asking Harper who was the oldest sibling, but she didn't really need to. She knew that he was without having to be told. It was the way he guided his crew, the way he nudged them along like delinquent ducklings wandering away from the group. The older brother who'd lost two of his younger siblings already. She couldn't imagine him at the back of a crowd, and certainly not in the middle—he would always be in front, always leading, protecting those who came behind.

Sully thought of her brief and beautiful life as an only child. The taste of desert grit on her tongue, the pinpoints of light against the velvety black night. She knew that if she closed her eyes she could be there, lost in memory, lying next to her mother, tracing Ursa Minor, the first constellation she'd learned to find, their heads propped against the back tire of the El Camino—but she didn't. She kept them open, trained on the man across from her, anchoring herself with the texture of his face, his neck, his hands. Gray had infiltrated Harper's sandy hair, blending into the neutral tone like silver shadows. His hair had grown unkempt since the last trim, which Tal had given him months ago, when they were passing through Mars's orbit. It stood up from his head in lopsided tufts, as if he'd just gotten out of bed. There was one emphatic curl that bobbed when he moved. Sully remembered the way her own daughter's hair had done something similar when she was very small. It was almost impossible not to fall backward, to lose herself thinking of what she'd probably never see again.

The hand ended, and as they counted their cards Harper eked out a narrow victory. He looked relieved. "Phew," he said. "I thought if I lost one more time I'd have to show some modesty. Not the case."

He swept the cards into a heap and began tapping the deck together, squaring the edges. "Another?" he asked.

She shrugged. "Maybe just one more."

She watched him deal. With his sleeves pushed up above his elbows she could see the thick blond hair that lined his forearms and the sturdy knobs of his wrists. He was wearing his watch, the same one he'd been wearing the day she met him, the same one he always wore, with the watch face nestled against his pulse, the clasp facing out. His hands were broad, the skin on his palms and the pads of his fingers tough, his fingernails cut close to the quick. Sully wondered who he missed, what he'd left behind. Who he thought about in these idle moments. A friend, a lover, a mentor? She knew his résumé by heart, as she did everyone's, but knowing that he got his PhD in aeronautics and astronautics after two tours in the Air Force wasn't the same as knowing him—knowing whether he'd admired his father, or how many times he'd been in love, or what he'd dreamed about when he watched the Montana sunsets as a teenager. She knew that he'd traveled through the earth's atmosphere and back more times than any other human being in history, that he could cook better than she could, that he was terrible at rummy, okay at euchre, and almost good at poker. But she didn't know what he wrote about when he scribbled in his spiral-bound journal, or who he thought about as he fell asleep.

She imagined answers for him instead of asking: He'd loved his father very much, and had been missing him since his death with a yearning he'd never felt before. His mother was still alive, but it wasn't the same with her. He'd been in love a few times—once as a teenager, and it had burned hot and steady until it went out like a light, then again in his late twenties, when he asked a woman to marry him. She'd said yes and then slept with one of his colleagues, leaving him heartbroken and careful.

The third time was written all over his face, but Sully couldn't see it.

Instead, out of all the other questions spinning through her head, Sully picked, "What do you miss the most about home?"

She arranged her cards in her hand without looking to see what she was holding. Instead, she kept her eyes on his face, the jump in his jaw as he clenched his teeth together, the wistful shrug of his mouth.

"My dog, Bess," Harper said. "She's a chocolate lab, had her for eight years and her mother before that. It's stupid, but I miss her like hell. I leave her with my neighbor—he loves her almost as much as I do. I never did get on with humans as well as I got on with ol' Bess."

Halfway around the centrifuge they heard Tal turn off the gaming console, shuffle into the lavatory and then out again. He gave Sully and Harper a solemn, sleepy nod before he climbed into his bunk and drew the curtain.

"What about you?" Harper asked.

"My daughter, Lucy. Also hot baths."

He laughed. "I think I'd go with mountains over a bath. Or big, empty fields." He lowered his voice and said in a dramatic whisper, "I'd push Ivanov out the airlock if I could walk through a field for five lousy minutes."

Sully chuckled under her breath. When Ivanov dropped in through the entry node a few seconds later, with uncanny timing, she imploded with laughter. She hid her face behind her hands as Ivanov walked past and strode along the ring. There was a sullen stare already fixed on his face, and he went to bed without saying a word to them. Harper gave Sully a stern look.

"Get it together, Sullivan."

She nodded, her lips pressed together against any further eruptions. She suddenly remembered what Devi had said, about Ivanov being frightened, and the laughter left her completely. She wondered if she sometimes mistook sadness for sullenness. If he was more vulnerable than she realized. Ivanov's light went off behind his curtain.

"What about the husband?" Harper asked, drawing a card.

"Ex," she corrected, and was going to add something, but realized there was nothing she could say about him that would make sense. Jack was a minefield, planted with resentment and deadly shards of joy. No sooner had she alighted on a bright, comforting memory—Jack asleep on the couch with a two-year-old Lucy facedown on his chest, the two of them snoring in concert—than she was blown back by the unexpected detonation of a deeply buried bitterness a few inches away. Lucy had stopped falling asleep with Sully when she was eight months old. She changed the subject.

"I can just see you galloping around on some big piece of land in Montana, on your black stallion or whatever, ol' Bess running alongside. You know, I always wondered . . . why are you still hanging out with all these geeky scientists? You broke the damn record—retire already."

He smiled. "I guess I always think, just one more ride, you know? One more, then I'm done. Then they'll ask me to do another one and I'll think, what the hell. You are pretty geeky, though. If I had realized what I was getting into this time around I might have stayed home."

Sully let her jaw hang slack in mock horror. "I can't *believe* you!"

"I know, I know, outrageous. But I'm definitely retiring after this one—promise. I've got the land all squared away. You're gonna visit me and Bess when we get home, right?"

When we get home. The words hung in the stagnant, recycled air. Sully let them drift away and played along with the fantasy of the invitation.

"I suppose I will," she said. It was a nice thought. She'd never seen Harper's house, but she pictured something small, off the beaten path, with a big front porch and a long driveway, surrounded by acres and acres of empty space. There was his muddy truck parked in the driveway and Bess sitting tall by the front door, waiting for her. In her imagination this became her home, too. In reality, she didn't have a home anymore, she'd left her things in storage and given up her apartment for the two-year trip. It felt good to pretend she had somewhere—someone—to return to. She caught Harper looking at her.

"What?" she said.

"Nothing," he replied, "just wondering."

"Wondering what?"

He shook his head. "I'll ask you when we land."

"You're kidding."

"Not kidding. I need something to look forward to." He winked at her. "We all need something to look forward to."

They passed another hour playing. "It's getting late," Harper said.

Sully began to put the cards away. He held out his hand and said "Good game," in that half-chivalrous, half-wisecracking way of his. She took it, but instead of shaking they just held hands for a moment. She felt the pressure of his grip, the scratch of his callused palms, the dry heat of his skin against hers. The moment passed and he didn't let go; neither did she. He looked down at her and suddenly she was terrified—of what, she wasn't sure. She flipped his hand over to look at the watch on the inside of his wrist.

"I should go to bed," Sully said, and let go. "Sleep well."

She climbed into her bunk without looking back at him, knowing that if she did, he would still be watching her. She shut the curtain and sat hugging her legs to her chest, her forehead resting on her knees as she listened to him moving through the centrifuge, brushing his teeth, switching off the light in his bunk. *When we get home.*

-ᴧᴧᴧ-

THE NEXT MORNING, Sully didn't rouse herself until hours after the alarm buzzed. The lights were at full strength beyond her curtain. The rustling of the others entering and exiting the lavatory, opening and closing their curtains, shuffling around the centrifuge in their rubber slip-ons, made it impossible for her to go back to sleep, though she would have liked to. She could have slept all day, she was so tired lately. After running a brush through her hair she began to braid it, and her arms were aching by the time she finished. She felt weak, as though she were ending the day instead of beginning it.

Everyone had retreated to a separate corner of the ship. There was only Tal left on Little Earth, looking at a radar tablet showing the local activity in the asteroid belt. The belt was in fact sparsely populated, millions of asteroids spread out across such an incredible distance that they'd be lucky to see even one on their way through. Their passage through the belt had been scheduled around a particularly inactive window, a Kirkwood gap, when all the larger asteroids were swept up into the orbital resonance created by Jupiter's massive gravity. The chances of colliding with an asteroid were infinitesimal, but it was Tal's job to make sure they didn't beat the odds.

"Clear skies?" Sully asked as she took a protein bar from a cabinet in the kitchen area.

"The clearest," Tal said, looking up from the smudged tablet screen. "Nothing but dust and pebbles for a couple thousand miles."

Sully peeled back the wrapper from the bar like the skin of a banana and leaned over Tal's shoulder. "I'd hate to get creamed by Ceres."

Tal snorted. "Yeah, me too. But—not to worry, I'll keep an eye on things. Anyway, I think we're two weeks or so away from Mars's orbit—so, getting there."

She put a hand on his shoulder for a moment and then left Little Earth, climbing up the exit node's ladder, her protein bar clamped between her teeth. After a few rungs she felt the weight slip from her body and she let go, kicking off to float the rest of the way. A few crumbs detached from the bar and drifted in front of her. She snapped them up like a hungry fish and propelled herself down the greenhouse corridor. She grabbed an overhead rung to stop herself in front of one of the tomato plants, where she rubbed a few leaves between her fingers, releasing the smell into the air, and then checked the late bloomer she had told Devi about yesterday. She noticed that the little flowers were gone, replaced by tiny green nubs, and she immediately began looking forward to sharing her observation with Devi—looking forward to anything had become so rare. She continued past the entry to Ivanov's lab, where all the rock samples were being categorized. Through the doorway she glimpsed him peering into the enormous microscope built into the wall, pulling one piece of rock from the viewing drawer and replacing it with another. He spent most of his time in there these days.

Before turning into the comm. pod, Sully drifted straight ahead, onto the command deck, where she hovered in front of the clear cupola for a moment. The view had lost its novelty, but not its magnificence. The deep black of space, studded with bright pinpoints of light: burning steady red, or

pulsing blue, or faintly glimmering like the wink of a co-
quettish eye from beneath the dark lashes of space and time.
Sully could smell the sticky sap of the tomato plant on the
pad of her thumb as she gazed out into the void, breathing in
the earthy smell of photosynthesis to quiet the accelerated
beat of her heart as she took in the overwhelming, infinite
space that surrounded her. No beginning, no end, just this,
forever. From here, the idea of Earth seemed like an illu-
sion. How could something so verdant, so diverse and beautiful and sheltered, exist among all this emptiness? When
she pulled herself away from the cupola she spotted Thebes
working behind her, a tablet in one hand and one of the
engineering apertures open in front of him, a hive of knobs
and wires and switches.

"Hey, Thebes," she said, and he looked up from the cir-
cuit map.

"Morning, Sully," he said. "Just doing a systems check. I
noticed the temperature programming in the comm. pod is
off quite a bit, actually, running hot—did you reset it?"

"No," she said, "I didn't. But I've noticed it's really warm
in there lately. Isn't the environmental system one of Devi's
projects?"

Thebes sighed. "It is," he said, "but she's finally getting a
little sleep this morning, and it's no trouble."

She lingered on the command deck, watching him tweak
the controls.

"Is she . . . doing any better?" Sully asked hesitantly, already knowing that she wasn't but wanting so badly to hear
that she was. Thebes shrugged, unable to give Sully what
she wanted. They looked at each other for a moment, in a
shared, knowing silence.

Finally Thebes announced, "All set. Seventy degrees on the dot."

As he fitted the aperture cover back into place, Sully continued on to the comm. pod, suddenly consumed with worry. How much longer before one of Devi's mistakes proved fatal? Before Ivanov and Tal came to serious blows? Before their precarious routine fell apart completely and something went really wrong? And if everything went right, if they somehow made it home without mutiny or casualty, what then? What would be waiting for them? What kind of life?

In the comm. pod, Sully gently collided with the only surface not occupied by some sort of equipment, a padded storage compartment opposite the entryway. After steadying herself and making her initial rounds, checking in with the receivers' memory banks, taking stock of the probe uplinks, then sending a few commands back to the Jovian system, she settled into the daily task of scanning the airwaves for remnants of Earth's noise pollution. It was tedious, and so far unrewarding, but she kept at it. To stop would be to give up—to inhabit the bleak possibilities that had been lurking at the edge of her thoughts for months—and that she would not do. Every now and then she picked up the handheld microphone and transmitted something, quietly, so that none of her colleagues would hear her talking. The faith that there was someone left to answer her kept smoldering. The odds for making contact would only increase the closer they came to Earth, and so even in the silent emptiness of space she felt hope grow as the days passed and the distance shrank. The crackle of the empty sine waves filled the pod and the data backlog from the Jovian probes kept stacking up, raw and unprocessed, but she didn't care. Hours passed.

It wasn't until she began to think about going back to the centrifuge for something to eat that she heard it. A cacophonous bang, and then, nothing—not even static. She hurried to reboot the machines, checking all the connections and the stored telemetry as they restarted. All was well in the pod. She didn't understand.

In the sudden, ominous silence she propelled herself out of the comm. pod, through the corridor and onto the command deck, where she looked out the cupola. A small cry escaped her. What appeared to be their main communications dish floated past, drifting playfully in a gust of solar wind, a severed arm waving goodbye as it receded into the darkness.

SEVEN

ONE MORNING AUGUSTINE woke later than usual. The sun was already high, the snow's blinding albedo shining in through the windows like a floodlight. Augie lifted his head from the pillow and squinted at the tangled bedding beside him, gently poking it until he established that Iris was no longer there. The sleeping bags were cold, despite his own body heat, the bright sun shining in through the windows, and the sturdy furnace. The cloud of his breath bloomed above his face. He sat up and looked around for her, first to the table where she sat with her books, then to the chair where he sat with the radio equipment, then to each of the windowsills where she sometimes perched. She was in none of these places. She had been with him constantly since his illness, and Augustine realized it had been weeks since he hadn't been able to find her. The incessant hiding he'd become accustomed to in their earlier days had ceased.

He got to his feet and began wrapping himself in clothes in preparation for the search. Having slept in woolen socks and a full suit of long underwear, he layered a flannel shirt, a fleece-lined sweater, and an insulated vest over his winter silks, then jammed his legs into a pair of flannel-lined work pants. Next came the scarves, two of them, and the parka and the unwieldy mittens, which he put on prematurely in his rush to get outside, then had to remove again in order to get his boots on. In the stairwell, a blast of cold air ruffled his white hair. He cursed and trudged back to the desk to snatch his hat from where it lay draped over the backrest of the chair. Getting dressed for the Arctic outdoors, even in spring, was an ordeal. And then, as he pulled the hat down over his ears, he looked out the window and saw her. He took the stairs as quickly as he could, the sounds of his haste reverberating in the empty stairwell: the waxed canvas of his pant legs rasping, the thud of his boots landing heavily on each stair tread, the whiz of his mittens skidding down the handrail, the throb of his breath pounding inside his eardrums.

He burst out onto the blinding white mountain, snapping a pair of mirrored ski goggles over his eyes to dull the brightness. He could see the shape of her, down the mountain path, just beyond the outbuildings. It looked as if she was lying on the ground, but he couldn't be sure, he only knew that the color was wrong—she was dressed in bright blue, the color of her long underwear, not the color of her parka. Spring was coming, but it was still devastatingly cold. Augustine ran down the path, past the cluster of outbuildings, and arrived at her side out of breath and half-blind with the white glare. Iris was sitting up, cross-legged in the snow, wearing only her thin winter silks and the thick wool socks she slept in. He collapsed next to her—the adrenaline that had gotten him this far this quickly was nearly spent. He began taking off his own parka to give to her.

"Are you all right?" he asked as he struggled with the toggles. "Where's your parka, my god, your *boots*? How long have you been out here, are you *crazy*?" His voice steadily elevated in volume until he was practically shouting. He finally got his parka off and wrapped it around her like a blanket. Taking her tiny hands in his, he felt the hot but not-too-hot flush of healthy circulation. He leaned back and looked her over, carefully this time. She smiled, an uncertain slant to her brow, as if she was worried about him—as if he were the one acting strange. She extracted her hands from his grip, reached out, and touched his bristled cheek with her warm fingers.

"Look," she said, pointing toward a nearby valley. He followed her finger and saw the small herd of musk oxen they used to watch, back when the sun was just beginning its return. The herd had been away for the last week or two, having undoubtedly found some other valley to graze in. Augie had barely noticed their absence, but clearly Iris had. She paid attention to things like that.

"They're back," she whispered with rapt excitement. Augie watched with her for a moment as the animals nuzzled the snow for the grass just beneath it. He closed his eyes and caught his breath, listening to the soft squeak of their hooves in the snow and the scrape of their horns against the frozen ground. When he opened his eyes, Iris's expression was full of wonder, her face illuminated with curiosity. He pulled her onto his lap and she didn't protest, just made herself comfortable, laying her head against his shuddering heart. Augie wrapped his arms around her. His lungs finally relaxed, his voice left his throat and sank back into his sternum. He exhaled, long and slow. Somewhere a wolf howled, but it was far away and Augustine wasn't scared. He was just tired and worried, feelings he was beginning to grow accustomed to.

"Please, can we go back now?" he asked her.

She nodded, her eyes still on the herd, and together they rose to their feet. He looked down at her socks, crusted with snow, and asked, "Shall I carry you?" They both knew quite well that he was barely able to haul his own weight back. She shook her head, wordlessly pressing his parka back into his hands, returning it to the person who needed it more. She waited until he had redone the toggles, then they plodded back up the mountain, between the outbuildings, along the zigzag of the steep mountain path, to the observatory.

In the control room Augie checked her extremities—every toe, every finger, even the tip of her nose, searching for the frostbite he was certain must be lurking. She humored him. He tried to remember the symptoms he'd read about before he came here: discolored skin, a waxy texture. When he found nothing amiss, he began to doubt the dependability of his own mind. He went over the details again: the sight of her from the control room, the brilliant blue of her winter silks against the white of the tundra, the crust of snow and ice clinging to the wool nap of her socks, the sensation of her warm hand against his cheek and her compact body on his lap. The herd before them, the sounds of their grazing. There was no room for doubt in his recollections.

His mind rewound, back to the beginning. He envisioned finding her just after the evacuation, alone in one of the outbuilding dormitories, sitting on a bottom bunk with her arms wrapped around her knees. He thought of the first time she spoke, to ask how long the polar night would last; of them walking together under the vivid stars; their trip to the hangar, the wolf, the sounds of her anguish and the severity of her distress; his fever, the sickly dreams, her ministrations throughout. Had she gotten sick, too? Was she ill in some way that he couldn't see? Was he? Perhaps he was still in bed—still fevered after killing the wolf down by the hangar.

He held her wrist and found her pulse, beating briskly. Her hair was tangled and greasy, thick clumps of matted curls hanging around her neck and a halo of softer, shorter wisps framing her pale face. He pressed her forearm and watched the brief white thumbprint appear and then fade to pink. She was an ordinary, healthy girl. Iris watched him knowingly, as if she could read his mind, which both comforted and unsettled him. He asked her not to leave the observatory without him and she shrugged, a gesture that filled him with irritation. He hadn't asked for this, hadn't wanted a companion, had never signed up for another life to care for, especially now, at the end of his days, but—she was here. And so was he. They were stuck with each other.

He considered her for a moment, her unkempt hair, the way the curls were threatening to merge into lumpy dreadlocks. There was something feral about her, he realized, and he was suddenly ashamed of himself. Carried along by a gust

of proprietary resolve, he went to fetch the wooden comb
he ran through his beard occasionally. When he wordlessly
offered it to her she didn't seem to know what to do with it,
looking at it like a foreign object. The comb was inadequate,
and the task of untangling her hair was enormous, but Iris
was patient with him and he was determined to make this
child—a child he had somehow ended up responsible for—
look more like a little girl and less like a musk ox. He did his
best. In the end there were a few pieces he had to cut off,
and he tried to even out the ends in some semblance of a
hairstyle. The dark curls ended abruptly just below her ears
and a short set of bangs had become necessary when the
tangle that flopped into her eyes proved impossible to disen-
gage. Iris ran her hands through her new hair and nodded
her approval. There was no mirror, but she seemed to enjoy
the bounce and sudden lightness, whipping her head back
and forth to test the movement of her new 'do.

They ate together afterward, among the snippets of dark,
matted hair: soup, saltines, and a can of ginger ale between
them. After he had swept up the clippings and washed the
dishes, Augie moved to his ham radio station and turned
on the equipment, sinking into his chair. It had become a
daily routine. He watched Iris open her astronomy book and
begin to read, pressing her lips together and holding the covers tightly, as if the tome might run away. Occasionally she
reached up and took a curl between her fingers, testing the
texture of it, rolling it around her pointer finger and then
releasing it. There was still something wild about her, Augustine thought, as he watched her play with her hair, but
it was harder to pinpoint now. She looked like a recently
adopted stray—unaccustomed to care, but no longer abandoned. Neither of them moved from their seats until the

sun had sunk and the daylight had dripped down behind the mountains, moving off to saturate some other skies.

—ᴧᴧᴧ—

AUGUSTINE'S RADIO SEARCH had proceeded with the antici-pated level of success—none. But he persevered anyway. It was a familiar momentum, the fierce determination that had guided him over the years, the cutthroat struggle to achieve, to possess, to understand; his coldhearted quest for knowl-edge. But it was different this time: here, at the end of it all, he had given up on triumph and was persisting for reasons beyond ambition, for reasons he didn't fully understand. In the control room on the third floor he set up shop in front of the south-facing window, looking out over the tundra that stretched down toward warmer climes. While he scanned the frequencies he reclined on a wheeled chair upholstered with supple black leather, appropriated from the director's office on the first floor. With the heap of outdated radio equipment in front of him and the sepia globe he'd salvaged from one of the outbuildings to his right, he would settle in for the day, prop his feet up on the filing cabinet just beside the table and lazily spin the globe as he scanned the airwaves, letting his finger drag through the oceans, across the continents. Initially, he made notes about which bands he'd searched, but as time wore on and he'd searched them all several times over, he let his method become more whim-sical, tuning the frequencies like picking tarot cards from a fortune-teller's deck.

Most of the time, Iris read at the table across the room. He guessed that she had read the Arctic field guide from cover to cover a few times over before she put it down, and from there she moved on to an astronomy text he'd found shoved into one of the research assistants' lockers, the cover laminated and marked with a Dewey decimal sticker, forgotten in the chaos of the evac. A rogue library book, far from home—*how fitting,* he thought, as she buffed the smudged covers with the sleeve of her shirt, then smeared them with new fingerprints as she read. Their silence was companionable as they sat at opposite ends of the control room, engrossed in their solitary projects.

He let his mind wander to the mystery of her proximity: sitting with him in the control room, and more broadly, joining him here at the end of civilization—the edge of humanity, measured in both time and space. He wondered how it had happened, how she had arrived here and how she had stayed, where she came from, whom she belonged to, whether she had any feelings on these subjects; she never once said anything about it, and it was somehow unimaginable that she ever would. She was a puzzle, but she was his puzzle, and her presence kept him working, kept him striving without rational expectation of success. It was possible, he mused, that she was what had kept him alive this long.

AUGUSTINE DIDN'T SLEEP that night after he and Iris returned from the tundra. He tried, but by the time Iris began to make her wordless sleep sounds he knew it was futile. He extracted himself from the sleeping bags as quietly as he could, the synthetic whisper of the fabric hushing him as he slithered out onto the cold floor. At the ham station he plugged his headset into the receiver and switched the equipment on. Outside the window the tundra glowed blue under the yellow-pink blush of the full moon. He settled into his chair to listen to the white noise from the radio waves.

Now and then he glanced at the swell beneath the sleeping bags to make sure she was still there, her chest still rising and falling, perhaps accompanied by the slight twitch of an unconscious mind tickling the nerves of an arm or a leg.

The tuner scanned automatically. Augie pulled out one of the Arctic atlases that had been gathering dust in the control room, holding it on his lap while he listened, flipping through the pages. He eventually came to the well-worn map of Lake Hazen in the center of the book, an enormous body of water roughly fifty miles east of the observatory, where the researchers used to fish in their free time. Augie could recall a number of trips being organized, trips he never went on, though he was always invited, and countless stories being told, stories he never listened to. *Fishing trips are for terrestrials,* he would scoff to himself, and return to the images of some distant galaxy. When he needed time off, he preferred the exotic glamor of other places—tropical beaches, expensive resorts, dense jungles. Yet now—the journey was feasible. The destination was desirable, in fact. Perhaps a journey was just what he and Iris needed: an adventure to welcome the strengthening light. The year-round snow and ice of the mountain would give way to wildflowers and warm breezes down by the lake, closer to sea level. Perhaps the change would do his small companion some good. Perhaps it would do them both good. Supposedly some of the warmest temperatures on the archipelago had been recorded there: as balmy as the low seventies in high summer. Augie let his finger drift along the length of the blue outline in the atlas, tracing the long slope of its western shore. And why shouldn't they go? He had been listening to white noise and transmitting into the void for long enough. Hope dwindled in the face of probability. He needed a change. If they left soon they could use one of the snowmobiles from the hangar. The snow cover wouldn't last forever, but there was time.

He lifted the ear of his headset and listened to Iris breathe for a moment before letting the earphone slap back against the side of his head. Augustine felt like an animal awakening after a long wintry sleep. Perhaps they would even find something useful at the lake, something like—and suddenly he remembered. He slid the headset down to hang around his neck so that he could hear his own thoughts without the stuttering static. The shore of Lake Hazen had boasted a small seasonally staffed weather station for decades, since the 1950s, back when radio communication was their only option. He recalled the aerial array he'd seen in more recent photographs of the station—vastly superior to his own antenna here at the observatory. It followed that their transmitting equipment would be more powerful as well. He snapped the atlas shut. Another reason. It was settled. They would go.

He was scribbling plans and supply lists when the sun came up and Iris began to stir. She stood up with a sleeping bag wrapped around her like a long, hooded cloak and shuffled over to where he sat, her new hairdo jutting out in unexpected directions. She touched the pad he was writing on and then let her hand rest on his shoulder, shrugging as if to say *What gives?* He covered her hand with his and turned his chair to face her.

"Let's take a trip."

EIGHT

"WHAT THE HELL have you done?" Ivanov shouted at Tal. Tal was brandishing his radar tablet like a weapon. Their voices boomed around the centrifuge, drawing everyone toward them.

"I haven't bloody done anything," Tal shouted back, his face beet red. "I've been looking at this screen all morning and there's been *nothing*—no debris, no asteroids, nothing within fifty fucking miles."

"Well, *something's* collided with the antenna, no? Perhaps

as we're in the main asteroid belt it was a *fucking* asteroid, no? Or do you think the dish just fell off?"

"Enough!" Harper shouted. "That's enough."

Tal threw the tablet onto his bunk and walked over to the cooking range, turning his back to the group while he collected himself. The veins in Ivanov's neck still bulged, but he folded his arms across his chest and kept his mouth shut for the time being.

Harper stood up straighter, as if to physically invoke the power of his command in front of the assembled crew. "I want to be talking about how to fix our communication capabilities, and at this moment I don't give a damn how it happened unless it's relevant to that goal. At this point the retrieval of the antenna is probably impossible. Other options."

The crewmembers were silent, staring at the floor. Tal kept his back turned. Sully could hear the quiet, shrill squeak of Ivanov's teeth grinding together. Thebes cracked his knuckles one at a time. Devi drew a circle on the floor with the toe of her shoe.

"Other options," Harper repeated, and this time there was a warning in his voice. "Now."

"We can make a new antenna," Sully suggested. "I think I have all the main components, especially if we take the paraboloid from the landing module. The gain won't be as high, but it should work."

Thebes laced his fingers together and began to nod. "A replacement antenna is plausible, I agree," he said. "But the installation will require a great deal of EVA work—probably two space walks, one to assess the damage and prep the site, another to actually install it. The risk is unavoidable. I think we have to go ahead and do it, but we needn't rush—Earth wasn't saying much anyway."

"That's a good point," Sully said. "The scheduled uplinks from the probes are lost as long as the receivers are dark, but they're not high on our list of priorities right now. I'm not even sure the new system would be strong enough to pick up those signals, and in the meantime Earth has been silent this whole time—no noise pollution, no satellite activity, nothing. I've been checking. It's all been spooky quiet. So might as well take our time and do it right."

Tal finally turned back to the group. "If I have a few days I can try and up the radar sensitivity. I don't know if it will work, but it might. If we're sending warm bodies out there I'd like to have a handle on the micrometeoroid population."

Ivanov's teeth squeaked again and Sully cringed at the sound. Devi still hadn't said anything. Harper sighed and ran his hands through his hair, making an unconscious *tsk tsk* sound with his tongue against the back of his teeth while he considered. He crossed, then uncrossed his arms. Finally he spoke.

"So we'll assess the damage as best we can from inside and get to work on the antenna replacement. Sullivan, Devi, Thebes—I'd like the three of you to work on this together. Sully, let's not worry about the Jovian probes. If we can pick up their signals, great; if not, Earth is the focus. Tal, I want you to work on the radar system, see what took a bite out of us and what we can do to prevent or at least anticipate a repeat. Ivanov, you and I will take stock of the damage from the EV cams. Thanks, everyone—take your time, do it right, but let's get moving."

Devi hadn't said anything since the meeting began, and Sully wasn't sure she had been paying attention. But as they left the centrifuge to go look at the equipment in the lunar module, Devi turned to Sully and started chattering. She was brimming with ideas for the replacement they were about to cobble together. Beneath Devi's nonstop stream of consciousness, Sully let out a soft sigh of relief. If there was anyone who could make this plan work, it was Devi.

-ᴧᴧᴧ-

THERE WAS FINALLY work to do again. Important work. *Aether* was abuzz for the first time since leaving Jovian space, four months ago. Sully, Devi, and Thebes began by raiding the rest of the ship for the components that could be spared. They appropriated the dish from the lunar landing module, and the comm. pod was full of redundancies they could pilfer. The replacement was well under way by the time Harper and Ivanov reported back on what little they could glean from the installment site. Sully and the engineers used the table in Little Earth as a staging area so that their tools wouldn't keep floating away.

They were still at it when the main LED lights on Little Earth automatically dimmed, signaling the end of the day. Each of the individual bunk lamps was illuminated, giving the centrifuge a soft, candlelit glow. It was midnight by their watches, but the constraints of time no longer seemed relevant. They were tired, but also invigorated. The problem had woken them up, snapped them into the moment. They finally had something to do, a reason to pay attention. Even Ivanov rose to the occasion, acting more amiable than he had in months.

Sully and Devi were doing most of the construction, while Thebes handed them tools and prepared the components they needed.

"Drill," Devi said, and Thebes put it into her hand before she had a chance to look up.

"Wire cutters," Sully said, and Thebes was already at her elbow.

The construction of the new dish was moving along faster than anything had since they'd worked on the logistics of the Jovian moon landings. After Thebes and Devi left, Sully stayed at the table for another hour, making a few more adjustments but mostly thinking. After tidying up the area, Sully walked back toward the sleeping compartments. Tal was on the couch studying a notebook full of dense calculations while he fiddled with the tablet on his lap. Harper and Ivanov were conferring quietly near the lavatory. Harper said something she couldn't quite hear, and a genuine smile appeared on Ivanov's lips. Ivanov laid his hand on the commander's shoulder for a brief second, then disappeared into the lavatory while Harper continued on to his own compartment. Sully noticed that Ivanov had left his curtain open. Looking in, she saw a panorama of photos showing rosy faces and white-blond heads—his family, every one of them smiling—on every surface. Ivanov returned sooner than expected and caught her staring. She blushed, ready to be scolded, but he didn't seem to mind.

"It is a bit much, no?" he asked.

Sully shook her head. "Not at all," she said. "I think it's perfect. I wish I'd brought more things from home, but I didn't . . . well, I didn't anticipate wanting them so much."

"You have one daughter," he said, not a question but a statement. "And your husband—he didn't understand?"

She was surprised, first at his boldness and then at his accuracy. Ivanov understood her, in some essential way, and she was surprised. He hadn't spoken to her in weeks, but suddenly he saw her more fully than she could see herself. She remembered watching him have dinner with his family in Houston at the outdoor café, the tender way that he cut his daughter's food into little pieces, the rapt attention he paid to his wife as she told a funny story, the love visible on all their faces.

"No, he didn't," Sully said.

"My wife also did not understand, but she tried to, and I believe this makes me lucky." Ivanov patted her arm. "Not everyone has a calling," he said, and shrugged. "It is difficult for them to comprehend, I think. Good night." He climbed into his bunk and closed the curtain.

The lone photograph of Lucy seemed so small where it was pinned to the wall, the empty space around it like an ocean. Sully reached out and touched her daughter's face, already smudged with fingerprints. She turned out the light and lay back in the darkness, but even when she closed her eyes, the negative image of the photograph burned on the inside of her eyelids. She didn't think she'd be able to sleep, she was so energized by the renewal of their work. But eventually she did, and dreamed of fireflies dressed as little girls.

-vvvv-

THE STRENGTHENING DAWN light beyond her curtain pulled her out of her dreams, but it had been only a few hours since she'd gone to bed. She closed her eyes, ignoring her alarm, and when she opened them again it was almost 1100. As she wriggled into her jumpsuit and braided her hair she'd already begun thinking, planning a mount for the replacement antenna. Harper was sitting at the long table with a set of *Aether*'s blueprints laid out in front of him and a cup of instant coffee. He didn't look up as she slid onto the bench beside him.

"Morning," she said brightly. The lids of his eyes were

puffy, their rims red. He kept his gaze down. "Did you sleep at all?" she asked.

He seemed startled. "Hm? Oh, no, I guess not. Preoccupied."

She looked more closely at the blueprints and saw that he had begun marking them up with notes for the spacewalks. "Who will walk? Have you decided yet?"

Harper sighed and ground the heels of his hands into his eye sockets. "It has to be you," he said slowly, letting his hands drop into his lap, "and it has to be Devi."

Sully nodded. There was something strange in his body language, something reluctant. Did he think she wouldn't want to walk? Or was he worried about Devi? She waited to see if he would add anything, and after a moment he did.

"I'm not sure Devi's up for this—emotionally. But I'm also not sure Thebes will be able to improvise out there as well as she can. I've been going over it for hours. It has to be Devi."

"She can handle it," Sully said, but when she looked at the helpless expression on Harper's face she suddenly shared his doubt. She thought of Devi's nightmares, of her recent failings as a caretaker of the ship. She'd never seen Harper look so uncertain, and it frightened her. He was their commander, after all. "I'll be there with her, we'll have you and Thebes talking us through it. This will be fine, Harper. We can do it. You should get some rest, you look ragged."

He laughed. "An understatement, I'm sure."

Sully had an urge to reach out and smooth down the lick of hair that stood straight up from the crown of his head, as she might've done for Lucy, but she didn't. "It is. I order you to sleep for a few hours. We have time, don't burn yourself out on this."

Harper nodded. "I know, I just—I'm worried about . . ."

He looked at her for a long moment and then let his gaze drop. She waited, but this time he didn't finish his sentence.

Sully reached out and squeezed his shoulder and then stuffed her hand into the pocket of her jumpsuit, as if to stop herself from touching him again. "I'm worried too, but she's smarter than you and me put together. If she can't do this, no one can." She said it lightly, but Harper wasn't smiling.

"I know," he said. "That's what worries me."

~~~

TWO DAYS LATER, the replacement antenna was finished and the first walk was scheduled. Sully made her way to the comm. pod out of habit before realizing she had nothing to do there with no antenna. She ran her fingers over the knobs and buttons of the machines that lined the walls, displays dark, speakers silent. The pod seemed more like a tomb than a communication hub. The longer she stayed, the more sinister the quiet became. Eventually she drifted out of the pod and moved down the corridor, toward the command deck and the cupola.

Devi was floating in front of the cupola's many-paned view, her hands pressed against the thick silica glass. The loose knot of hair at the nape of her neck drifted away from her head, hovering like a black cloud between her shoulder blades. She wore a dark red jumpsuit, the same as always, the legs cuffed above her ankles, an inch or two of skin visible between the bright white of her socks and the red of the suit. She wasn't wearing shoes. Beyond the panes a great blackness hung, a darkness full of depth and movement and stillness and a hundred million pricks of light, too far away to illuminate anything, too bright to ignore.

"What do you see?" Sully asked, propelling herself head-first into the cupola to float next to Devi.

"Everything," Devi said, nervously toying with the zipper of her jumpsuit. She pulled it up to her neck, then back down to her sternum in rapid succession until the heather gray of her shirt caught in the plastic teeth. She didn't bother to dislodge it. "And nothing. It's hard to say."

They hovered together in silence, looking out into the vast emptiness. The prospect of entering it, of inhabiting the vacuum, made home seem even farther away. Out there, there was no safety net, nothing to anchor a floating astronaut to the ship other than the thin tethers and each other. Sully started to say something about the spacewalk, then stopped, not wanting to speak out of turn, suddenly unsure if Harper had even told her yet.

"I know," Devi said suddenly, "about the walk. He told me last night. He's worried, yes? Because I've been so . . . disconnected. And you. He's worried also because he's in love with you. He doesn't have to worry. We'll fix it."

Sully was stunned, silent for a long beat. She was used to Devi's ability to see through the surface of things—most of the time she used this skill on inanimate mechanical objects, but on the rare occasions that Devi turned her mind to human affairs, she spoke alarming truths with robotic precision. It was unnerving. Sully could feel warmth creeping up her neck and she willed it to cool. Devi had said it so simply, so matter-of-factly. She didn't question the verity of the statement, and it was a relief, in a way, to hear those words aloud. To know that her thoughts about what things might be like between her and Harper when they returned to Earth were based in something real, something quantified, qualified, and named by an outside person—by the smartest person she knew. And yet this wasn't the time. She couldn't think about Harper right now, not like that. It might never be the time. She pushed Devi's words away and focused on the spacewalk instead, gazing through the cupola with a determined single-mindedness. After a moment they heard Thebes calling out for Devi. Before she left, Devi took Sully's hand and squeezed it.

"You needn't worry either," Devi said.

With that she pushed off with her feet and disappeared into the corridor. Sully stayed for a long time, thinking. She considered the unfamiliar orientation of stars before her until she was quite certain she had picked Ursa Minor out of the chaos. It was from an unusual angle, but it was definitely the little bear she knew so well. She was sure of it, and it felt good to be sure of something.

SULLY AND DEVI went over the mission plan with Harper dozens of times, reciting their actions like actors reciting lines. The two women were at ease; the training in Houston had prepared them for all manner of extravehicular repair work, and the first walk would be fairly simple. Thebes was checking the suits while Tal was glued to the radar system. Ivanov kept himself busy pointing out errors in Tal's updated computer code, poking holes in Harper's mission plan, and offering Thebes what-if suit malfunctions with infinitesimal probabilities—a one-man red team showing them the gaps in their strategy, the flaws in their approach. For once they were glad of his criticisms.

As the preparations were checked off and the crew readied themselves for the walk, the good-natured camaraderie they had developed in Houston returned, that feeling from the bar before the launch when they had listened to the jukebox and done shots together. Tal began making jokes again and Ivanov actually smiled at one or two of them. Devi was talking nonstop, thrilling to the project at hand, engaging with the crew and the mechanical tasks before her, and Thebes seemed to breathe a sigh of relief just watching the crew converse. They all felt the momentum pulling them forward. Sully felt more hopeful than she had in months. Maybe, just maybe, the frequencies of Earth would carry more than silence once the comm.s were back online. Only Harper seemed hesitant. Even as the rest of the crew thrived on the challenge of bringing the communication system back to life, Harper oversaw the work with an air of apprehension.

The eve before the walk, Harper pulled Sully aside on the command deck. As he spoke to her, the bright blackness of the cupola's view behind him transfixed her. It was intoxicating. Knowing she was hours away from stepping out of the airlock and into the vacuum, she struggled to focus on his face, to move her gaze away from the subtle movements of swirling atoms just outside the glass and to meet his eyes, which were boring into her.

"Sully," he said. "Sully." She had no idea how many times he'd already said it.

"Yes, sorry, I'm listening."

"I want you to promise me that if something seems off, if anything goes even the slightest bit awry, you'll abort and come straight back to the airlock. I know how it feels once you're out there, but please. Not having the comm.s online won't kill anyone. We can always try again. We can always wait to dock with the ISS. We can always—I don't know, but there are other options, okay? I know we've been friendly these past few months, you and I—shit, Sully, there's little enough fun to be had—but I need to know you're going to follow my orders when you're out there. Tell me you understand."

"I understand, Commander."

"All right, then. Get some rest. We open the airlock at 0900 tomorrow, let's be ready."

Harper turned and floated back toward Little Earth, leaving Sully alone on the command deck. She watched him go and then let her gaze drift back toward the cupola. She reflected on Devi's words, wondering what it would feel like to love him back—wondering if she already did. Unsure, she tried to reject the possibility, and instead let the black glow of space fill her imagination with its emptiness.

NINE

AUGUSTINE WALKED DOWN to the hangar alone. Iris stayed behind, packing. The hike was difficult for him, but that felt right somehow, like penance for his many sins. At the hangar, everything was as they'd left it. The bay doors were open, the snow piling up inside in wind-carved slopes, the constellation of ratchet heads still strewn across the oil-stained concrete. The two snowmobiles were uncovered, and the flashlight he had carried with him on their last journey out here lay exactly where he'd left it. He tried to start the snowmobile he'd gotten running the last time, but during the commotion he had left the key in the On position and now the battery was dead. Augie tried the other snowmobile, and after some coaxing he got it going. He fed it a little gas every time the engine slowed and eventually it hummed peacefully, its sleek gray body vibrating and a fog of white smoke rising off the tailpipe, no longer needing his ministrations.

Augie slid onto the seat and took stock of the controls. He was accustomed to being a passenger on this particular machine, but after a few moments he decided he'd figured out the main features. As a young man he'd ridden motorcycles—how hard could a snowmobile be? No double yellow line, no traffic, nothing to run into, just forward movement across the vast, empty tundra. He backed it up out of the hangar without much trouble and retrieved some of the full fuel canisters while it idled, lashing the containers to the luggage rack with a bungee cord. He thought of the pink-stained grave just a few yards away, marring the pristine runway. He had avoided looking in that direction, had kept his gaze trained on the hangar, but now, as he prepared to ride away, he found he couldn't leave without at least casting a glance toward the fallen staircase and the mound of bloody snow.

The unlocked wheel of the staircase still spun lazily in the wind, while a thin layer of powder on top of the hard-packed tundra moved across the ground in intricate wind-driven spirals. Swinging his leg over the seat of the snowmobile, Augie turned away from the grave and felt the vibrations of the vehicle enter his bloodstream, shaking his organs as he lay on the gas and sped away from the hangar, back up the mountain.

Iris pushed open the control room door and came bound-

GOOD MORNING, MIDNIGHT | 135

ing down the stairs to meet him halfway. "Are we riding?" she asked, out of breath. It was a reaction he'd never gotten from her before, this kind of delight. Her entire face seemed to change, to become more childish and less feral. He remembered that she was only a little girl, and that recollection kindled emotions he didn't quite recognize. Tenderness, perhaps, but something else as well, something darker—fear. Not of her, but for her. Was the journey safe? Had he thought it through? Should he be more careful with this tiny spark of life that had somehow ended up in his care? He wondered what her father would do in his place, and the thought was so outlandish, so incomprehensible, that he pushed aside the fear and the tenderness and occupied his mind with other things.

In the control room, they went over the packing. There was so much they needed to bring, so much they had to leave behind, so little they knew about the weather station on the lake. There was no way of knowing what they would find there. They made a pile of necessities: the tent and the subzero sleeping bags, food and water, extra fuel, one very warm set of clothing each, helmets and goggles, a camp stove, a map, a compass, and two flashlights. Everything else was deemed luxury items that they would take only if there was room: Iris's books, spare clothes, extra batteries, and a second fuel canister. They hauled the luggage down to the snowmobile and strapped it all on. With a passenger and all this gear, the load was heavy, but Augie was shrinking in his old age and Iris had been pocket-sized from the start. The vehicle was rugged, built for steep, roadless terrain and substantial weight. It might not handle perfectly, but it would take them where they needed to go.

They shut the observatory down, leaving just enough heat

on to keep the pipes from freezing and the telescope from cracking. As Augie adjusted the furnace, he wondered whom he was leaving it on for—perhaps them, if they had to turn back, or perhaps no one if Lake Hazen proved to be a more hospitable home. The furnace would run out of fuel eventually, of course. The cold would creep into the building, the pipes would freeze, the giant telescope lens would crack. Frost would creep across the windows, and eventually it would consume their cozy control room sanctuary, just as it had the rest of the outpost. Soon enough, winter would live here for good.

Iris wrapped her little arms around Augie's waist and they rode down toward the tundra, veering east before the hangar came into view. Iris tightened her grip, clinging to him as snow-covered rocks jolted them this way and that. Her helmet was a few sizes too big and he had insisted that she wear three hats to pad it out. The goggles were also too large—the single wide, yellow eye engulfing most of her face—but she wore them with a safety pin to tighten the elastic band around her tiny head. Once they made it down to level ground, the ride became smoother, and Iris relaxed her grip. The journey was already under way—no point second-guessing things now. After four or five hours riding into the white stare of the distance, Augustine let the snowmobile roll to a stop.

They climbed off to have a drink of water and eat a few crackers. Iris's face was a vigorous red, imprinted with the white outline of her goggles, wisps of dark hair escaping her many hats and curling wildly around her cheeks. She seemed thrilled by the adventure so far. Augustine looked back the way they had come, but the outline of the observatory was no longer visible. The air around them was opaque, shimmering with a curtain of snow that rippled in time with the wind. He had been on edge since they left, counting the miles as they passed, resisting the urge to make a U-turn and speed back toward the safe haven they'd left behind. He clung to the faint hope that lay ahead, that they were doing the right thing. The empty stillness around them felt ominous.

After they finished eating, Iris put her goggles back on, and then her hats, one by one. Augustine crumpled the plastic wrapper the crackers had come in and tucked it into the pocket of his parka as Iris climbed back onto the snowmobile. He pressed the starter button, but nothing happened. He pressed it again. Nothing. His heart began to beat faster and he inhaled a long, slow, icy breath. *Stay calm,* he thought. *It was working five minutes ago.* He tried again, then fiddled with the key, the throttle, back to the starter button. He pulled his goggles down to rest around his neck, staring at the silent snowmobile in disbelief. He got off and took a step back, as if he might see the problem better from there, but all he saw was a machine he didn't understand. A sour panic rose in the back of his throat. They were stranded, miles from the observatory, even more miles from the weather station. There was nothing in between—no oasis, no shelter, nothing but empty, endless tundra. They would probably freeze to death if they tried to walk. Iris was shifting on the pillion seat of the snowmobile, waiting to see what he would do next. Augustine collapsed down into the snow—not because he decided to, but because his legs would no longer hold him. He'd been so foolish to leave the one sanctuary on this forsaken island. He leaned his head back against the flank of the snowmobile and stared up into the white swirl of sky. Already the wind was erasing their tracks. This was it: the quiet, cold death he had only just decided was unacceptable. Iris's tiny foot tickled his shoulder, and without thinking he reached up and took her boot in his mittened hand, holding it against his cheek.

"I'm sorry," he said, but the wind snatched his words away before he could be sure he'd spoken them. He closed his eyes and felt the sting of the snow-heavy wind against his exposed skin. Behind his eyelids he watched prickles of light sparking across darkness, and when he opened his eyes the intense white of the snow momentarily blinded him. It would be a quiet end—they could either trudge onward, trudge back, or stay here beside the motionless snowmobile. In every direction Augustine saw the same conclusion. The same outcome. He imagined Iris's eyes sewn shut with frost, a bruised blue seeping into her cheeks. It was his fault. He had brought them here, taken them away from the safety of the observatory into the white, menacing wilderness.

He'd been staring at the fuel valve tucked beside the right footwell for some time before he realized what he was looking at: a switch turned halfway between Off and On. Augustine got on his knees and brought his face up to the valve. The lettering was unmistakable—perhaps Iris had kicked it when she climbed down? He twisted it all the way to On and slowly got to his feet. He said a silent plea as he reached for the power switch. The snowmobile roared to life and relief flooded his body. His hands shook as he placed them on the handlebars, and he tightened his grip to ease the tremor. He felt the menace of the landscape more keenly than ever, but he guided the snowmobile forward despite it—into the blank distance, covering finite miles disguised as infinity beneath a low, indifferent sun.

When the light began to fade they stopped and unpacked

the tent for the night. Augie had been on the lookout for a boulder, a small tree, even a tall snowdrift to block the wind and make their camp feel less exposed, but there was nothing in any direction, so he pitched the tent beside the snowmobile. The tent was tepee-shaped, a cone of orange in the middle of a white vista. The fluorescence of the fabric brought out the bluish tones in the snow. As they settled in for the night, Iris took off her helmet and two of the three hats, keeping the emerald-green cap with the pompom and her yellow goggles on throughout dinner. There was nothing to make a fire with. They huddled together inside the tent while the wind howled around them, pulling the orange fabric taut against the aluminum poles. The tent pegs squeaked in their shallow holes. Augustine hoped that they would hold through the night, that the tent wouldn't go skittering across the smooth, slippery expanse of the tundra as they slept. He had pounded the pegs as deep into the packed snow as the can of baked beans he'd been using as a hammer had allowed. They heated those same beans over the little kerosene stove, the tent flap open for ventilation. Darkness fell.

Iris hummed along to the sound of the wind against the tent. There was no need for words, nothing to say. Augustine chewed and listened to the desolate moan of the wind, which suddenly seemed ominous, and he wondered again if they should turn back. If he had made a mistake taking Iris away from the known safety of the observatory. After dinner, they crawled out the flap of the tent to look up at the stars. The sky was full of them, but on that night the constellations were only a homely backdrop for the rippling river of the aurora borealis that flowed through the air, green and purple and blue streams of dancing light. The two of them walked a little way from the glow of the electric lantern that burned in their tent, transfixed by the aurora, ready to follow one of the shimmering paths of light—to climb right up into the sky. After a while, the lights dimmed and slipped away. Augie turned, not sure how long they'd been watching, and saw the illuminated orange shell of the tent and one last thread of green glowing above it, gradually fading from view.

They slept soundly that night, their breath rising from their nostrils as steam, their thickly bundled bodies curling toward each other, unconsciously searching for warmth as the wind continued to howl and sing around them.

~~~

IN THE MORNING they ate another can of beans, this time one with pieces of pork mixed in, then took down the tent. They wiped the tundra clean of their night and rode east once more. The day spread out before them, pale and in-finite. It seemed as if they weren't moving across the dis-tance at all, but riding on an invisible treadmill. Late in the day they saw an Arctic hare bouncing across the tundra, jumping vigorously on its hind legs like a pogo stick, more interested in height than distance. When they made camp again that night they saw another hare, or perhaps the same one, bouncing nearby. Augie pointed it out as Iris slurped a mouthful of creamed corn, heated on the kerosene stove.

"It's so they can see farther," she said. He was speechless for a minute. She spoke so rarely that it always took him a moment to respond. Her knowledge of the Arctic wildlife would be extensive, he realized, and thought back to the field guide she'd reread so many times she probably had the whole thing memorized. He felt a small twinge of regret that he had never bothered to learn a single thing about this environment he'd spent the past few years living in—

not on purpose, anyway. The child beside him knew about the wolves, the musk oxen, the hares. Augustine knew only about the distant stars, billions of miles away. He'd been moving from place to place his entire life and had never bothered to learn anything about the cultures or wildlife or geography that he encountered, the things right in front of him. They seemed passing, trivial. His gaze had always been far-flung. He'd accumulated local knowledge only by accident. While his colleagues explored the regions of their various research posts, hiking in the woods or touring the cities, Augustine only delved deeper into the skies, reading every book, every article that crossed his path, and spending seventy-hour weeks in the observatory, trying to catch a glimpse of thirteen billion years ago, scarcely aware of the moment he was living in.

There had been other camping trips, other nights spent stargazing, but whether it was because of the liquor that fueled him in those days or his preoccupation with the sky above him rather than the moment itself, Augustine barely remembered those trips. He had always craned his neck up to the heavens, had always looked away from so many incredible vistas on Earth. It was only the data he gathered, only the celestial events he recorded that had made an impression on his memory. When he considered how long he had been alive, it seemed remarkable how little he had experienced.

There was another aurora that night, pure green, and it lasted for a long time. He and Iris sat in the mouth of the tent with their lantern turned off until the last ripples faded from the sky. When they finally crawled back into their sleeping bags, his mind was ablaze. The look of wonder on Iris's face had been almost as incredible as the aurora itself. As he drifted off to sleep, he forgot about how far they'd ridden and how far they had to go. He thought only of the sound of Iris's breath next to him, the moan of the wind, the tingling cold in his toes and fingers, and the sharp, unfamiliar sensation of being alive, aware, content.

～～～

THERE WAS ANOTHER full day of travel, one more night out on the tundra, and then, on the morning of the fourth day, they came to the edge of the mountains. The terrain had grown progressively rugged around them, Paleozoic rock erupting from the snow cover in dark, jagged shards, and by midmorning it was difficult to find a path for the snowmobile to traverse. On the other side of the mountain range, Lake Hazen would be stretched out beneath the craggy peaks. Having never made the journey before, Augustine was surprised and dismayed by the terrain. Was there a mountain pass? An easier route he had missed? The way forward was treacherous, but they forged on, the sharp studs biting into the snow and ice as they made their way up the mountain. They made cautious progress on the snowmobile for hours, and when they found a straightaway, the ground evening out into a gentle slope, Augie let out a sigh of relief and allowed the machine to gather momentum, whipping past the scenery as if they were back on the smooth, empty tundra. The skis sliced through powder, sending up a crest of white in front of them, like the froth of a wave. Both the relief and the momentum were short-lived. When the terrain grew rough once more, Augustine couldn't see beyond the snow in the air. It wasn't long before a hidden boulder caught them by surprise and threw both passengers from the saddle of the snowmobile. As he hurtled through the air, over the handlebars, Augustine wondered if his body could take the landing, wondered if they should have turned back, wondered if he would ever get up again. The impact knocked the wind out of him, but as he waited to recover his breath he moved all his limbs one by one and was relieved to find nothing amiss. Turning his head, he saw that Iris was nearby, already on her feet and inspecting the snow angel she'd made where she fell. As he sat up and took stock of his surroundings, he realized that the snowmobile was totaled. The machine was on its side and one of the skis had shattered. He got to his feet slowly and went to see if anything could be done, but the engine only croaked when he tipped the snowmobile over and tried to start it again. *There will be no return trip.* Where had Augie heard that before? He struggled to remember. Gathering what gear they could carry and leaving the rest, Iris and Augie continued on, stumbling over exposed rock and sheer ice with heavy loads and sore limbs.

They hiked for hours. The terrain steepened once more, and by the time they reached one of the lower peaks of the range, they were exhausted and the day was ending. But there, at the top, they caught their first view of the lake below them—an enormous sheet of ice. Beneath a setting sun, they could see the weather station down below, at the foot of the mountain, just a few huts and a tall antenna array, but an encouraging sight nonetheless. Their new home—no turning back now. They camped for the last time, and in the morning they began their descent. Hours later, when they finally stumbled across the plateau to the camp, the light was just beginning to fade.

The camp wasn't much. A low half-cylinder-shaped tent of green canvas next to two larger white tents of a similar shape, each with a little stovepipe chimney, nestled by the lake on a flat, snow-covered terrace. To the right of the huts rose a garden of tall, slender antennae and a little radio shelter. The shores of the lake were still snowbound, but the rocky earth was beginning to poke through. In the middle of the lake was a small island, and even from where he stood, Augie could see a few Arctic hares leaping high into the air, staring back inquisitively over the frozen lake. The ice creaked and chimed like frozen bells scraping against each other. It was a new and welcoming sound to replace the ravaging howl of wind sweeping across the tundra. The frozen gusts they had lived with for so long were absent at the weather station. As Augustine surveyed the tiny camp beside the vast lake, a warm, gentle breeze ruffled his frozen beard. Spring was on its way. The thaw had begun.

TEN

THE AIRLOCK OPENED. Sully watched as the mechanical door swung back to reveal the gaping hole of space just outside, bottomless and empty. Devi climbed out first, and Sully followed. She took a moment to breathe and observe her surroundings as she clung to the rim of the airlock chamber, then stepped out into the void. *Aether* seemed enormous from the outside, but so much of it was storage tanks, radiation shields, solar panels, the propulsion system— components the crew never saw from within. She turned her gaze to the whirling centrifuge, so small next to the rest of the ship. It was amazing that all six of them had lived there for so long, jammed together in the midst of all this space. She propelled herself past the greenhouse and life support areas, past the research pods, to the front of the rounded cupola, where she waved her massive white glove at the four faces pressed against the glass.

"Good so far," she said into her helmet comm.

She turned to see Devi a few yards away, looking not at *Aether* but out into the depths of space. Sully turned to look too, and suddenly the ship didn't seem large at all. It seemed microscopic. She heard Harper in her ear, asking Devi if she was good to go.

"Copy, good to go," Devi repeated.

Devi and Sully slowly made their way toward where the base of the comm. dish had been connected to the hull of *Aether*, at the aft of the ship, in front of the propulsion system and behind the storage tanks. The remote modification tool, a long, flexible arm, was at the other end of the ship, where it could work on extravehicular problems that arose in the living and working quarters, but the arm was not long enough to reach the site where the dish had been. Devi and Sully moved slowly, crawling over the enormous hull like climbers on the face of a mountain, fastened to the ship by their tethers, lengths of steel cable floating behind them like the silvery thread of a spider. From the command deck, the rest of the crew was following along via the EVA cameras mounted in their helmets. Harper kept them on course, occasionally making suggestions about their route when they hesitated, but mostly staying silent, letting them move at their own pace.

Sully appreciated Harper more than ever in that moment,

when all that separated her from the void was a thin cable. The last commander she'd served under, on her last space mission, had directed her nonstop as she worked, issuing orders as if she were his avatar in a videogame instead of an expert in her own right. That was when she was living on the International Space Station, her first time up, a dozen years ago, just after she'd graduated from the AsCan program. It was a ten-month research mission. She was green, not stupid, but she kept her mouth shut. At that point she had already heard the rumors that the *Aether* selection committee was beginning their search, and rumor was that anyone going up during the search was basically auditioning. She wanted a spot on their list so badly it hurt.

That first trip into space had convinced her that she would do anything in her power to get a place on *Aether.* The planning had been under way for years by then, and the craft itself was already being assembled in space, orbiting the planet while they built the components on Earth. At the right time of day she could see *Aether* from the ISS, the sun glinting off its hull, shining in the distance like a man-made star. When *Aether* eventually returned from its long voyage, to Jupiter and back, it would dock with the ISS and become a permanent addition. There wasn't an astronaut in the program who wouldn't have traded their soul for a place on its maiden voyage—a place in history, right next to Yuri Gagarin and Neil Armstrong. No one knew for sure when the team would be selected or even when the mission would launch, but veterans and newcomers alike had been buzzing about the possibility for years by the time Sully graduated from candidate to astronaut.

Floating from mark to mark, scrabbling for handholds on the tin can that had been her home for almost two years, she remembered the day they announced the search for *Aether*'s crew, seven years ago. She also remembered the day they offered her a spot on the crew, sixteen months later, and the look on Jack's face when she told him. They were living separately by then, but no one had said the word *divorce* yet. She couldn't recall Lucy's expression because she hadn't been the one to tell her. Jack had done it. They agreed that the news would be easier coming from Jack, but they both knew the real reason—that Sully was the one who couldn't handle telling her only child that she would voluntarily be spending more than two years apart from her. Was it worth it? Would she do it again? All the hard work and sacrifice and endless training had landed her here: the loneliest place in the solar system. She almost laughed out loud. If only she could have warned her past self how it was all going to turn out. But even if she had known—she wouldn't have done a thing differently. Ivanov's words returned to her: *Not everyone has a calling.* Out there, floating in the emptiness, she felt a sad serenity: she had followed hers. She hadn't been outside the spacecraft since Callisto and it was a beautiful day for a walk, just like all the days, and all the nights, that had come before. She let her memories recede, and she let the future spin away from her. None of that mattered anymore. There was only the next handhold, and then the one after that.

"Try the fourth storage pod—there should be a ladder on the side facing away from you." It was Harper, mistaking her pause for indecision. She glanced over her shoulder and caught a glimpse of Devi, making her way across the row of storage pods on the other side of the ship.

"Copy," she said, and leaped out across the smooth, cylindrical pods labeled with tall black numerals. She grabbed hold of the rungs she hadn't quite been able to see. The two women arrived at the aft, where the comm. dish had been ripped away, at the same time. Sully laid her white hand on Devi's shoulder and Devi flashed her a thumbs-up.

"Good so far?" Sully asked.

"Good so far," Devi repeated.

They tethered themselves to the site and set to work inspecting the damage, prepping for the installation.

~~~

SULLY PULLED THE airlock shut behind her and they waited for the chamber to pressurize before they began taking off their suits. They'd been outside for more than five hours. The rest of the crew was crowded against the other side of the lock, waiting for them to reenter the ship. Eventually the interior airlock hissed and Harper pulled it open. Devi and Sully went through to join the others in the greenhouse corridor. Ivanov shook Sully's hand. Thebes and Tal hugged her. Harper's expression of worry collapsed into one of relief, and Sully draped an arm across Tal's shoulders so that she didn't have to decide whether to hug Harper like a friend or shake his hand like a colleague. Thebes didn't seem to want to let go of Devi; he held on to her for a long time, like a parent reunited with his child. The others followed Harper back to the observation deck and gathered in the cupola as they discussed the next spacewalk. They went over the footage from the helmet cameras.

The walk had been successful in that they'd made a viable plan for the replacement installation and had sent a few pieces of the old system that were too damaged spinning out into the asteroid belt, where they would drift for more than a million human lifetimes. There were compliments and cheers all around as they fast-forwarded through the footage of the day, letting the more complex moments play in real time; but when the screen went dark, the mood grew somber. The success of the second walk was less certain. The repair work would be improvised as they went. There had been no training in the underwater facility for what came next. Concerns for the second walk were raised, solutions brainstormed, but after a few hours Harper called an end to the session. The crew was exhausted, the sudden burst of activity over the past days had begun to show on their faces.

"Take a day," Harper said. "I want everyone rested for round two. Let's get some dinner started and go over the fine print."

Ivanov insisted on making dinner, which he never did. They sat at the long table and watched as he threw together an odd-looking stew of canned tomatoes, potatoes, kale, and frozen sausage, which in the end tasted quite good. Tal picked up his bowl to slurp down the vivid red broth and came up for air with a smear of orange across his mouth.

"Not bad," he said, and served himself a second bowl.

Ivanov shrugged. "Old recipe," he said, and almost smiled—not quite.

As they ate, they revisited plans for the second spacewalk. The new comm. dish was much smaller, reaped from the lunar module, but with a few adjustments and a couple of attachments, they had figured out how to make it work. Thebes would recalibrate the system from within while Sully and Devi installed it outside. The trickiest part would be getting the thing out the airlock and over where it needed to go.

Tal, Thebes, and Harper cleaned up after dinner while Ivanov had a go at the gaming console. Sully and Devi were falling asleep at the kitchen table and went to bed almost immediately after dinner. Sometime in the night Sully awoke to the sound of Devi whimpering in her compartment. She pulled back her curtain, shuffled across the centrifuge, and slipped inside the bunk. Devi was having a nightmare, and when Sully shook her awake, the terror in her eyes was so deep and wild that it unsettled Sully too.

"What is it?" Sully whispered. "Bad dream? You're safe, Devi, you're safe."

Devi scrabbled at Sully's shirt, pulling at the thin gray fabric as if she were drowning. It took Devi a moment to realize she was awake. Eventually she lay back against her sweat-drenched pillow, her breath shallow and her muscles tense.

"Tell me about your dream," Sully instructed.

Devi curled against her and shuddered. "We failed."

"What happened?"

"We lost the dish. I let it go and it drifted into the sun, and then we—we drifted into the sun too. It was my fault."

Sully began to stroke Devi's hair, as she might have done once for Lucy, combing her fingers through it and stopping to gently undo each tangle she encountered. Devi sniffled beneath her hands, her chest shivering with unexpressed sobs. Sully imagined the dream Devi had described to her, and it frightened her too. Not only that they might fail, or that they might all die without ever returning home, without ever knowing what had happened to Earth and everyone on it—but that it would be her fault. Sully realized anew how much responsibility she and Devi had in their hands.

Devi drifted back to sleep but Sully stayed with her, the younger woman's head nestled into the curve of her shoulder. Her arm ached but she kept still, waiting and thinking, until the artificial dawn began to creep over Little Earth. Finally she slipped out of Devi's bunk and returned to her own, padding across the quiet centrifuge, bare feet and bare legs, her long hair limp and wavy from yesterday's braid. In her bunk she changed her underclothes, slid on her jumpsuit, and tied the arms around her waist. She set about combing her hair into sections with her fingers and opened her curtain while she wove them together, watching the lights glow, then strengthen, then shine.

THAT DAY WAS full of preparation. Thebes was going over the suits and EVA toolkits, testing for weak seals and possible malfunctions. Ivanov was giving Sully and Devi a full medical workup before round two while Harper and Tal rigged the communications dish for transportation. In addition to his duties as an astrogeologist, Ivanov was *Aether*'s doctor. He hadn't practiced medicine in decades and his bedside manner wasn't much to speak of, but he made the blood work quick and painless. The second spacewalk would take at least eight hours, maybe more—about twice as long as yesterday's outing. After Ivanov had finished Sully's medical exam she left the lab and went to the command deck, where Harper and Tal were watching the footage of the first walk.

"Fellas," she said. "Not worried, are you?"

"Hell no," Harper scoffed. Tal pursed his lips while he shook his head with comic certainty, arms crossed, eyebrows scrunched. The bravado was a joke. Everyone was worried.

"Good, me neither." Sully floated toward the cupola and looked out. In the distance she could see Mars, still just a pinprick, lost among the stars. At the control board Harper and Tal went back to their reconnaissance, rewinding and replaying the video until they were satisfied, then moving on to the next piece of footage. Sully stayed in the cupola, communing with the darkness just beyond, the savage landscape she was about to inhabit once again—dangerous and beautiful and unknown. She knew she was ready; she'd gotten the physical okay from Ivanov, and the playbook for the walk was firmly imprinted on her brain, but there was an emotion stirring that didn't belong. Devi's dream—it must be fear. A thick-rooted fear, growing in the part of her where reason didn't live. Someone else might have called it intuition, but not Sully. She wrote it off as nerves and turned away from the window, back to the ship, back to the plan.

ELEVEN

AUGIE AND IRIS reached the small camp by the lake as darkness fell, and they stumbled into the first tent they came to, a sparse but welcome respite from the raw cold of the outdoors. Despite the dilapidation, the crisp scent of frozen mildew, and the minimal furnishings, it felt more like a home than anywhere Augie had lived in years. There were four camping beds with canvas mattresses, an oil-burning stove, a gas range, and a few sticks of furniture. The aluminum rods that held the vinyl shell of the tent in place curled overhead. Augie felt he was sitting inside the belly of a whale, admiring its rib cage. In the center of the room was a card table with a few folding chairs, and beyond it a desk covered with meteorological maps and weather records, a small generator, a few wooden crates used as bookshelves. A dozen kerosene lamps with blackened glass chimneys were clustered in the center of the table, and a mismatched collection of ragged carpets lay on the plywood floor. There was a comfort in that one room that the entire Barbeau outpost had lacked—a sense of personality, of coziness. It was clear that lives had been lived here. Meals had been made, novels had been read, games had been played.

They put down their gear and began to look more closely at what had been left behind. The crates were packed with paperback books, mostly romance novels, along with a few mysteries and one or two basic cookbooks. The mattresses on the cots were sheathed in protective plastic, and upon unwrapping the first one, Augustine found a few wool blankets, a crumpled sheet, and a mealy pillow stuffed inside the plastic case. He shook out the sheet and stretched its elastic to cover the corners of the slim mattress. Plumped the pillow. Refolded the blankets.

At the table, he lit a few of the lamps, then propped the front door open to let in the last of the natural light. The musty smell of abandonment stirred around him and started to trickle out into the open air. Iris had gone back outside and was sitting in the snow a few yards from the edge of the lake, drawing figure eights with a rock. Augustine found a boulder to sit on and stayed with her there for a moment, taking in the view. He was filled with a sense of relief. The journey had been worth it. They had made it. There would be no return trip, and yet—he felt safe there. Without the shadow of the evacuation, the looming emptiness of the hangar and the runway, this place felt more like an oasis than a place of exile.

The sun was already gone, captured by the mountains that circled the lake, and the sky had deepened to a dark blue. There would be plenty of time for exploring in the coming days. They sat in silence and listened to the ice. A wolf howled somewhere far away, and then another answered from the other side of the lake. Still they sat. Full darkness settled and a snowy owl swooped overhead, landing on one of the antenna poles, where it watched the two humans with curiosity. Stars began to prickle in the sky above them.

"Hungry?" Augustine asked, and Iris nodded. "I'll make something," he said, and slowly, stiffly rose from his boulder. He was looking forward to sleeping on the cot—it would be no worse than the nest they'd made in the observatory and much, much better than the frozen ground they'd spent the last few nights on. As he approached the hut, he saw the glow from the kerosene lamps illuminating the walls and the flicker of their flames from just inside the threshold. He was glad they'd come.

Inside, he started the oil stove, but he left the door unfastened so that Iris could slip through when she was done communing with the first body of water she'd seen in—well, he didn't know how long. He hadn't seen water since flying over the fjords on his way back to the observatory outpost after his last vacation, over a year ago now. The frozen lake was a reminder of a gentler season fast approaching. He closed his eyes and imagined how it would look in a month, when the midnight sun had risen and the trickle of spring had found its way to them. He imagined the softness of the mud, the virility of grass poking up through the barren land, the liquid glass of the melted surface, and it filled him with a sense of serenity. He could stop fighting the landscape, just for a moment, just this once. Since the evacuation, since Iris, he had felt more earthbound than he had in years. There was a time when the changes in the sky meant more to him than the ground beneath his feet, but not right then. He had been looking up for long enough; it felt good to think of the dirt instead, to imagine the life that would soon return to the land.

As the stove began to warm the hut, Augustine shed a few layers and rummaged through the boxes and packages stacked around the gas range. There was an abundance of food, and he suspected that one of the other huts would have an even larger store packed away for the long winters and rare supply runs a location like this would get. He found a skillet, sticky with old grease and dust, and rinsed it in a tin basin with water from the big insulated tank in the corner of the tent. When he set the skillet down on the hot range, the moisture began to spit and crackle. He emptied a can of corned beef hash into the pan, and when the hash was brown and crisp, he flipped it out onto two plates and scrambled some powdered eggs. There was an enormous can of instant coffee and both condensed and powdered milk—*what riches*, Augie thought—and while Iris began to eat he set some water to boil for coffee, then sat down beside her.

"Is it all right?" he asked her, and she nodded her approval between big bites of hash.

When the water was ready, Augie made himself a mug of coffee, sweetened with a generous helping of condensed milk, and decided it was the most delicious drink he'd ever had—better than whiskey, even. They continued to sit at the table after eating, their dishes stacked in front of them and the oil stove humming beside them, not saying anything, just enjoying the tones of silence. The kerosene lamps illuminated the hut and the stove kept it surprisingly warm, even as the temperatures outside plunged. Augustine set the dishes down in the basin and left them for the morning, then unwrapped another one of the cots for Iris. They weren't accustomed to sleeping so far apart; in the observatory, they had curled up in the nest together, for warmth. Iris watched Augie fold the plastic and shake out the sheet, then fit it to the mattress. They took out their subzero sleeping bags and laid them on top of the beds.

In the night Augie woke to hear the howls of a pack of Arctic wolves. They sounded close—in the mountains behind the camp, he guessed, perhaps sniffing around their abandoned snowmobile and marking it as theirs. *They can have it,* Augie thought, and drifted back to sleep.

--vvv--

IN THE MORNING, he lay on the cot for a few extra minutes, enjoying the warmth of the oil stove still chugging away. When he got to his feet, he shuddered to hear the cartilage in his joints cracking, his bones clicking against each other like dominoes falling down the length of his body. He was sore from the tumble he'd taken off the snowmobile the day before, but he'd live. He found a scouring pad and soap, warmed up some water, and washed the skillet and tin camping plates from last night's dinner. When he was done he wandered outside and looked back at their hut to see the smoke curling up through its slim silver chimney and disappearing into a pale blue sky. The sun had already climbed well past the tips of the surrounding mountains. He heard

Iris before he saw her, the hollow beat of improvised percussion accompanied by the keening hum that could only be hers. He followed the sound and found her sitting on top of an upturned dinghy by the edge of the lake, tapping out a rhythm on the hull with a piece of wood, her skinny legs crossed beneath her, the green pompom of her hat jiggling in time with the beat. Augie waved to her and she waved back before returning to her composition. Something about her was different, and it took Augie a moment to realize— she looked happy. He left her to her music and turned back to the camp.

There were the three huts, two large white ones, one smaller green, set in a row, a cluster of oil, kerosene, and gas drums gathered behind them. Augustine inspected them in turn. The other white hut was more barren than theirs, but mostly the same. It had two more cots—a backup dormitory, he thought, perhaps for the summer season when the population of the little camp swelled. In the green hut he found the food stores and more cooking supplies. This seemed to be the cook tent, presumably used as such in the warmer, busier summer months. During the winter the operation probably shrank down to the one tent they'd taken up residence in. The cook tent was packed with canned and dehydrated food, a huge array of it—more fruit cocktail and instant coffee and creamed spinach and mystery meat than they could consume in years. The variety was staggering, the quantities ample, the quality questionable, but it was vastly better than what they'd had before. They would not go hungry here, nor would they freeze to death—that much was clear.

Back outside the cook tent, the air was incredibly still.

The sun had warmed the basin surrounding the lake and the temperatures were almost balmy—about 35 degrees Fahrenheit, he guessed. He loosened his scarf and stood still, letting the light soak into his old, battered skin. He couldn't remember the last time he'd felt this good. On the small island toward the center of the lake, he saw the Arctic hares bouncing up and down on its banks, watching him. He wondered whether they summered there or bounded across the ice to the mainland before it was too late and the ice turned to water, trying their luck in the mountains that ringed the lake. Or perhaps—he smiled to think of it—they were swimmers.

There was one more building that he hadn't looked in yet. It was the control shed next to the radio antenna array, and he was saving it for last. A solid structure of wood and metal, it was set apart from the cluster of tents, nearer to the array than to the living quarters. Augustine walked to the radio shed and put his hand on the knob, then paused without knowing why. *Surely this can wait,* he thought, and let his hand fall back to his side. The radio was the reason he'd come here—a chance to contact what was left of the outside world—but suddenly it seemed secondary. They could build a home here, and wasn't that what he'd really wanted? He turned to look at the camp and saw Iris lying on her back on the overturned dinghy, staring up at the sky, her crude wooden drumstick clutched across her chest like a funeral bouquet. He left the building and returned to her.

"Walk with me?" he called to Iris.

She lifted her head and swung her legs off the dinghy. She shrugged—a yes. Augie took her hand and pulled her to her feet.

"Come on," he said, "let's explore."

~~~~~~

THE ICE WAS still solid despite the creaking sounds it made. They skated back and forth, falling occasionally, attempting to race and spin and jump on its thick, slippery surface. Iris wanted to walk out to the island, but halfway there Augustine began to stumble. It was as if his legs weren't obeying him. The second time he fell to his knees they turned around and headed back for the camp. The Arctic hares watched the two humans go with perked ears and quivering noses. He stopped to rest two hundred yards from shore and Iris waited by his side, attentive and mute, laying her palm against his forehead as though she were playing doctor.

Back at the camp, Augustine lay down on his cot and Iris made coffee. It was watery and black—she hadn't used enough of the instant powder or any of the condensed milk—but he drank it gratefully and closed his eyes. When he opened them again the light outside was fading and Iris was sitting at the card table reading one of the romance novels. Her lips moved as she scanned the page. Two lovers in gauzy silks clutched each other on the cover.

"How is it?" he croaked, and his voice came out rusty, as if he hadn't used it in days. She shrugged and made a teetering motion with her hand: *so-so.* She finished the page and turned the book facedown on the table, then got to her feet and began to root around the kitchen area. He gradually realized she was replicating the meal he'd made them last night. He felt a kernel of pride that she had paid attention, that he had taught her something useful without even intending to. *Perhaps this is how fathers feel,* he thought. The smell of the corned beef made him hungry, and when the food was ready he dragged himself to the table, where they ate in front of the kerosene lamps. After he finished washing the dishes, he turned around to find Iris asleep on his cot, curled around the paperback novel like a crescent moon. He fastened the door, just a little latch to make sure it didn't blow open in the night, and warmed his dishwater-damp hands in front of the oil stove. Then he blew out the kerosene lamps and lay down beside her, the two of them nestled in the narrow cot. Iris shifted slightly and the book fell off the cot, but she didn't wake. As he drifted off he focused on her breath and finally identified the source of the nagging fear that had been plaguing him all this time: love.

~~~~

AUGUSTINE DRIFTED THROUGH high school and most of college under a cloak of social invisibility. He was quiet and smart and watchful. It wasn't until he was a senior in college that he realized the two girls sitting on either side of him in his thermodynamics class were smitten with him—that he could have either of them, perhaps both, if he wanted. But did he want them? What would he do with them? He'd already had sex once, in high school, and he had found it pleasant enough, but too messy and awkward to be worth pursuing it again. And yet—this kind of romantic charge was new to him. It was beyond the puzzle pieces of human bodies; it was an emotional mystery. An experiment he'd never had the variables to conduct before. Not one to back down from an intriguing research project, Augustine didn't hesitate to sleep with both girls in quick succession. It came out that they were in a sorority together, and they immediately became vicious, to him and to each another, when they realized they were dating the same boy. The semester ended with tears and nasty letters and one of the girls dropping out, but to him the experiment had been a success. He'd learned something, and he'd realized there was so much more to learn.

During the years that followed, he continued to experiment with these emotions. He developed new and more effective techniques for attraction. He would woo his test subjects diligently, sparing no expense, no compliment, and when they had finally fallen in love with him, he would reject them. It was gradual at first—he stopped calling, stopped sleeping over in their beds, stopped whispering flattery into their lovely ears. The subjects would begin to suspect they were losing him, just after they'd decided they wanted him, and they would double their efforts to keep him. The sex would become more adventurous, and he would enjoy these gestures as they came, then shame them later for offering themselves so freely. The invitations to dinner or the cinema or the museum would become one-sided. Eventually he would stop seeing them altogether, would scorn them without ever saying so, without ever saying goodbye or even offering the conventional "It's not you, it's me" line. He would simply disappear from their lives. If they had the gall to go looking for him, he would make them feel insane—as if he had been halfhearted all along, or as if he'd never wanted them at all. He never felt guilty about any of it, just curious.

These women Augustine experimented on called him the usual names: asshole, jerk, son of a bitch, dirtbag. Then there were the more clinical terms: pathological liar, sociopath, psycho, sadist. He was intrigued by these names, and there were moments when he wondered if they were correct. Asshole, certainly, but sociopath? In his twenties and early thirties, before his post in New Mexico, it seemed possible. He was observing emotions in these women that he'd never felt before, witnessing pain he'd inflicted with barely a flash of sympathy. He tried to remember: Had he loved his mother, or had he only manipulated her for his own comfort? Had he, even then, been experimenting on her to see what worked and what didn't? Had he always been this way? The fact that he wasn't particularly troubled by that possibility seemed to make it even more probable.

It wasn't personal—it was never personal. He wanted to understand love's boundaries, to see what sort of flora grew on the other side, what sort of fauna lived there. And infatuation, lust—were they different? Did they manifest with different symptoms? He wanted to understand these things clinically, to experiment with love's limits, its flaws. He didn't want to feel it, just to study it. It was recreational. Another field of study to explore. His real work was far loftier, but his questions regarding love were not easily answered. He never felt satisfied. And Augustine was accustomed to satisfactory answers, so he persevered.

His behavior wasn't without consequence. Eventually he would overstep the mark. The women—the test subjects—would become too hazardous, too plentiful. He would run into them in cafés, see them at work or walking in his neighborhood. And they all knew each other, because what better way to leapfrog from one woman to the next than by exploiting the fringes of a lover's social circle? Augustine didn't care enough to apologize—it was easier simply to leave, to find a new observatory, a new fellowship or adjunct teaching position, and begin again. It was only a side project to him, an off-the-books experiment that was dwarfed by his real work, among the stars. He enjoyed the variety of bodies, different breasts and bellies and legs to explore when he needed a break from his research, but that was all. Occasionally he felt pity, but never compassion—he couldn't understand the reactions he was confronted with. They seemed overblown, ridiculous.

His father was dead by the time he got his PhD, his mother in the locked wing of a mental hospital. He had no other family, no other examples of love to draw from, only blurry memories of dysfunction and an unhappy childhood. He had never been interested in television or novels. He wanted to learn from life, from observation. And he did: he learned that love was concealed by a swirling vortex of unpleasant emotions, the invisible, unreachable center of a black hole. It was irrational and unpredictable. He wanted no part of it, and his experiments only confirmed, again and again, how distasteful it all was. As time wore on he grew more fond of liquor and less fond of women. It was easier. A better, simpler escape.

In his thirties, he accepted a position at the Jansky Very Large Array in Socorro, New Mexico, home to some of the best radio astronomy opportunities in the world. Augustine was well known by then, among his colleagues, but also farther afield. He was young and photogenic, which made him popular with the media, and his work was revolutionizing his field. But he knew his contributions wouldn't be remembered until he truly made his mark. He was at the edge, almost there, but he still needed the theory that would put his name alongside those of the pioneers of science. His reputation as a womanizing asshole preceded him wherever he went, but so did his reputation for groundbreaking, meticulous research. All the facilities wanted to host him, and he had his pick of the tenure-track posts. But Augustine hated teaching. He wanted—no, needed—to discover.

The Jansky Array was a rare departure from Augie's optical research, but the funding practically landed in his lap, with no tedious paperwork or bureaucratic schmoozing required. Perhaps a few years of radio astronomy would be just the thing to take his research to a new level. He booked the ticket and packed his suitcase, just one, the enormous piece of distressed leather baggage that he'd been toting across oceans and continents since his undergraduate days. In Socorro they gave him a warm welcome and he settled in quickly, glad of the change of scenery and impressed with the scope of the VLA. He stayed for almost four years— longer than he'd anticipated, longer than he'd stayed anywhere since college—and it was there that he met Jean.

TWELVE

"NICE MORNING FOR a walk," Devi said, grinning at Sully through her helmet. *Aether*'s reflection moved across her mirrored visor. Although she could barely see Devi's face beneath the reflected image, Sully could make out her teeth as she smiled, wide and white beneath the glare. The stillness of the space around them was complete, like the quiet of morning before the birds begin to chirp, before the sun wakes the earth—only out here there was no daybreak, no high noon, no gloaming hour. Just this eternal moment of hush. No before, no after, just an endless sliver of time between night and day.

She felt peaceful. She felt capable. Propelling herself and the comm. dish through empty space, feeling the soft vibration of her propulsion unit, hearing the occasional transmission from Devi or Harper. The aft of the ship was looming closer—almost there. The minutiae of the installation would take hours, but she had time. She had tools. She had a plan, a partner, a team; she had a damn jetpack. It would be fine. She saw Devi touch down on the installation site in front of her and brought the payload in for a gentle landing. Devi was ready with the tethers, clipping them into place as soon as Sully got close enough, so that the new dish could float a few yards away from the ship while they reconfigured the wiring and then connected its mast to the hull. The dish swayed against its restraints, a long arm with a big round paw, waving at them. Devi and Sully tethered themselves to the site too. Loose wires floated out from the connection point like Medusa's snaky curls. Devi arranged them meticulously and intuitively, splitting and splicing them to match the mechanics of the new comm. dish. Sully supplied the tools as Devi asked for them, clipping the spares to her utility belt.

Hours passed as they worked, mostly in silence. Occasionally, Devi would reach out and request a tool from Sully's belt, but there was no chatter between them. Devi was immersed, as she should be, and Sully was alert, as she should be. Everything was progressing as planned. And yet—something was not quite right. Sully took a gulp of water from the straw inside her suit and rolled her neck from side to side within the cramped confines of her helmet.

"*Aether*, time check, please," she said.

"Six hours since EVA commenced," Harper responded. "You're doing great, guys."

"Almost ready to connect," Devi said. "Sully, could you bring the mast down to, say, four inches above the connection site?"

"Copy," Sully said, and began to reel in the dish with the tethers. When she could reach it she grabbed the mast and let go of the tethers, tugging it down toward the hull of the ship and letting it hover just above the area Devi was working on.

"Perfect," Devi said. "Now keep it right there while I hook it in."

It was another hour before the electrical connection was established. By then Sully was beginning to feel antsy. Together the two women lowered the dish, Devi packing the wiring back into the aperture, Sully directing the movement of the mast, until finally the new system was in place and ready to be secured, bolted onto the hull of the ship. Nearly finished now. Sully took another sip of water and laid her oversized glove on Devi's shoulder.

"Good work," she said. Devi didn't respond. She stayed motionless beneath Sully's hand, and the cloud of apprehension that had been following Sully since they began the walk solidified, condensed into real fear. "Hey, are you okay?" Sully kept her voice steady, but inside her head she was repeating *no, no, no* over and over, like thumbing the beads of a rosary.

There was a blast of static over the ship's frequency and a muffle of expletives, poorly disguised by a hand over the microphone.

"Devi? What's the matter?" Sully maneuvered herself closer, still holding on to the mast of the dish, so that she could peer behind the mirror of Devi's visor. There was that static again.

"We've got a carbon dioxide problem in Devi's suit showing up here—Devi, are you feeling okay?" Thebes asked from inside the ship. "The oxygen level in your suit just took a nosedive."

Sully looked past the reflection of the ship on Devi's visor and knew that something was wrong. Devi seemed dazed, her eyes beginning to lose focus, to roll back in her head. She was already fighting to stay alert.

"Respond. What's going on out there?"

The two women looked at each other for a long moment, Devi struggling to enunciate her words. "It's the scrubber," she whispered. "The lithium hydroxide cartridge failed. I didn't notice, because—" She inhaled as deeply as she could, but there wasn't enough oxygen to sate her lungs. She was suffocating inside her helmet. "I should've noticed."

"Get back to the airlock," Harper said, almost a shout.

"I don't think there's time," Devi said. Her arms had begun to convulse, twitching and shivering, and Sully watched as the tool she had been holding fell from her thickly padded fingers and spun away from them, out into the emptiness. It was happening so quickly, Sully barely had time to react before Devi was unconscious, swaying against her tether like a tree following the whims of a breeze. Sully froze, her hands locked around the mast of the new comm. dish.

"Devi. *Devi.*"

Sully squinted past the reflections on Devi's visor and saw her face, her features more relaxed than they'd been in months, as though she were asleep, having pleasant dreams. No more nightmares. No more fear, no more loneliness. Shocked silence from *Aether* as the rest of the crew checked her vitals. She knew it even before Thebes's voice confirmed it in her ear.

"Sully—she's gone. She was right, it's too late. You couldn't have . . . There's nothing you could have done."

She was only vaguely aware of the words that followed, anxious demands coming from within the ship, from Thebes, from Harper, but she couldn't make sense of them. The words meant nothing to her. She stared into Devi's helmet, watching her friend dream. She kept her hands locked onto the mast, instinctively keeping the dish secure, but there wasn't room for anything else. Waves of shock rolled through her, pressed her thoughts down, muffled the voices, and by the time the undertow released her, the voices had ceased, she wasn't sure how long ago. Minutes? Hours? And yet—there was still work to do. She had to finish.

"Aether," she said.

"Sullivan," Harper responded immediately.

"I need . . ." She stopped and swallowed. Took a sip of water. Swallowed again. "I need you to tell me what to do now."

She could hear his measured exhale on the other end of the comm. and Thebes mumbling something she couldn't make out.

"You have the drill?" Harper asked.

She checked her belt. "Yes, I have the drill."

"And the bolts?"

She checked her utility pouch, patting it with her free hand.

"Yes, I have the bolts."

"Just like we practiced. The first two will be tricky because you need to keep hold of the mast, but after that you can let it go and use both hands. Copy?"

She couldn't move. "I think—" she began, but Harper interrupted her.

"No," he said, "no thinking. Just one bolt at a time, Sully."

She did exactly that, and when she was finished she detached Devi from her tether without asking Harper's permission. She knew it was what her friend would have wanted—what any of them would want.

Sully stared after her as she drifted away, growing smaller and smaller, shrinking to the size of a star and then disappearing altogether. Would she drift forever? Or would she fall into the sun? A distant star? Sully thought of *Voyager,* breaching the solar system and embarking on an infinite sojourn. She hoped that Devi might follow—that she might remain intact, somehow, her lifeless body traversing the universe on an infinite, incomprehensible journey. Sully didn't move for a long time, just looked out into the dark emptiness, silently asking the void to hold her friend close.

THE NEXT MORNING she woke up screaming. A terror more intense than anything she'd ever felt before. It clung to her long after she opened her eyes, humming in her bones. She watched Devi drift, a tiny speck of white in an endless black void, over and over. At first, she tried to reimagine it, envision a different ending to the story—conjuring scenes in which she rushed Devi back to the airlock just in time, in which she sensed that the CO_2 scrubber was failing long before it became poisonous—but there was no solace in these reenactments. Devi was gone and Sully was still here. It seemed nonsensical, but it was the way things were.

She had done as Harper told her, put aside her thoughts and installed the bolts, one by one—an hour of work masquerading as a lifetime—then gotten herself back to the airlock. She had slipped out of her suit and into the ship, where the remaining four waited for her in silence. She'd propelled herself past them without a word, back to the centrifuge, back to her compartment, and drawn the curtain. She'd slept and not-slept. She'd thought and not-thought. The nightmare of the spacewalk followed her mind wherever it hid, unconscious, subconscious, conscious. She couldn't escape it because it was literally all around her: the vacuum she had tumbled into just hours ago. The poisonous, frozen, boiling blackness that was their road, their sky, their horizon, surrounding *Aether* and everyone inside with violent indifference. They were not welcome here. They were not safe. After a while Sully stopped trying to escape the terror and let the throbbing ache of it align with her heartbeat, let it ebb and flow with her breath. It sank into her physiology and became part of her. She would never be safe again. She knew that now.

Devi's death had stirred something deep and dormant in Sully's subconscious. No longer moving chronologically, her brain began to replay everything horrible that had ever happened to her, everything that had ever wounded her. Lucy's tiny heart-shaped face looking back, framed by Jack's shoulder as he walked away from her in the airport—the day Sully left them behind for Houston, hoping that the separation might work, knowing that it couldn't, and leaving anyway; boarding her flight with the damp of her daughter's tears still soaked into the collar of her shirt. Then leaving them behind again just before the launch of her first spaceflight, when Jack had already served her with divorce papers and Lucy was so incredibly grown-up, speaking in full, eloquent sentences, the blond in her hair beginning to darken, the innocent trust in her eyes beginning to fade; the knowing slant of her eyebrows when Sully couldn't help but say things like *I'll be back before you know it.*

Then her return: knocking on a front door that used to be hers, being greeted by what's-her-name, although of course she knew all along her name was Kristen, those letters emblazoned on her brain as permanently and painfully as an unfortunate tattoo. Watching her daughter fold herself into what's-her-name's lap, feeling Lucy's reluctance to leave the house with her when they went out to a movie, the slight but discernible roll of Jack's eyes when she said she had to be back in Houston by Monday, the sight of the three of them sitting on the sofa together in the living room as she showed herself out, knowing that her family was loved and safe and appreciated and that she had absolutely nothing to do with any of it. Knowing that she had been replaced, and that her replacement was an improvement—a better mother, a better spouse, a better person than she could ever be.

She had visitors that day. Each of the other crewmembers stopped by her compartment, some more than once, but their voices, the tap of their knuckles against the wall, seemed far away. Harper and Thebes went so far as to sweep aside the curtain and look at her with mournful eyes, but all she could say was "Tomorrow," because what she really needed was to finish this day and get to the day after. It was the only way she could escape the day *of* and move beyond it—not even a real day, just a sliver of silence between light and dark when she'd held tight to the radio dish while Devi died beside her. She was vaguely ashamed to dismiss her crewmates, her friends, seeing the hurt hiding in the lines around their lips, above their eyebrows, and turning them away with just a single word: *tomorrow.* It couldn't be helped. Today was full.

～～～

WHEN HER ALARM clock buzzed at the usual time she was exhausted from a sleepless night, but she got up anyway. She couldn't spend another day in hiding, not that she knew how to spend it any other way, but something had to give. They had work to do, a mission to complete. She needed to configure the new comm. dish—the reason all of this had happened. She sat up and changed her shirt, her underwear. She scooted into a fresh jumpsuit and zipped it up to the neck. Running her fingers over the stitching of her monogram, she traced the initial of her first name—a name that not even Jack had called her. She'd been Sullivan since college, Sully for short. The name she'd inherited from her mother. She closed her eyes and pictured Devi's monogram, white thread against the burgundy she'd always favored for her *Aether* uniforms: *NTD.* N for Nisha.

"Nisha Devi," she whispered. Then she said it again. And again, like a chant—or perhaps a prayer.

In the kitchen she found Tal, eating oatmeal paste straight from one of the nonperishable pouches that most of their food came in. His black hair rocketed away from his head in unwieldy curls, so thick and wiry that it looked the same in Little Earth and zero G.

"Hi," he said cautiously.

"Morning," she responded, and sat across from him with her own serving of oatmeal paste.

"I'm glad you're up," he said.

She nodded. They ate in silence, and when Tal had finished his breakfast and disposed of the wrapper he stood behind Sully and laid both his hands on her shoulders.

"It was awful, and it wasn't your fault," he whispered, then squeezed, gently, and let his arms fall to his sides. Sully forced herself to keep eating the oatmeal even though it tasted like mud and she felt sick to her stomach. There would be plenty of things she didn't want to do today, things that made her feel ill, but she would do them. All of them. She owed Devi that much.

On the table in front of her sat the deck of cards she and Harper used to play with. Used to? She wondered if this feeling would ever lift, if she would ever be able to laugh with her whole body or exchange silly banter with Harper again, shuffling the deck into a waterfall as they had just a few nights ago. It didn't seem possible. She remembered again that day in Goldstone when her mother taught her how to play alone. *How to stay occupied,* she'd said at the time. It was useful—the hours Sully had spent playing alone in her mother's office seemed to overshadow the rest of her childhood. School was a blur, her elementary school friends faceless, nameless entities that wove in and out of her memories. It was only that office that was crisp in her recollection, the mornings at the kitchen table listening to her mother read the newspaper headlines, the nights driving out into the desert. It was only the snap of the plastic cards against the plastic desk, the groan of the air-conditioning, the muffled voices emanating from the control room that seemed real. She had been so proud of Jean, never for an instant begrudging her the time that could've been spent teaching Sully how to swim the breaststroke or ride a bike or cook an egg sunny side up. One year Jean got a promotion, and it was a thousand times better than any A+ or gold star, it was *their* hard work, their joint sacrifice, coming to fruition. Sully didn't mind being sequestered in the dark, dusty office because she knew that Jean was doing important work—practically changing the world, just down the hall. As a child, she admired Jean more than anyone else. From the moment she understood what her mother did for work, Sully knew that she wanted to follow in her footsteps.

The mythos of her nameless, faceless father was similar. The work he was doing was bigger and more important than any one family. Whenever Sully asked about him, Jean would tell her he was a brilliant man, that he was so smart and so dedicated to his work that he didn't have any room left in his heart for them. Jean told her to be proud of his calling—to know that she didn't have a father because the world needed him more than they did.

"Little bear," Jean would say, "your daddy is too big for one family, but you and me, we're the perfect size for each other."

Then she turned ten, her mother got married, and the ratio shifted. Shattered. They moved to Canada with her new husband and Jean was pregnant before the year was out, giving birth to twins a few months after Sully turned eleven. Jean stopped working, gave up her research, and fell into motherhood, became immersed in it. She was absorbed by her newborn twins in a way she had never been absorbed by her firstborn. The pride Sully felt in her mother dissipated. What had all those afternoons alone been for, if this was what came of it? All the work, all the sacrifice? The twins got bigger and bigger—they started talking and Jean taught them to call her *Mommy*. Sully had never called her that. There was nothing left for her, no room for an angry teenager in their new family, so she applied to boarding school and returned only when the dorms were closed and there was nowhere else she could go. At first she hoped for some kind of argument from her mother, pleading phone calls, groveling letters—some recognition of Sully's anger—but her absence was accepted without disagreement. Sully graduated, skipped the ceremony, and went south for college, back to where she'd been happiest.

Jean died before Sully got her degree—an unexpected fourth child, stillborn. She never woke up from the surgery and Sully didn't make it back in time. The embalmers made her up to look like someone Sully didn't recognize. At the funeral she sat next to the twins, little girls with honey-brown eyes and auburn hair, like their father. She realized she was an orphan. What remained of this family had never belonged to her.

Harper sat down next to her. He slid a cup of black coffee toward her. She jolted back to attention, ashamed; she was mourning the wrong person.

"You look like you might need this," he said.

She smiled, to make him feel better, but the expression felt foreign on her face, like a mask that didn't fit.

"I do," she said, and took a sip. It burned the roof of her mouth, but she didn't mind. It was a relief to feel something tangible, something immediate and uncomfortable to distract her from everything else, even if it was only for a moment.

"I'm sorry. About yesterday," she said, and took another sip.

He shook his head slowly, his lips pressed together. "That's not something for you to be sorry about. We all need different things. You needed time. You seem better today. I'm glad."

She shrugged and wrapped her hand around the mug in front of her. "I guess I'm coherent, if that's what you mean."

"Ha," he said, a joyless laugh cut short. He chewed on his lower lip, embarrassed. Laughing was not allowed, not yet. "It'll do for now."

Sully stood up and left her coffee mug on the table, still full. She hovered for a moment, unsure what to do next, where to go. "I'm going to work," she finally said.

"Work," Harper agreed, nodding. "I think Thebes is already in the comm. pod. He'll be glad to see you."

"Then that's where I'll be," Sully replied.

THIRTEEN

THEY'D BEEN AT Lake Hazen for almost two weeks—long enough to explore every corner of the camp—and yet something about the radio shed still made Augustine uneasy. He avoided it, as though there was too much power behind the door, too much reach; an ear to hear things he didn't want to know. There was no telescope here, no window to the stars, so instead of working he spent his time playing with Iris. They walked out to the little island in the middle of the lake and sneaked up on the Arctic hares, laughing as the hares bounded across the ice in a panic, leaping onto the shore and disappearing into the mountains that ringed the basin. He taught her chess with an old plastic set they found, a few pennies in place of missing pawns. They made snow sculptures.

And they feasted. The abundance and variety of nonperishable foods in the cook tent were thrilling after the monotony of the survival rations at the observatory. It was a museum of cans—canned pot roast, meat loaf, whole roast chickens soaked in brine, tuna fish, every kind of vegetable he could think of, even eggplant and okra; energy bars, protein bars, granola bars, shortbread bars, meat bars; powdered eggs, powdered milk, powdered coffee, powdered pancake mix; a shocking amount of butter, lard, and Crisco. Iris fell in love with fruit cocktail, treasuring every syrupy cherry with her eyes closed and a small smile on her lips. Augie was more enthused with the baking supplies, the possibility of conjuring something fresh and warm, and he began to experiment with pound cakes and scones studded with chocolate chips and raisins, then progressed to loaves of bread. The supplies of baking soda and baking powder alike were enormous, a stock that would last a dozen men a dozen years, and there were similarly vast quantities of onion and garlic powder, cayenne, cinnamon, nutmeg, curry, salt, black pepper. He'd scarcely used an oven since he was a boy, when he'd kept his mother company, but the pleasures of measuring and mixing and greasing the pan came rushing back to him. His mother had often begun ambitious projects in the kitchen and usually failed to finish them, leaving the chaos and the raw ingredients for Augie to deal with while she became distracted by something new. He'd forgotten he was good at finishing these projects, but more than that, he'd forgotten he enjoyed it. It was an unfamiliar feeling. He struggled to remember the last time he'd actually enjoyed something.

The days continued to lengthen and the snow around them to shrink. Grass sprouted on some of the lower hills surrounding the camp, then a few wildflowers popped up, crowding together in clusters of color, bordered by the remains of the snow. The equinox slipped past, and before Augie knew it the solstice was bearing down on them—the arrival of the midnight sun. He'd never been in the Arctic for a full polar day before; he had always fled south when the cargo planes began arriving on their biennial supply runs in the summer, when the stars disappeared from the sky for the season, leaving him with nothing to do and no reason to stay. As the weather warmed and the snow melted he began to realize how much he had missed.

When he'd chosen the Barbeau Observatory as a research destination five years ago, he was already an old man, near the end of his career, beginning to understand what a mess he'd made of things. He was drawn by the isolation and the punishing climate, the landscape that matched his interior. Instead of salvaging what he could, he ran away to the top of an Arctic mountain, nine degrees shy of the North Pole, and gave up. Misery followed him wherever he went. This fact didn't faze him and it certainly didn't surprise him. He had earned it, and by then he expected it.

Now, as he watched Iris dart along the shore, skipping rocks over the ice sheet, a strange sensation came over him, a muddle of contentment and regret. He had never been so happy and so sad all at once. It made him think of Socorro. Those years in New Mexico were the sharpest, the most vivid memories he had. Only now, decades later, did he finally understand that Socorro had been his best chance to have a life that felt like this—sitting by the edge of the lake, smelling spring, watching Iris, feeling grateful and complete, feeling alive. When he met Jean all those years ago, she lobbed him out of cool contemplation and into the heat of emotion. He couldn't observe her; he had to have her, to be seen by her. She was more than a subject, a variable to be quantified. She unnerved him, confused him. He'd loved her, of course he had, he could admit it now, but it wasn't so easy back then. She was twenty-six and he was thirty-seven when she told him she was pregnant. All he could think of were his parents and his own cruel experiments. He didn't want to be in love. He told Jean he'd never be a father. *Never,* he said. She didn't cry, he remembered that because he'd expected her to. She'd only looked at him with those big, sad eyes. *You're so broken,* she'd said. *I wish you weren't so broken.* And that had been that.

He'd found a position in Chile, in the Atacama Desert, where he'd lived once before. He got out of New Mexico as quickly as he could and forgot Jean as completely as he was able. It wasn't until years later that he allowed himself to think of her, of what could've been and what already was—a child, with his genes and maybe his eyes, maybe his mouth or his nose, but without him in its life. A child without a father. He tried to banish the idea from his consciousness, but it crept back, again and again. Eventually he made a call to Socorro and found out what little there was to know. Jean had left New Mexico shortly after he did, but she'd stayed in touch with some of the other research fellows. Augustine was told she'd had a girl, born in November, somewhere in the southern Californian desert. He tracked down a work address for her and kept it tucked in his wallet for months, just behind his driver's license.

He waited until the baby's birthday, and then he sent the most expensive amateur telescope he could afford. No note, no return address. Jean would know who it was from, and she could decide what to tell her daughter. He wondered what she'd already told her about her father, whether she'd lied and said he was dead, or a military POW, or a traveling salesman, or whether she'd told the truth and said—what, exactly? That he didn't want her? That he didn't love either of them? He kept sending things for a few years, never a card, just an occasional investment in his genes. Gestures that he couldn't actually claim were thoughtful, but that seemed better than nothing. Now and then he sent Jean a check. He knew she cashed them, but he only heard back from her once: a plain white envelope with a photo in it. She'd sent it to an old address, the observatory in Puerto Rico after he'd already moved on to Hawaii, and it took an extra few months to find its way to him. The girl looked like her mother. Probably a good thing. The next year his gift, sent to the same place in southern California, was returned and labeled *Invalid Address*. He never heard from them again. It was almost a relief to lose them; sending the gifts every year was just a reminder of his inadequacy to be anything more than a blank return address and a medium-sized check. The passionate, promising focus he'd begun his career with had narrowed into lonely obsession. He'd known this about himself for years. He didn't need more proof.

⌇⌇⌇

A PAIR OF Arctic terns had begun to build a nest on the ground, not far from the camp. They were apparently under the impression that they had the entire lake to themselves, so whenever Augie ventured closer for a look at the nest, he was regaled with swooping and screaming, little gray and white bombs with red feet and beaks emerging from the feathery masses. Iris didn't seem to provoke these wrathful displays, but Augie could hardly walk in their direction without giving rise to an attack. More than once he received a vicious peck to the crown of his head, and eventually he took to shielding himself with a square of plywood he'd found lying around camp. After a few collisions with a creature decidedly larger and more solid than they, the terns gave up their offensive and let him look. He wondered at their easy surrender, but reasoned that birds who spent their entire lives making the trip between the Antarctic and Arctic regions—more than forty-four thousand miles of migration every year—probably weren't the most innovative of creatures. The nest progressed nicely. What sights had they flown over on their long journey? How had they survived to make the same nonsensical trip every year? Augustine looked at the terns preparing for the arrival of their chicks and marveled at their tenacity—hatching new life at the end of the world. One of the terns swiveled its head to stare at Augustine with one eye. *What do you know that I don't?* Augustine asked it. But the tern only ruffled its feathers and hopped away.

One morning the sun rose and decided not to set. For a couple of days it sank below the mountain ridge in the evening but never dropped behind the horizon, and soon it stayed high and bright without pause. Within a few days of the midnight sun's arrival, Augie and Iris lost all sense of time. He had long ago lost track of the days, but he knew it must be mid-April if the midnight sun had risen, the same way he would know late September had arrived when the lake was bathed in twilit days, the sun hovering just beneath the horizon before it set completely and plunged the Arctic into another long, dark night.

Time didn't matter anymore. The only reason to keep track of time was to stay connected with the outside world, but without any sort of connection it was meaningless. Light and dark had always been the earth's clock, and Augie saw no reason not to abide by it now, even at this strange latitude. The winter had laid him low—his joints, his immune system, his temper had all been slow and dark—but with the endless light in the sky he felt a kind of buoyancy, a charge of electricity running through his nerves. His life took on a pleasant rhythm: he slept when he was tired, cooked when he was hungry, visited the terns when he felt like a stroll, and set up a little open-air porch at the mouth of their hut, with a lopsided Adirondack chair some previous resident had constructed from spare pieces of plywood, an empty packing crate for an ottoman. Augustine bundled up and sat in his chair, squinting against the bright albedo of the snow on the lake, waiting for the cold air that lingered on the plateau to be stirred by warmer currents.

Iris adapted with ease too. She began to favor short naps instead of longer, uninterrupted sleep. She ate when Augie set a plate in front of her; otherwise, if she found herself hungry, she took a shortbread bar from the cook tent or foraged among the other nonperishables. She spent a lot of time on the ice, skating back and forth, sometimes making the trek out to the island to startle the hares. She looked for more bird nests, which were always on the ground because there were no shrubs or trees, only low-lying vegetation and rock. The snowy owl they'd seen on their first day became a fixture, as did the faraway howls of the wolves in the mountains behind them. One bright night, or day perhaps, it didn't matter anymore, Augie awoke to the sound of a large furry body brushing up against the side of the tent. He sat straight up to check that Iris was napping also. He realized it was a wolf scratching an itch on the hut, separated from Augustine's head by mere millimeters of vinyl and insulation. He shuddered a little at the thought but was largely unperturbed and went back to sleep. The other habitants of the lake and the surrounding mountains had become accustomed to the new human presence there. Gradually, Augie grew to accept their neighbors too.

They woke up in the brightness one day to discover the snow had finally vanished. The lake ice began to get louder, to shift and groan against the shore. Meltwater puddles multiplied and the ice's pale blue color became dull and gray. Eventually the ice sheet broke apart and gentle winds blew the fragments against one another with sounds like glasses being clinked, a toast to summer. One day—Augie guessed it was early July—a gale howled along the surface of the lake and pushed the shards of candled ice out of the water and onto the muddy shore, where they crashed against the earth like solid, splintering waves of white quartz. The water washed over the soft brown earth and the basin of the lake began to warm. Before long, it was mild enough that Augustine sat in his homemade Adirondack chair wearing only his long underwear while Iris walked barefoot along the stony beach.

Soon after the lake cleared, following a long sleep and a slow breakfast, Augie walked out to the upside-down dinghy and flipped it over. He'd noticed an outboard motor, two oars, and some fishing gear in the unused sleeper hut. He gathered up everything but the motor, which he wasn't sure he could carry, and dragged it out to the edge of the lake.

Iris looked on with excitement and began pushing the dinghy toward the shore, inch by inch. Together they pushed it
halfway into the water.

"Char for dinner?" he said with a wink, and she made
a high-pitched squeal he'd never heard from her, hopping
from one foot to the other as if the ground had become too
hot and the boat was her only refuge. It had been a long time
since they'd eaten anything so fresh. The rod was strung; he
had an orange spinner in his pocket, and a sharp hunting
knife on his belt. He went inside to grab a container for the
fish and scooped up some of the candled ice from the shore
to put in the bottom. Iris was already waiting in the boat,
alert with excitement. Augie gave the dinghy a good push,
then leaped in as it floated away from the shore.

Augustine rowed while Iris sat in the bow, facing the island and running her hands through the water. Had she ever
been in a boat before? he wondered. She seemed so small,
dwarfed by the scale of the mountains before her, the island,
the lake itself. Her shoulders seemed too narrow to hold a
human together. When they'd rowed far enough out, he put
down the oars and took up the rod. He'd fished before, as
a boy, but now he felt clumsy and uncertain. He toyed with
the reel for a moment and the mechanics of casting came
rushing back to him. His first cast wasn't very good, but his
second went farther and landed with a soft plop. He began
to slowly reel it in, just enough to keep the spinner dancing
at the end of the line. Iris watched him closely to see how he
did it. After he'd reeled it in, he cast again, then handed her
the rod. She took it without hesitation and began reeling.
They passed the rod back and forth, Augie casting, Iris reeling, but they didn't have to wait long. There was a jerk on

the line and the tip of the rod bent toward the water, softly at first, then sharply, until the rod was inches from the surface of the lake. Iris's eyes widened and her grip tightened. She looked to him for instruction.

"Hold tight and keep reeling it in. Looks like you hooked a good one."

The fish fought harder the closer she dragged it to their little boat. At first Augie thought he should take the rod from her and reel it in himself, but she was doing well. Soon the fish was splashing against the side of the boat, churning up white froth. He got out the net and scooped it up, guessing it to be a five-pound Arctic char, longer than one of Iris's arms and twice as thick. It flopped in the bottom of the dinghy, exhausted but determined to fling itself back into the water. Augustine got out his knife and was about to plunge the tip into the char's brain in order to sever its spinal cord. He paused and looked up at Iris, remembering her tenderness toward the wolf that night at the hangar.

"You might not want to watch," he said.

She shook her head gallantly and kept her eyes trained on the fish.

He severed the char's spine with the knife, slid the hook out of its mouth, then ran his knife through the gills, a short cut on either side. He held the fish over the side of the boat while it bled out, dark, thick streams running down the length of the tail fin and into the clear, cold lake water. He looked up at Iris and caught her wrinkling her nose.

He laughed at her expression. "Sorry, kid," he said. "Can't eat live fish."

"I'll do the next one," she said in defiance.

Augie laid the char down in the container he'd prepared,

a pink stain spreading across the ice. He rinsed his hands and his knife in the lake and folded the blade back into the handle.

"All right," he said. "How about you cast this time?"

He passed her the rod and showed her how to hold the line with her pointer finger and release it at the last minute.

She nodded impatiently. "I know," she said, and waved him off. "Give me some room."

~~~~

AFTER A FEAST of baked char and canned peas and powdered mashed potatoes with plenty of powdered garlic mixed in, Iris and Augie sat outside their tent and watched the ripples on the lake, curling across the surface like ribbons of light. When Augustine woke in his Adirondack chair later, it was impossible to tell how long he'd been out—the water continued to ripple, the sun still blazed down on his bare feet. Across the lake he saw a small herd of musk oxen drinking at the shore. He tugged the broad-brimmed hat he'd found in the cook tent down over his eyes and squinted across the water. There were eight of them, and almost hidden in the great shaggy layers of their half-shed winter coats was a ninth, a tiny calf pressed against the side of its mother as she drank from the lake. He turned to Iris, but her chair was empty and she was nowhere to be seen. Maybe she was asleep. Augie struggled to his feet, pulling himself up by the rough plywood arms of the chair, and went down to the edge of the water.

The musk oxen continued to bury their noses in the shallows. He watched the little calf become impatient, braying and scuffing its hoof on the soft earth, nudging its head against the hindquarters of its thirsty mother.

"*Umingmak,*" he murmured under his breath. It was the Inuit word for musk oxen; he couldn't say where he'd learned it or how he'd remembered it. *The bearded ones.*

He raised his hands to his face and felt the clumps of wiry hair on his chin and neck, the long tufts on his head—still thick after all these years. He smiled, and felt the corners of his mouth with his fingertips, just to be sure he was doing it right.

FOURTEEN

THE WORK WAS a relief. Sully didn't want to take a break and lose the single-minded concentration that was keeping her thoughts corralled, but she was so exhausted that her concentration was slipping anyway. Thebes had been working alongside her in the comm. pod for much of the morning. They hadn't spoken about the spacewalk—they hadn't spoken about anything except the task at hand. Sully was grateful for the silence. Getting the new comm. system online was all she could manage. She feared that the slightest empathetic gesture would undo her and she'd wind up back in her bunk, the curtain drawn, staring at her hands but seeing Devi, hidden beneath the bulk of her white suit, becoming smaller, smaller, and vanishing. Thebes was the one to suggest they break for lunch.

She watched him slip down the entry node ahead of her. For the first time she noticed that even in zero G the shape had gone out of his shoulders. Thebes seemed half-empty, like a tube of toothpaste that's almost used up, and she realized she hadn't given any thought to the rest of the crew. It wasn't just her tragedy, it was theirs too. All of them had watched Devi float away: Sully might have been there in person, but the rest of them had seen it all through the helmet cams. The same moment was stuck on replay in everyone's head, not just in hers. She had to remind herself that she wasn't alone. She went down the entry node after Thebes and landed on Little Earth, feeling the weight of her body return to her.

The rest of the crew—Thebes and Harper, Tal and Ivanov—were sitting around the table waiting for her. She saw tears sliding down Ivanov's cheeks and realized she was crying too—silently releasing the water that had been building behind her eyes since she woke up that morning. She licked a salty tear from her lip and sat down with them. They passed around the last tinfoil dish of shepherd's pie, one of the premade meals they'd been saving for a special occasion. They ate in silence, passed the dish again, ate some more. When it was empty and the trays had been scraped clean, Ivanov took Tal's and Harper's hands, and the others followed his example. They bowed their heads together, chins tucked into their chests.

"*Aether* has lost her youngest daughter. Protect her," Ivanov said.

They stayed like that for a long time, and when their necks began to tire, Thebes raised his head and added, "She was loved." It wasn't much, but it was true, and it helped. Their time aboard *Aether* had been long and difficult and beautiful, but through it all, Devi had been well loved by everyone at that table. Sully looked at her crewmates and it dawned on her that they were her family—that they had been all along.

THAT AFTERNOON, THEY received the first signal since the main comm. dish had broken away from the ship a week earlier. Sully spun the volume knob so that she and Thebes could revel in the static telemetry of their probe on Europa, alive to them once again, whispering through the speakers. Sully went around to all her machines, checking that they were receiving properly and saving everything to the hard drive. The spacewalks had accomplished their directive—at least the loss had been worth something instead of nothing. Sully thought of Devi fighting to stay conscious. Telling her it was too late. She could feel her clumsy grip on the mast, could see the mirrored glint of her friend's visor. She felt again the helplessness as she clung to the antenna and watched Devi expire: unable to move, unable to fix the horrifying problem happening right in front of her, inches away. And she wondered, not for the first time, how Devi hadn't noticed sooner—whether she'd seen the oxygen levels in her suit falling, sensed the problem, but not said anything. Sully would never know.

She turned back to the fuzziness coming out of the speakers and the wavering signal. There was still work to be done and she threw herself into it headfirst, moving from machine to machine, testing the gain, tinkering with the squelch settings. The signals grew slightly clearer, the feedback slightly softer. By the time the day was done, she and Thebes had calibrated the new comm. system as best they could. The reception was as good as it would ever be. If there was anyone out there trying to call them home, they would hear it.

Sully stayed to listen after Thebes left. She felt . . . *connected* wasn't the right word, because there was nothing out there to link to, but she felt less alone. She'd done her part, she'd extended the electromagnetic red carpet. If no one took advantage, if their welcome was left hanging, unmet even after all this time and work and sacrifice, then it wouldn't be her fault. She would have done her best. *They* would have done their best. She was moving beyond the turbulence of loss and isolation, into a quieter space—a space where Mission Control's signal was already speeding toward them, where she was ready and willing to see what came next.

It was late by the time Sully returned to Little Earth. She found Tal in his usual place, his thumbs poised over a gaming controller, but with one notable difference: Ivanov sat beside him, with another controller in hand. She'd never seen them play together. Ivanov's blond hair was combed back from his forehead, his ruddy cheeks glowing with competition, the usual stoniness in his features softened to a more manageable stiffness. Tal looked wild with excitement, his brown eyes wide, his teeth bared at the screen, the thick black beard that had taken over his face even bushier than usual, as if even his hair follicles were responding to the acute novelty of having a real live opponent, one he wanted very much to beat. The two men didn't look up at her, immersed in the challenges of their avatars. Sully moved along the curve of the centrifuge toward the long kitchen table. Harper and Thebes sat across from each other playing five-card draw, betting nuts and bolts from Thebes's toolbox. Sully sat down next to Thebes and watched.

"Thebes tells me we're up and running again," Harper said as he laid down a full house. Thebes whistled through the gap in his teeth and threw his hand down.

Sully nodded. "We're back. Not much chatter out there, though."

"Shall I deal you in?" Thebes asked her as he shuffled the deck with his elegant black hands, the pale pink of his fingernails skimming over the cards like tiny butterflies.

"No, thanks," she said, "I think I'll just watch."

"We're piggybacking Mars's orbit any day now," Thebes said as Harper cut the deck. "Then the slingshot back to Earth. I think we'll have a better chance at picking up something faint as we get closer."

She looked over at Ivanov and Tal, still intent on their game, united in concentration and competition, then back to Thebes and Harper. Harper noticed her still staring at Thebes's hands as he looked at his cards, tilting them up without taking them off the table.

"Are you sure you don't want to play?" he asked.

"I'm sure," she said. "I think I'm going to go back to the comm. pod for a minute. I forgot to do something." She got up from the table.

"Aren't you going to eat anything? We've all had dinner already," Harper said. "Some lasagna thing. We saved you some." Thebes let the edges of his cards snap back to the table. She took a serving of fruit leather from the kitchen and held it up for him to see before she put it in her pocket. She wasn't planning to eat it, but Harper was appeased. As she left Little Earth she heard Ivanov shout with triumph, followed by a low groan from Tal.

She passed through the greenhouse corridor slowly, letting the vivid green of the aeroponic plants fill her. They pressed out the thoughts and refilled her mind with color, saturating the nooks and crannies of her brain—green, the color of home. She wondered if she might be able to sustain it, to make this verdant peace permanent, but no sooner had it occurred to her than all the rest of the thoughts came rushing back in and the blazing viridescence faded away. It was too much. She was just a tiny point of consciousness lost in an ocean of chaos, not unlike *Aether*. Tunneling through the vacuum of space, thin walls weakening beneath the violent forces of the cosmos, losing pieces of herself along the way, just like the ship they lived on.

Sully paused at the entrance to the control deck but didn't go in. She stayed away from the swimming blackness just beyond the cupola. She turned and propelled herself to the comm. pod instead, raising the volume on the muted speakers and letting the sounds wash over her. *It's been silent in here for too long,* she thought. After a few moments she began to scan, seeking out some of their fellow wanderers. She found an old robotic surveyor, still circling Mars. Then Cassini, one of Saturn's first explorers. And then there it was, the wanderer she always hoped to hear: *Voyager 3,* heading toward the edge of the solar system, through the heliopause, into the Oort cloud and beyond, to interstellar space. The incoming telemetry was sparse and basic; since she'd last searched it out, some of *Voyager's* functions had shut down. From the plasma readings she could guess that it had moved beyond their solar system—had crossed over into a new one.

She stayed in the comm. pod for hours, listening and

watching her screens. When she returned to Little Earth the others were either asleep or concealed in their compartments, the glow of their reading lights shining against the curtains. Before she had a chance to shut herself in her bunk, Harper swept his curtain back. He was half inside his sleeping bag, propped up against the wall with his tablet illuminated on his lap.

"You're back," he said. "What did you forget?"

She couldn't think of something credible, something that would have occupied her for this long. The truth was easier. "I didn't forget anything. I just . . . wanted to listen for a while."

He nodded. "But you're all right?"

"Yeah," she said. "Just tired." She caught hold of her curtain. "'Night," she said, and drew it shut.

"Good night," he murmured, and she heard the click of his light going off.

She lay in the dark for a long time, on her back with her eyes open, inspecting all the shadows in her compartment. At the foot of the bed, the craggy mountain of clothes she'd worn today and would wear again tomorrow. On the wall, the square of the photograph of Lucy. Above her, the dark round globe of her reading light. After a while she fell asleep and dreamed she was traveling in the other direction on *Voyager* 3, away from home instead of toward it. Her feelings in the dream were untroubled, tranquil. She was nestled into the cup of *Voyager*'s parabolic dish, curled up like a sleepy cat while she looked out into the blackness and realized she'd gone farther than she'd ever expected to. She realized she'd come to the end of the universe, and she was pleased.

‑∿∿∿‑

THE FIVE OF them gathered at the long table for breakfast and a rundown of the next phase of their journey. Sully sipped orange juice through a straw and arranged a screen of attention onto her features while Tal spoke about the trajectory plan. While they were traveling past Mars, jumping on and off its orbit as if it were a celestial highway, they would be a relatively short way from Mars itself. Tal went on to explain the complexities of Mars's orbit and how exactly they would use its gravity for their own purposes, but beyond that Sully lost track of what he was saying. She was contemplating the texture of the cabinet behind his head when she realized that she'd reached the end of the orange juice and was making a rude sucking noise with the straw. Tal had stopped talking and was looking at her. She froze in midslurp, and he continued.

"So I know we've been seeing Mars from a distance for some time, but if you'd like a better look, the next few days would be the ideal time."

Her mind drifted out of focus once more. Harper took over and got everyone squared away on their tasks for this final leg of their journey, as *Aether* drew closer to Earth. Sully nodded in the right places, and when they were finally dismissed she went straight to the comm. pod. She had lost time to make up on the Jovian probes, and she wanted to be sure the incoming data was recorded and filed correctly. The straightforward labor of data entry soothed her, even if the conclusions she was drawing and the hypotheses she was forming still didn't have an audience. It helped distract her from the unknowns of their journey. Sully was a few hours into her work before she realized she was ravenous and hadn't eaten since yesterday. She remembered the fruit leather she'd tucked away in her pocket the night before and ripped into the package while she cataloged the telemetry.

She thought of Mars while she worked. She pictured its cratered red earth, orange dust, and dry, empty riverbeds. She thought of the plans for colonization—an American mission had already been there and back a few years ago, mostly to do a geological survey but also to look for potential habitat sites. Before *Aether*'s departure, a private space travel company had been entrenched in the logistics of building a permanent colony on Mars. It was supposedly only a few years from realization—too late, apparently.

She was excited to see the red planet so close. Their view on the way out almost two years ago had been fleeting and from a distance. They had been focused on other things—the pull of Jupiter, the planet no one had ever seen up close. Now Mars's significance lay mainly in its proximity to Earth. The last signpost before their destination: nearly there. When Sully had done a few more hours of work with the Jovian telemetry, she changed her receiving frequency to *Voyager 3*, still thinking of her dream from last night. She alighted on the signal just in time to hear a shrill whistle, and then silence. She couldn't get it back, no matter what she tried—found only empty sine waves where the signal had been just a moment before. It was late by the time she gave up. The probe was gone. Perhaps the power had finally quit, perhaps something else had malfunctioned and rendered its comm. system unusable, or perhaps it had traveled so far it was simply beyond their reach. It was possible that she would get it back another day, that something had blocked the signal—a planet in the way or even an asteroid—but she thought not. She floated in the silence of the comm. pod for a long while, remembering her dream. In the end she wished *Voyager* well and let it go, for good.

It was time to turn her attention back to Earth—not the Earth she'd left, the Earth she was returning to. The long months of retrospection and grief, thoughts of people she'd left, people she'd lost, were too heavy for her to carry anymore. She had been looking backward long enough. Now, finally, she gave herself permission to look forward. She didn't feel hope, not yet, but she made room for it. Sully adjusted her wavelength and began to scan the frequencies: mostly listening, occasionally transmitting, but constantly searching, from one band to another. When she had scanned both the UHF and the VHF spectrums she began again, from the beginning. There had to be something out there. There had to be.

FIFTEEN

THEY BEGAN TO spend a lot of time in the little dinghy, out on Lake Hazen. Augustine would row them out, halfway to the island, and then they would take turns casting. It never took long—the lake was teeming with char that would snap at anything and the little orange spinner was too tempting to ignore. They would catch one, maybe two if they were smaller, pith and bleed them, then row back and gut them on the shore. Iris grew skilled at casting, and she was getting good at the gruesome parts, too, at severing the spine and removing the guts—she refused to leave the fish for Augie to clean.

The tiny wildflowers grew in thick, colorful carpets across the tundra. As mantles of color popped up among the new grass and the soft brown earth, Augie and Iris started to venture farther and farther from the camp to explore the unfamiliar abundance of summer. The surrounding hills and mountains were full of lemmings and Arctic hares and birds. The musk oxen and caribou kept to the tundra, eating all the tiny, rare botanical specimens like canapés at a fancy cocktail party. During one such hike, Augie rested on a boulder while Iris scrambled on ahead. A caribou approached and carefully snapped up the patch of marsh saxifrage that Augustine had been admiring, fitting its clumsy lips around the little yellow flowers and chomping off their stems at the root before sauntering off to sniff out more delicacies. Augie could see the whorl of fur in the center of its forehead, could hear its teeth clicking together, could smell the rich, musty odor of its breath. He'd never been so close to a wild animal—not a living one. It was enormous, with antlers that towered over him, so tall they seemed to disappear into the brightness of the sky, like the branches of a tree.

Augustine thought of the radio control building, as he often did. He still hadn't gone inside, and as time passed he began to wonder why. What was he avoiding? He was curious to see what kind of equipment it might offer, what he might or might not hear, but everything else was so pleasant, it subsumed his curiosity. He didn't want to disturb the tranquillity of their life at the lake. He didn't know what he would find, and whether it was nothing or something, he was in no rush to risk the brand-new happiness they'd forged. For once, Augustine was content not to know. And yet—this search for another voice wasn't about him. His own happiness wasn't the most important thing to him anymore.

When they first arrived, he'd been fooled into thinking his health was improving—the calm of the lake, the relative warmth, the stillness of the wind made him feel stronger. But as time wore on, he came to understand that his days were as limited as ever. Comfort didn't mean improvement. Life was easier here, but he was still growing older. The long night would come again, and when it did, the temperatures would plummet and his joints would seize and ache just as they had before. His heart would beat a little slower, his mind would not operate quite so nimbly. The polar night would seem to last forever. He both feared and hoped this year would be his last. He was old—wildflowers and gentle breezes would not make him young again. He looked up the incline to see Iris skidding back down, jumping from rock to rock like a mountain goat.

"How was the view?" he asked her. Instead of answering, she handed him a bouquet of mountain avens, a small white flower with a burst of yellow stamen in the center, frothy with pollen. A few of the blooms were spent, their seed heads sprouting long white tufts of fuzz, some still twisted in a glossy bud shape and others already blown out by the wind like the wiry white hairs of an old man's beard. He laughed.

"Are these meant to look like me?" He gave one of the seed heads a poke and Iris nodded with her best serious-not-serious face.

"Things could be worse, I suppose," he said, plucking one of the spent flowers and sliding it into his buttonhole. Iris smiled in approval and continued down. Augie struggled to his feet, scrabbling against the smooth surface of the boulder to haul himself up, crushing the flowers against the rock by accident. As he watched Iris make her way back toward the camp, he cradled the crumpled, half-dead bouquet in his hands and followed her. It was time.

-ᴧᴧᴧ-

With his coffee in hand, he ambled across the rock-strewn plateau and gave the doorknob of the little radio shed a try. It was stubborn, so he set his coffee mug on the ground and gave the door a hard shove with his shoulder. Inside the shed he found exactly what he'd been expecting: a well-equipped base station. With a few stacks of radio components, various transceivers for HF, VHF, and UHF frequencies, two pairs of headsets, speakers, a tabletop microphone, and a sleek generator in the corner, the station was complete—just ready and waiting for an operator. The trouble with the observatory had been its reliance on satellite communication—radio was used only as a backup or for local transmissions—but here the setup was built for radio frequency. He noticed a lone satphone on the desk, a few handy-talkie sets beside it.

Augie started the generator and let it run for a few minutes before he checked that the equipment was connected to the power source, then he started turning things on. Orange and green displays flickered. A low, even static emanated from the speakers, as if there were a hive of bees inside. Some survival gear was tucked under the desk—bottled water, emergency rations, two sleeping bags—and he realized that as the sturdiest building at the camp, this must be the emergency shelter as well. The three tents were durable enough to make it through Arctic winters, year after year, but they weren't indestructible. The Arctic was anything but gentle to its inhabitants.

After a few moments of fiddling, Augustine plugged in the headphones, slipped them on, and began to scan. *Here we go again,* he thought. But it was different from the observatory—the aerial array outside was going to allow him to reach farther with his voice and his ears than he ever had at Barbeau. He ran an admiring hand over one of the transceivers and wiped the dust from the glowing green display with his thumb. He flicked the microphone on and pulled it close to his chin in anticipation, then chose a VHF amateur band and began to transmit, *CQ, CQ, CQ,* over and over as he scanned the frequencies. Nothing—but then, he hadn't expected an answer. He kept transmitting, moving from VHF up to UHF, then down to HF, then back to the beginning. Eventually Iris appeared in the doorway, which he'd left open to let in the summer air. She shook a fishing rod at him. He looked from her to the equipment and back again.

"You're absolutely right," he said. "I'll meet you at the boat."

She disappeared from the doorway, leaving the slender rectangle of lake and mountain and sky unbroken. He began to switch everything off, the generator last, then unfastened the headset from where it hung around his neck and coiled the cord. He shut the door behind him, letting his eyes adjust to the blaze of the sun reflecting on the water.

Iris was sitting on the upside-down hull, tapping out a jazzy rhythm with the butt of the fishing rod.

"Ahoy," he called, and she jumped up.

Together they flipped the boat over and shoved it into the shallows, a smooth and effortless movement by now, after all of their fishing trips. Augie went to get the oars and the net, and then they pushed off from the shore. He let them float for a few minutes, closing his eyes, listening to the lap of the water against the earth, against the hull, and feeling the heated gaze of the midnight sun on his face. When he opened his eyes, Iris was hanging her legs over the side of the dinghy, the tips of her toes dragging on the lake, leaving brief ruts in the water: there and gone, there and gone. He dipped the blades of the oars beneath the glassy surface and began to row.

SUMMER SEEMED TO fade faster than it had arrived. The warmth seeped out of the valley and a cold front crept in, chilling the delicate wildflowers and icing the muddy shores of the lake with frosty crystals. Augustine continued to sit in his Adirondack chair by the lake, watching the progression of time, the descent of the sun, but now he bundled himself again in woolly layers. The cold returned to his bones, his joints, his teeth. He didn't leave the camp anymore. Iris wandered the tundra and the mountains alone. They still fished together, taking the dinghy out for as long as the lake would allow it, but rowing had grown difficult for him in the cold air and the frosts fell heavier with each passing week. *It won't be long now,* he thought.

Augustine continued to scan the bands once a day in the radio shelter, but the silence was perpetual, the isolation complete. He listened only out of a need for work, for purpose. As the days passed and grew colder, getting from his chair to the shelter and back again escalated from a pleasant stroll to a challenge. Augie hoarded his energy for the short walk, unwilling to give it up. He became unable to row the dinghy even a short way. Eventually a thin rind of ice formed at the edges of the lake. *It's just as well,* he thought. Not long after, the sun finally reached the horizon and dipped beneath it before climbing back up. The sunrise/sunset concert it created was magnificent and lasted several hours, bathing the mountains in a fiery orange glow and sending spurts of violet cloud into the sky before fading back into vivid blue. These moments of day's end and day's beginning, pressed together into a continuous event, became a regular marker of time's passing.

The lake froze, then melted, then froze once more. One afternoon, as the sun dipped behind the mountains and hid there briefly, a cold drizzle began to fall. In the cool twilight, the rain hardened into sleet and then softened into thick, white flakes of snow, which drifted slowly down and covered the brown landscape. Augie had retreated from his chair when the drizzle began, but he returned to it when the sleet changed to snow. Iris joined him, sitting on his little footstool made from a packing crate, and together they watched the contours of the land disappear beneath a blanket of white. When the sun cleared the mountains a few hours later it bathed the freshly covered peaks in pale fire, and as it climbed higher the tundra burned brightly, a field of white flame. The familiar cloak of the Arctic had returned and would not be shrugged off for many months to come.

The stars also returned. One night, after the color-soaked mountains had dimmed and then darkened into black peaks set against a sleepy blue sky, Augie walked down to the edge of the frozen lake to test the ice. He tapped it with his boot, and when it held he took a few cautious steps, giving it another tap and finally a good hard stomp. It was firm. It would hold him. He walked back to the shore and headed toward the radio shed. He noticed a set of fresh tracks in the snow, illuminated in the starlight, leading down from one of the hills and then disappearing at the edge of the lake. The prints were enormous and widely spaced, with the pricks of long claws indented around the impressions: polar bear prints. Here? He was surprised—forgetting the radio for a moment he doubled back, following the tracks to the shore, where they disappeared onto the ice. He bent down to examine the shallow scratches on the surface where the bear had dug in as it crossed the frozen water. Perhaps it was on its way to the fjord, he thought. Perhaps it was lost. He shrugged and turned back toward the radio shed.

Slipping the headphones over his ears, he began to scan, adjusting the controls in the soft glow of the flickering kerosene lamp. The static was soothing—it obscured the utter silence of the Arctic, a silence so complete it seemed unnatural. The lapping of the water had ceased, the air was still, the birds had all gone. The silence of winter had descended. The terns had left their beautiful nest, flying south toward the other pole, and the musk oxen and caribou had returned to the wide-open tundra. Every now and then the quiet was punctuated with the long, trembling howl of a wolf, but otherwise the lake was wrapped in hushed stillness. The white noise of the radio waves was a relief, a soft crackle to obscure the loneliness. He set the receiver to scan automatically and closed his eyes—let his consciousness drift. He'd fallen asleep when he heard it: a voice, slipping through his eardrums and into his dreams. He bolted upright and pressed the headphones against his ears. It was so faint Augie wasn't sure he'd really heard it. But no, there it was again—not words, just syllables, interrupted by static. He strained to make out what they were saying and pulled the microphone toward him, suddenly unsure how to respond. The language of amateur Q codes abandoned him in his excitement, but it didn't matter. The FCC wasn't listening anymore.

"Hello?" he said, then realized he was practically shouting. He waited, straining to hear a response. Nothing. He tried again, and again, and finally, on the third try, he heard her. A woman's voice, clear as a bell.

SIXTEEN

MARS WAS BEHIND them and the pale blue dot of Earth was growing larger by the day. They began to spend their spare moments in the cupola, watching the color of the atmosphere become more vivid as they moved closer—everyone except Sully. She kept long hours in the comm. pod, dividing her time between tracking the Jovian moon probes and listening for signals from Earth as they drew closer to home. She barely interacted with the others. She usually slipped out of the centrifuge early, as the artificial sunrise began to dawn, and returned to it late, when the others were already in their bunks. There was nothing, not so much as an errant cable news broadcast or a Top 40 countdown, but she kept listening. The nearer they came, the more likely it would be for their antenna to pick up a signal. In times of disaster, ham operators were always the first to get information flowing along the airwaves; surely, she thought, there would be some chatter. There had to be. There was still no theory that made sense, no possible explanation for the silence. But gradually they had accepted it.

They were close enough to see the moon circling their little blue planet when Sully finally lost track of her probe on Io. It wasn't unexpected—the conditions on Jupiter's closest moon weren't kind, and the probe had already outlasted its expected life span. It was an overachiever, yielding extraordinary data, but Sully was nonetheless saddened by the silence. There were only so many signals out there, and having one less to keep track of—first *Voyager*, now this—made her feel even more lost. There were so few things to hang on to. The universe was an inhospitable place, and she felt fragile, temporary, lonely. All of their tenuous connections, their illusions of security, of company, of camaraderie, were disappearing. Judging by its last transmission, the probe had strayed into volcanic territory, away from the sulfur dioxide snowfields they had set it down in. Its final temperature readings suggested submersion in lava—and even NASA didn't design things that could survive that.

Sully left the comm. pod for the night and floated down the corridor toward the cupola. At least they were nearly home. Regardless of what waited for them, it was good to see their little planet through the heavy glass, its silvery moon whirling around and around like a lazy pinball. Tal and Ivanov were floating in front of the view side by side when she arrived. They made room for her in the cupola. The three of them drifted there, suspended in space, watching the blue dot where they'd begun their lives loom closer. There was a barely discernible prick of brightness near the surface of the planet, there and then gone, and Ivanov's hand shot out to point at where it had just been.

"Did you see?" Ivanov said. "Just there—the International Space Station, I think. It must have been."

The spark had disappeared over the edge of the earth before he could even raise his hand. Tal shrugged and buried his fingers in his beard in contemplation.

"Could be," he said.

"Could be?" Ivanov sputtered. Two drops of indignant saliva left his lips and hovered in front of his face. "What else would it be?"

Tal shrugged again. "I dunno," he said, "a satellite, maybe. Hubble. Space trash. Could be a lot of things."

Ivanov shook his head. "Not possible. Too big for that."

Sully began to back out of the cupola, not interested in playing the referee, when she saw Tal put his hand on Ivanov's shoulder. "You could be right," he conceded. "I'm just saying—we'll wait for it to come round again, yes?"

Ivanov nodded and they continued their vigil, watching their looming planet. Sully was surprised to see them compromise this way, surprised and pleased—a new connection, in the midst of all this loneliness. She slipped out of the cupola. Neither of them noticed her go.

When she arrived back at the comm. pod Harper was waiting for her. She felt ambushed. She tried to hide the irritation she felt at finding him there, in what she thought of as her private space. He pointed at the last transmission from the Io probe, the telemetry she had left on her main screen when she wandered away.

"The Io probe finally kicked the bucket, eh? Death by volcano?"

Sully nodded. "Yeah, it quit on me yesterday."

"Wanna take a break? Make some food? Play some cards?"

"I don't think so," she said. "I have some things to do in here, and I just took a break. But thanks."

"I get it. It's just that I haven't really seen you in a while. I wanted to ask how you were doing." Harper's face was wide open, an invitation for her to unload, to emote, scrawled across his forehead. He wanted her to talk to him, but somehow it was infuriating. She didn't want to be rude, or unkind, but she didn't know how to respond, and the question itself irked her. How was she? How were any of them? They were in an impossible situation, doing whatever they could to get through—to pass from one moment to the next in a single piece: staring at Earth, listening to Earth, playing games while they thought of Earth.

The pause dragged on. Finally she said, "I'm a little out of sorts for all the obvious reasons, but I think you know that. Otherwise, I'm fine."

"Sure, sure." He seemed uncertain all of a sudden, as though the script he'd rehearsed in his head was no longer relevant to their conversation. "I just miss seeing you. But, you know. Take your time. Maybe we'll see you for dinner." He pushed past her and out of the pod. One of her machines chirped to signal an incoming telemetry delivery. The rest buzzed softly—nothing but empty sine waves.

Sully stared after Harper, immediately sorry that he'd gone. Did she have to be so brusque? So cold? Why couldn't she articulate how she was feeling? She was ashamed but also angry—that he'd bothered her, that he'd stirred up this unexpected vortex in her chest. Her mind started spinning through memories of Devi, of Lucy, of Jack—even as far back as her mother, Jean. She had lost them all, in one way or another. Each loss returned to her as she floated in the comm. pod, adding to the whirlpool swirling over her heart until she wasn't sure what was old and what was new. She took a breath, then another. She visualized Earth, its hazy blue outline, its rugged topography, the wisps of cloud, but it didn't soothe her. She thought of Harper, Thebes, Tal, Ivanov—there was always more to lose. She tried to calm herself, to still the drift of her body, but the lack of gravity made it difficult to remain stationary. Her shoulder bumped one of the speakers, her hip nudged a screen, and the more she fought to be still, the more she drifted. She was fighting an absence instead of a presence, and it suddenly chilled her. Which way was up? As the floor dropped away to become the ceiling, she felt the thread of logic she'd followed throughout the mission, throughout her entire life, snap. Hard work and intelligence could not keep her safe—there was nothing she could have done, no amount of effort or foresight or skill could have kept any of this from happening. Nothing in this universe could possibly keep any of them safe. She felt her perspective darken, and again she was watching an astronaut drift away into the blackness, only this time it was her inside the suit—screaming, pleading, shaking, unable to breathe.

SULLY HAD ONLY ever had one other panic attack, after her stepfather called to tell her Jean was dead. Sully had never lost hope that they would find their way back to each other, that someday they would be in the desert together again, looking up at the stars, just the two of them. Jean would call her "little bear," the way she used to, and they would admire the luminous craters of the moon, the swirls of the Orion nebula, the misty sparkle of the Milky Way. They would heal. They would drive home on sand-strewn roads and they would forgive each other. After that call, the fantasy that had sustained her since she was a girl evaporated. Her mother had drifted away from her somewhere between the Mojave Desert and British Columbia, but there had always been that hope. There were times when it seemed right around the corner, and when it was finally, conclusively too late, the weight of loss was too heavy to hold all at once.

She remembered putting her phone down on the kitchen counter in her first real apartment in Santa Cruz and staring into the texture of the countertop—grainy silver-gray flecks—then slowly letting her back slide down the length of the refrigerator, her legs crumpling beneath her. She remembered staying there for a long time, choking on her tears, wondering how she was still conscious, still alive. In the morning she woke up with her cheek pressed to the tile floor. She kept her gaze on the white grout between the salmon pink of the tiles for hours, thinking that if she could only keep that pattern in her mind, nothing else, she could survive the day.

She reconstructed the pattern of the tile. She let it fill her. Diamond after diamond of pink framed with white. She remembered that she had eventually gotten up off the floor, had walked to the back door and opened it. She had sat on the stoop leading down to her tiny courtyard and looked up at the sky, the crisp blue dome of it. She had found a way through. She could do it again.

When Sully returned to Little Earth that night, the flood of adrenaline had subsided and in its wake a gnawing emptiness gripped her tender muscles. Harper was still up, sitting at the long table playing solitaire. He didn't greet her, and she couldn't think of anything to say. She got ready for bed and climbed into her compartment. She hesitated, left the curtain open, her bare feet still resting on the floor.

"I'm sorry about before," she said without looking at him. She heard the snap of a card being laid down.

"Don't worry about it," he said, but it wasn't a tone she was used to hearing from him. It was detached, as if he was issuing commands to a computer. As if he wasn't even speaking to a human being. She understood that she'd hurt him— that this was her penance. Losing a man who was still right in front of her.

"Okay. Well, good night," she said, and waited. He didn't respond. After a moment she drew her curtain and lay down. She would've wept if she'd had any tears left, but her eyes were red and dry. She turned out the light.

"Good night," he finally called, and he sounded like himself again.

She laid her cool palms against the pulsing heat of her eyelids. She would've smiled, but she didn't have any of those left either.

~~~

THE PLANET LOOKED the same as it had when they'd left it—no cloud of dust choking the atmosphere and obscuring the continents, no smoke billowing from the surface. An enormous round oasis in the midst of a parched black desert. It wasn't until they were nearly in orbit that Sully realized what was wrong. When they faced the dark side of the planet it was indeed dark—no illuminated cities, no tap-estry of twinkling lights. The sickening apprehension that had been growing since the receivers went dark, since be-fore Jupiter, grew larger still. All the lights in all the cities, extinguished. How could that be?

She kept scanning the frequencies, kept listening for something, anything, that might indicate the remains of hu-mankind. She began to transmit when she thought the rest of the crew wouldn't hear her. Her transmissions weren't exactly professional. They were prayers—not to God, who she'd never liked the sound of, just to the universe, or to the earth itself. *Please, please, just one voice. One answer. Any-body, anything.* There was nothing. Just a dark, silent planet circled by space trash and dead satellites and the ISS. They crept closer. Still nothing.

It wasn't until they passed the moon that she heard it. It was early in the morning, Greenwich Mean Time, and she'd been murmuring into the microphone almost without real-izing it, talking to herself. She was the only person she had much to say to these days. And then she heard it: so faint, so distorted she thought it was just atmospheric disturbance whistling into her receiver. She transmitted again, a cautious *Hello.* When the voice responded she almost screamed. She thought she must be crazy, delusional. It was like sitting down to a séance she didn't believe in day after day and finally feeling a presence. But no, there it was again, clearer this time, a man's voice, scratchy and old and unused. But a voice. A connection, reaching out to her. She brought the microphone right up to her lips. She pressed the Transmit button. Contact.

SEVENTEEN

IT LASTED BARELY two minutes before the signal cut out, but during that brief exchange, clouded with atmospheric disturbance, Augustine learned quite a bit. The woman on the other end of the signal told him she was on board a spacecraft called *Aether,* an ambitious deep space exploration project he remembered hearing about while it was being built in Earth's orbit some years ago, before he went north. She told him they were a little less than two hundred thousand miles from Earth, that they were headed home and had lost contact with their Mission Control team more than a year ago. He was the only radio contact they'd been able to make since then.

Augie told her he was at a research facility 81 degrees north, on the Canadian Arctic archipelago, that he'd been there for some time and had little information regarding the state of the world beyond his icebound island. He told her there had been murmurs of war, then an evacuation that he'd chosen to forgo, and then—nothing. Only silence and isolation. He wanted to tell her everything: how it felt to leave the observatory and cross the tundra, to make a new home for himself beside the lake, how it felt to kill the wolf and bury it in the snow, to take care of Iris, to feed her and teach her how to fish, to worry about her, to feel the stirrings of love; how it felt to watch the snow and the ice melt, to bathe in the light of the midnight sun and then watch it slip away. He wanted to tell her about these feelings—these overwhelming, disconcerting, glorious feelings that weren't always good, were often very bad, but which were always so vivid, so immediate, so new to him.

He had so much to say. He wanted to ask about her journey, to hear how it felt to be among the stars as opposed to looking up at them. He wanted to ask how Earth looked from out there, how long she'd been gone—but the connection faltered and then slipped away. Given the vast distance the signal had to travel, the rotation of the earth and the fluctuation of the atmosphere, it wasn't surprising. He saved the frequency and planned to monitor it for however long it took to regain the connection.

Over the next twelve hours he left the radio shed only once, to walk back to the tent and make himself a thermos of heavily sugared coffee. Iris was reading on one of the cots when he arrived, and Augustine told her everything that had happened—the woman, the spacecraft full of astronauts. She didn't seem to care. He tried to get her to accompany him back to the radio shed, but she declined and kept reading. She seemed happy for him but utterly uninterested in the development. He wondered whether she understood the significance of it. He shrugged and shuffled back to the little building, thermos in hand, trying to imagine why Iris hadn't leaped at the chance to hear a voice other than his, to talk to a woman not of this world.

Back in front of the equipment, his receivers trained on the correct wavelength and his ears pricked for anything unusual hiding amid the white noise, he leaned back in his chair and tried not to fall asleep.

~~~~

IT TOOK HIM a moment to realize that he was hearing her voice again, emerging from a foggy dream and into the freezing shed. When he did he bolted upright and let the empty thermos fall to the floor. He scrambled for the microphone.

"I'm here," he said, "KB1ZFI confirming receipt." He held the Transmit button down a second or two longer, wondering where to begin—what to ask, what to tell. He told himself to be patient. Let her respond. "Over."

A man's voice arrived in his headphones a moment later, gravelly and distorted by the distance it was traveling.

"KB1ZFI, this is *Aether*'s commander, Gordon Harper. I can't tell you how glad we are to speak with you. I'm here with Specialist Sullivan, whom you already know. Sully here tells me you're as confused as we are about what's happened. Confirm?"

"Confirmed," Augie said. "A pleasure to speak with you

also, welcome home. I'm only sorry it's not under better circumstances. The truth is it's been a long time since I've heard anything over the waves. Over a year since the evac. I'm guessing you have more information than I do, considering your vantage point. Over."

There was a long pause and Augie worried he'd lost the connection, but then the commander spoke again.

"It's too soon to tell. But we'll do our best to keep you informed. How are you faring on your own? Over."

"Surprisingly well. These research outposts are stocked to the gills. Not sure if things went nuclear or chemical warfare or what, but the effects in this part of the world are indiscernible, whatever happened. Wildlife is healthy, no sign of radiation poisoning. Over."

Augie wanted to know if they would reenter the atmosphere, if they even could, and if they did—what they would find. What else was out there, beyond his frozen home? What did the rest of the planet look like? He wasn't sure how to ask. They were still so far away. After so many months of just surviving, he was suddenly burning with curiosity to know—to know everything. There was an even longer pause this time, and he imagined what they might be saying to each other.

"KBɪZFI, this is Sullivan, I think we're about to lose—" And they were gone.

"Standing by," he said out loud to the emptiness.

～～～

AUGUSTINE HAD SEEN the last of the sun. It was officially autumn. The polar night began, and with it the temperatures grew extreme. It was time for hibernation again, for staying inside the main tent and keeping the oil stove burning hot. His short walks to the radio shed became more and more difficult; he felt his health failing, and breathing the subzero air hurt his lungs. The more he exerted himself the harder he breathed, and the harder he breathed the sicker he got.

Even so—he kept his vigil. He kept standing by, as often as he could. He fell in and out of dreams as he waited by the microphone in the little radio shed, dreams that grew more vivid as time passed, until he could no longer differentiate between sleep and consciousness. A fever kept him warm, heating his blood to a simmer within his veins. Eventually he heard the woman's voice again and shook himself awake. He wasn't sure how long it had been. Hours, or days.

"KB1ZFI," she was saying, over and over. "KB1ZFI, KB1ZFI," until finally he could rouse himself and find the microphone.

"Copy," he said, "KB1ZFI responding."

"I thought I'd lost you," she said, relieved.

"Not yet," he answered, his voice rusty, his throat full of phlegm. "Call me Augustine." He released the Transmit button to cough a deep, chestbound rattle. He wondered how much longer he had.

"All right, then, Augustine. I'm Sully. It's just me today. Tell me about the sky," she said, "or the animals. Hell, tell me about the dirt."

He smiled. It must have been a long time since she'd set her eyes on any of those things.

"Well," he began, "the sky is dark all day here. I'm guessing it's late October? No sun till spring, just stars."

"It's October all right. What about the animals? The weather?"

"It's cold these days—maybe twenty, thirty below. And the

birds, they're mostly gone. The wolves, though, they're still here, still howling, and Arctic hares, scampering around on the ice like that damn rabbit with the pocket watch, you know the one I mean. Oh, and there's a bear. He shouldn't be this far inland this time of year, but he is. Saw his prints in the snow myself. Between you and me, I think he's been following me."

"A polar bear? Following you? That doesn't sound so good."

"No, no, he's all right—he's easy company, keeps to himself. And the dirt—well, the dirt is frozen. Not much else to tell you here. Just hunkering down for the winter. And you?"

"Fair enough," she said. "We're in orbit now. Going to dock with the ISS if we can, see about rounding up the re-entry modules."

"And your trip? What did you see?"

"Jupiter," she said. She sounded wistful. "Mars. The Jovian moons. Stars. Emptiness. I don't know—it's hard to describe it all. We were gone so long. Augustine? I think I'm going to lose the signal in a minute, we're orbiting toward the Southern Hemisphere. But listen—take care of yourself, okay? I'm not sure what's going to happen next. I hope we talk again. I hope—"

She was gone. Augie turned off the equipment and struggled back to the tent. He collapsed on his cot fully clothed. It was hours before the stove thawed him enough that he could move again, and when he did manage to remove his boots and his parka, a slippery thought crept into his consciousness and then fell away into his subconscious, in and out, in and out, until he fell asleep.

-ᴡᴡ-

THE FEVER HAD its claws in him. He dreamed vividly of returning to the radio shed, of methodically turning on the
generator, then the transceivers, but then he'd realize he was
still on his cot, unable to move, and the dream would begin
again in a loop: his mind would wake and go to the shed, and
his body would remain. The rare moments of true wakeful-
ness were painful and brief. He was hot and cold, shivering
and sweating. For the most part he hovered on the edge of
consciousness, dreaming about waking up, dreaming about
dreaming about waking up. His brain was trapped in never-
ending layers of his subconscious: each layer he pulled back
led him to another and another.

Iris was there, in real life, or perhaps it was only in the
dreams, he couldn't tell. She was hovering over the cot with
anxious eyes. She laid cool, damp rags on his forehead and
steaming, hot rags on his chest. She sang to him; the wolves
sang along with their faraway howls. At times he mistook her
for Jean, at other times for his own mother.

When he eventually fought his way back to consciousness
the tent was dark and cold, the electric lamp had burned
out, and the oil stove had run dry. How long had it been?
Where was Iris? He found a small reserve of strength, went
outside and changed the oil drum, then rekindled the stove
before he collapsed once more. He drank half a gallon of
water, so cold it made his head ache.

He set the jug down and there was Iris, coming in the
door, latching it behind her. Lifting the glass chimney from
one of the kerosene lamps, then lighting the wick with a
match and lowering the chimney back into place. Adjust-

ing the flame. Carrying it to Augie's bedside, holding the light over him for a moment and then setting it down on the table. Laying her palm against his forehead, sitting down on the edge of the cot and smiling. Her eyes said *Go back to sleep,* but her lips said nothing at all.

EIGHTEEN

SULLY RUSHED BACK to Little Earth and started banging on all the sleeping compartments. She pounded on the frame of Devi's bunk for a few beats before realizing it was empty, then hurried along the curve of Little Earth to the long table. Thebes was already there, eating dried fruit and looking at her quizzically; the others quickly emerged from their bunks. The overhead lights reached their full morning brightness as she relayed the story of the contact—their first contact since Mission Control went dark. Their expressions of sleepy annoyance gradually gave way to excitement. When she reached the end of her story, however, her crew-mates looked more confused than enlightened.

"That's it?" Tal asked. "He doesn't know anything else?"

Sully shrugged. "I'm going to keep monitoring the frequency and I'm hopeful we can get him back, but yes, he doesn't know much about what's happened. He said it's been radio silence since the other researchers evacuated a year ago."

"Why did they evacuate?"

"I don't know—war rumors. But that's all he knew, rumors."

"So then, this guy is what, like the last person on earth? Is that what we're getting at here?" Tal seemed indignant.

"Don't joke," Ivanov admonished him.

Tal rolled his eyes. "I wish I were," he said. "Think about it. If this guy has been trying to make contact for all this time and hasn't been able to, not a peep till now . . . I mean, if something catastrophic happened, where would the safest places be—the least fallout? The poles, that's where. Exactly where he is. It's possible he's the only one left."

They all fell silent for a moment. Harper had been running his hands through his hair, over and over, as though by stimulating his scalp he might arrive at a new idea, a different angle he hadn't noticed. He dropped his hands into his lap and sighed.

"I don't see that we've really learned anything new. We're still looking at a lot of question marks. Sully, let's try to talk to him again—see what we can suss out. Otherwise, I want our docking seals checked. I think we should hook into ISS and go from there. Reentry sequence as planned. Not much point speculating, right? One thing at a time."

They all nodded and Harper went back to the comm. pod with Sully. The others trickled after them, and the search for the last man on earth began again—hours of static, Sully repeating his call sign over and over, until finally, hours later, they got their answer.

~~~~

THE SECOND CONVERSATION was even less enlightening than the first. Harper, Sully, and Thebes were crowded into the comm. pod while Ivanov and Tal floated in the corridor. All five of them were only more frustrated by the time they lost the signal, which didn't last long. They all drifted over to the observation deck afterward, where they could watch Earth moving beyond the glass cupola. Ultimately there wasn't a lot to discuss—the man on the other end had told them everything he knew, which wasn't much—but it didn't stop them from going over and over the meager facts. They would dock with the ISS and then the conundrum of reentry would be addressed. They couldn't orbit forever, but without a ground team to pick them up in the Kazakhstani desert, things grew complicated and uncertain. Sully went back to the comm. pod while the others continued debating.

She tried to reestablish a connection with the Arctic but couldn't. It had become clear that the man didn't have the information they were hoping for—an explanation—but there were other things she wanted to ask him. She wanted details of Earth: sunsets, weather, animals. She wanted to be reminded of how it felt to be beneath the atmosphere, housed within that gentle daylit dome. She wanted to re-member how it felt to be held by Earth: dirt and rocks and grass cradling the soles of her feet. The season's first snow, the smell of the ocean, the silhouettes of pine trees. She missed it all so keenly she felt the absence inside her abdomen, like a black hole sucking her organs into nothingness. So she waited. No more scanning. The frequency was locked in, it was only the many layers of atmosphere, the angle of the antenna, the rotation of the earth, and the vigilance of the radio operator below that occupied her now. She wondered if it was true—if she'd found the last man on earth.

In the days that followed, *Aether* arrived in Earth's orbit. Sully had no luck finding the Arctic survivor again. She wasn't able to keep her vigil as consistently as she would've liked to; as they circled the earth they had their work cut out for them, and the practical purposes for speaking with him again were minimal. The other crewmembers were focused on more pressing things. The plans for *Aether* had always been to dock with the ISS—the entire spacecraft was designed to eventually become an addition to the space station—so in that respect they were still within the parameters of their mission, following a plan set years ago. But without the other crew in the ISS to coordinate with, the procedure was difficult and uncertain.

As they drew closer to the ISS, she finally found him again. He was equally glad for the excuse to talk to her—about anything. He told her about the Arctic—the dark days and the frozen tundra. When he talked about the polar bear tracks he'd found, she recognized something in him: a stubborn loneliness. As though he couldn't say aloud, even now, at the end of the world, that he was lonely. That he craved connection without understanding how to obtain it; that finding a set of tracks, the merest evidence of another presence, was his idea of company. It went beyond the isolation of his situation, it was a part of him, and she suspected it always had been. Even in crowded rooms, even in busy cities, even in the arms of a lover, he was alone. She recognized it in him because it was in her too.

The connection broke before she was ready, if she would ever have been ready. She stayed in the comm. pod for a long time afterward. She flicked off the speakers and listened to the hum of the ship itself, the faint murmurs of her crewmates on the control deck. He was all alone down there, tracking polar bears and listening to the howls of wolves. He was older, she guessed from the gravel in his voice, and would be disheveled after so much time on his own in the Arctic wilderness. Long hair, shaggy beard. She pictured his eyes, ethereal blue, she decided, the same color as ice lit by the sun. At first she had imagined saving him—setting down the *Soyuz* pod on Ellesmere Island and finding his isolated camp—but the fantasy ended there. There would be no way back to warmer climates, and a very good chance they would end up in the freezing ocean or on the frozen tundra and never find him at all. No, the *Soyuz* pod would be set down in a more forgiving region, a place where the crew could hope to survive. The last man on earth would remain trapped where he was, and she would never know for sure what he looked like. He would always be a disembodied voice, a spectral wanderer. He would die alone.

From the control deck she heard Tal shouting in excitement—they had the ISS in their sights. She dried her eyes on the sleeve of her jumpsuit and wiped her nose with the back of her hand. She took a few deep breaths and rolled her jaw, shaking the grief-stricken grimace out of her face muscles. The ISS was good news. She tried on a smile and checked it in the silvery reflection of a transceiver casing.

Good enough. Propelling herself out of the comm. pod and down the corridor to the control deck, she ran into Thebes, approaching from the direction of the centrifuge.

"You ready?" he asked.

"Ready for what?"

"Ready to go home."

They drifted onto the control deck together, where Tal and Ivanov were already waiting. Tal had the docking controls ready and Ivanov floated in the cupola, watching the space station grow closer and closer through the window while Tal watched the port come closer and closer on his docking cam. The station's solar arrays spread out from the silver maze at its center like huge, illuminated wings. The vivid blue of Earth's oceans, swept with white ruffles of breakers and wisps of cloud, moved beneath it.

"I'm not sure," she whispered to Thebes, but he didn't hear her. Harper came in a moment later, and all five of them watched the two spacecrafts slowly approach, align, and then, miraculously, lock together and become one: a silver angel wandering in an empty heaven.

NINETEEN

AUGUSTINE STRUGGLED TO sit up. The flame of the kerosene lamp was burning low, the wick flickering inside the glass chimney. It seemed the tent was empty, but it was so dim he couldn't be sure.

"Iris," he called, and again, "Iris."

He heard nothing but the low moan of a gentle wind outside, pushing up against the shell of the tent, the hiss of the oil stove, the sputter of the lamp's flame. He tried to calculate how long it had been since he'd talked to the woman aboard

Aether—had it been yesterday, the day before, perhaps the day before that? He couldn't distinguish the passage of time from the blur of waking dreams he'd been caught up in. He wanted to talk to her again. He wanted to ask her more— about her mother and father, to learn how she'd grown up and where, if she'd ever had a family, children of her own. He wanted to know how she'd decided to become an astronaut, what it was about the loneliness of space that had made her leave everything behind. He wanted to tell her about his work, his achievements, but also his failures—to confess his sins, and to be forgiven. Here, at the very end of his life, he had so much to say and yet so little strength to say it. His head spun with the effort each time he raised it from the pillow.

He swung his feet to the floor and let his torso hang in his lap, head in hands, while the dizzying black clouds seeped away from his vision and he recovered his balance. He closed his eyes until his head stopped spinning and found a sense of stillness; when he opened them, Iris was in front of him, in the chair she had sat in throughout his illness, keeping watch over his fevered body. She blinked at him and didn't say anything.

"Where did you come from?" he asked. "Have you been there long?"

She nodded and continued to look at him, a blank stare on a beautiful face. He struggled to understand what he had known all along. His head ached from it.

"Why are you here?" he whispered. Iris cocked her head and lifted her shoulders as if to say *You tell me*. Augustine pressed the heels of his hands into his eye sockets, watching the dance of light and dark on the backs of his eyelids. He knew that when he opened them the chair would be empty. He opened them, and it was.

~~~

THERE WAS ONE night in Socorro that he hadn't thought about in years. He'd gone to every effort never to think of it again, but it came to him then, his breath rattling inside his dying lungs. It was soon after Jean told him she was pregnant, after he demanded she get an abortion. It was late, he was uninvited, but she let him in anyway, into the little adobe guesthouse she rented near the facility where they both worked. It was full of books and reams of fresh printer paper. Her dissertation sat on the dining room table in piles, her purple felt pen uncapped, a splayed legal pad full of indecipherable notes and a cup of tea beside it. Augustine stumbled to the table and threw himself down in the chair. He was drunk. The tea spilled somehow, an errant elbow, an oversized gesture, and began to soak into her work, the purple ink running down the page like tearstained mascara. Jean wasn't angry, she was—what? She was sad. She sat down next to him, righted the now-empty teacup, and threw a dish towel over the puddle as it traveled to the edge of the table and began to drip down onto the floor.

"Why are you here?" she asked him. He didn't answer her, only stared at the ruined pages in front of him. She waited. "Augie," she said. "What are you doing here?"

And then the most ridiculous thing happened: he began to cry. He went to the cupboard where she kept a few bottles of liquor, one of whiskey and one of gin, hoping she hadn't seen the tears. He remembered that he'd finished the gin last week, so he took down the whiskey and poured two fingers into her empty teacup. She covered her face with her hands as he drank it in one gulp. They were both crying then.

"What do you want?" she said, and he understood suddenly that he shouldn't be there. That she truly didn't want to see him—a flash of empathy for her that fizzled immediately.

"I want to try," he slurred. "Let's try."

She shook her head, slowly and firmly, and took the whiskey off the table. Put the bottle back in the cupboard.

"I want to fix it," he protested.

She looked at him and made sure he met her eyes before she answered him.

"No," she said. "Look at yourself."

She herded him to the door and he did—he looked at himself in the mirror that hung above a table where she put her keys and her mail when she got home, where she kept a little cactus in an aquamarine pot. He saw the way his features hung slack, as though the elasticity in his skin had already lost its snap, the way his eyes were rimmed with red, the corneas bloodshot and yellow. There was blood on the collar of his shirt. He wasn't sure who it belonged to or how it had gotten there. The man looking back at him was older than he expected—more broken and more lost than he'd ever allowed himself to acknowledge. The haze of a brain soaked in alcohol shimmered around his reflection like heat waves, and somehow, instead of seeing less, for once the haze let him see more. It sharpened the image. He saw that it was himself that needed fixing, and with crushing certainty he realized he didn't have the tools for the job, or even the conviction to try. He saw what Jean saw, and he understood that she and their unborn child were better off without him.

Augustine turned away from the mirror and left behind that brief shimmer of honesty—too heavy to carry with him, too blinding to look at for very long. Jean opened the door for him, and when he stumbled against the frame she guided him through the opening, gently but firmly, then shut the door behind him. Alone on her front step, he leaned back against her door and stared up at the overcast sky, dark and dense and impenetrable. No stars, just clouds. It was the last time they spoke.

—∿∿∿—

AUGUSTINE PULLED HIS outerwear on slowly and with great difficulty: scarf, hat, parka, boots, and finally his mittens. The tent was empty. The quiet sounds of his zippers being zipped, the clomp of his boots, the whisper of his parka rubbing against itself, all came together to create a soft symphony of incremental movement. Outside the wind still moaned, softly—Iris's melody. Augie was already breathing hard by the time he opened the door. The cold nearly knocked him down. The wind filled his lungs with ice crystals blown up from the ground, and his breath was already frozen on his beard before he'd gone more than two steps. He screwed up his strength, his determination, his sadness, and turned it into forward motion—one last burst. The radio shed was visible beneath a bright sliver of moon, and he stumbled toward it as fast as he could go.

He wasn't sure how he would begin when he spoke to her, or what he needed to say, but it didn't seem to matter. He only wanted to hear her and be heard. To have one honest moment, after all this time. Just one. He was halfway to the shed when he noticed a set of tracks in the snow and stopped. He followed them with his eyes, down to the edge of the lake, where he saw a small, snow-covered hill that seemed out of place. He followed the tracks, and when he came to the hill he realized that it was the bear that had been following him—after all this time, over all these miles. Part of him wanted to be afraid, to run for cover, but the rest of him—most of him—wanted to reach out and touch its haunch. He did, gingerly, and the bear chuffed softly. He walked around the huge animal to where its nose was pointed toward the lake, its neck and stomach laid flat against the snow, paws tucked beneath. He took off his mitten and touched it again, where its shoulder blades came together in a peak. The bear's fur was covered with a thin dusting of snow, but he let his fingers sink in and found a layer of warmth emanating from the bear's skin.

The bear chuffed again, but still it didn't move. Augie understood that it was dying. Its yellowing fur looked almost golden in the moonlight. Augie's legs gave way and he collapsed to his knees beside the bear, his fingers still buried in its fur. The radio shed could wait, he decided, it was this— this was the moment he'd been looking for. The wind picked up and began to sweep the snow into the sky, obscuring the radio shed and the other tents behind a curtain of white, till there was nothing left but Augustine and the bear.

He thought of Jean. The first time he had seen her was from across the parking lot of the research facility. She'd pulled up in her dusty green El Camino, her dark hair swirling around her shoulders as she unloaded her bags from the passenger's seat. Even from the entrance to the facility he'd noticed the red lipstick she was wearing, the sliver of skin that showed between her blouse and her jeans. He thought of the first time he'd undressed her, the first time he'd watched her sleeping, and wondered what it was that made her so compelling. So magnetic. He never did figure it out. And he thought of the photograph she'd sent him. That one snapshot: the child, the girl, their daughter. Standing still, arms crossed over her chest, wearing a pale yellow dress and no shoes, her dark hair cut just below her jaw, the straight line of her bangs ending above her eyebrows. Her mouth was slightly open, as if she wanted to say something, and her eyes were defiant—a bright, hazel glare.

The bear groaned and rolled onto its side. Augie moved closer. He wasn't afraid any longer, and as he fitted himself against the bear's warm stomach and felt its massive arms close over him, he was at peace. No longer an interloper, but a part of the landscape. He felt the bear's hot breath against the crown of his head and burrowed deeper against it, turning his face away from the wind and into the fur, where he found the quiet thunder of a heartbeat, slow and deep and steady as a drum.

TWENTY

ON BOARD THE International Space Station it looked as though the other astronauts had just stepped out for a moment: machines still turned on, half-empty food packets floating in the kitchen area. The only things missing were the *Soyuz* reentry pods—two of the three were gone. The equipment in the space station was archaic compared to *Aether*'s facilities, but the crew was already familiar with it, all of them having lived on the ISS at one point or another. Sully inspected its comm. station with curiosity, comparing the silence to that on *Aether*. Both stations were hearing the same signals—that is, none at all. She clung to the frequency where she'd found the man in the Arctic, but he wasn't there, and eventually she had to move on, scanning for other survivors. She wondered if she'd ever find him again.

After sweeping the station for habitants and clues, and finding neither, *Aether*'s crew came together near the remaining reentry pod. The last pod held three seats. Three of them would descend and two would remain on the ISS, circling Earth indefinitely. The options were murky: without a ground team to collect them, there was the potentially fatal possibility of landing in an ocean or a desert. The state of the planet below them was unknowable. Perhaps the dirt and the air and the water were poisoned, perhaps they weren't. Perhaps there were survivors, perhaps there weren't. In space, a finite amount of resources were available and it was unclear how long they would last. Neither choice was certain, and neither was safe. But they weren't ready to decide yet. They huddled together and talked about the docking procedure, the supplies, the equipment—anything but the question of who would go and who would stay. Anything but that.

～～～～

THEY SLEPT ON *Aether* that night, grasping at inane small talk over dinner. After two years of wandering the solar system they were home—almost. After two years, some of them would make the last leg of the journey and some wouldn't. All the waiting, the torturous uncertainty, had led to an impossible but still-unspoken divide. Sully lay awake in her bunk, and she guessed the others did as well, weighing the options and arriving at the same solution over and over: none. She turned from one side to the other, flopped onto her back, then onto her stomach, burying her arms under the pillow, laying them at her sides, throwing them over her face. Sleep was impossible. She thought of her daughter and touched the photograph pinned to the wall, just a dim square in the dark, but she could see Lucy's face anyway, her costume, the wavy dirty-blond hair—the curve of her smile burned into Sully's brain like a beacon.

And if the worst had happened? If her daughter was nothing more than hot ash floating in a bright sky, or even more horrible, a heap of decomposing remains returning to the dirt? She tried not to think these things, and yet—she had abandoned her entire family, she couldn't think about anything else. If only she had been a better mother, a better wife, a better person, then someone else would be lying in this bunk right now, replaying her own regrets. She would have stayed in Canada, she never would have applied for the space program or gone to Houston. The raspberry-red door in Vancouver would still be hers, and the copper pans that hung above the stove, and the task of folding her daughter's miniature T-shirts. There would be no divorce, no separation, no trouble finding a more recent photograph of Lucy when she wanted one. This picture of how her life could have been seemed so perfect, lying there in the dark, but it was pointless. She wasn't built for that life. She'd never been the woman Jack wanted, the woman he needed, she had never loved Lucy in the right way—she wasn't even sure what the right way was, only that the other mothers did it differently, that she could never seem to say the right things or do the right things or be the right person around either of them. The truth was, having her family had been even harder than losing them. There had always been something missing, and only now, after all this time and all these miles, could she begin to understand what it was: a warmth, an opening. The roots of something that had never been given the chance to grow.

-wwv-

LITTLE EARTH HAD begun to seem very small now that the actual Earth was filling the view from the cupola with its big blue girth. But they felt safe on the centrifuge, spinning inside their own familiar little world. They knew what to expect here, while their home planet had become a mystery in the time that they'd been away. After traversing the un-known, they'd only returned to more of the same. The mood over vacuum-sealed oatmeal and hot coffee was somber. It was time to discuss reentry.

"It'll have to be random," Harper said finally. "A lottery, drawing straws. Something like that. I'm not sure how else to go about it."

The rest of them nodded assent.

Harper made eye contact with each of them, gauging their support for the idea, then returned his gaze to the table, licked his lips, and swallowed. Sully watched the nub of his Adam's apple dip and rise in his throat, moving sluggishly, as if the effort pained him. "Okay," he said. "Let's bear in mind that we don't know what we're going to find down there. We might not even make it, but if we do, who's to say we won't be able to launch another *Soyuz*? So. Straws, I think. Might as well get on with it."

There was a stockpile of straws in the kitchen; Harper rounded up five of them and Thebes shortened two with his utility knife. Harper swept them off the table and into his fist. Short straws for a life sentence in space. Long for an uncertain descent.

"Okay," he said again. "Who's first?"

There was a pause and then Tal reached out across the table. He plucked a straw from Harper's hand and let out the breath he'd been holding when he saw that it was full length. He laid it down in front of him. Thebes, to his right, went next and drew another long straw, which he examined with an indecipherable expression. Ivanov chose, and it was short. The others gasped involuntarily and tensed, waiting for his reaction, but after a long moment of stunned silence he smiled. Gloomy Ivanov, smiling, like a marble statue suddenly altering its pose.

"It's all right," he said. "I think I'm relieved."

Thebes laid his broad hand on Ivanov's shoulder. Harper swallowed again and offered the two remaining straws to Sully. She drew. It was short.

~~~

THEY SCHEDULED THE reentry sequence for two days after the drawing. Tal needed time to figure out the trajectory of the pod, the angle at which they would enter the atmosphere, and the coordinates where they hoped to end up, all of which were incredibly complex without the assistance of a ground team. The crew decided to aim the pod for the Great Plains of Texas, where the weather would be temperate, the open space would be considerable, and they hoped to find some kind of answer from Houston. It seemed like their best chance—but for the first time in two years, the *they* had become fractured. Three would descend, two would remain. Their futures were suddenly divided.

After the meeting, Sully went to *Aether*'s cupola and peered through the swirling layer of feathery clouds as they zipped over the rich green of Central America, the deep, rippling blue of the Atlantic, the tawny deserts of northern Africa. She stayed there for a long time, watching the continents fly by—long enough to see the sun rise and set along the hazy rim of the planet's atmosphere a few times over. Maybe staying up here was for the best. Maybe she didn't belong on the surface anymore. She thought of Lucy, her glowing beam of know-it-all sunshine; she thought of Jack, the way he was before the divorce—mischievous, brooding, brilliant, and in love with her. She thought of Jean, pointing to the sky when Sully was little, the stars, the desert, introducing her to the electromagnetic spectrum and all of its magic. Her family. She watched the sun rise and set, rise and set, rise and set. As she watched the fourth sunrise flood the darkened planet with light, she let go. Somewhere over the Pacific Ocean, wisps of pink cloud moving over blue water, she released her memories and her plans for the future—she let them float out through the cupola and down to the atmosphere, where they sizzled against the hazy blue shell of a planet she would never return to.

That night, Sully returned to the centrifuge long after the others had closed their curtains and turned out their lights. She felt lighter than she had in years. She brushed her teeth and padded along the curve to her bunk, her feet whispering against the floor. As she passed Harper's compartment she heard him turn over inside, the rustle of his bedding and the frustrated sigh unmistakably his. She stopped short. Sully stood still for a moment, not thinking, just pausing, then adjusted her direction. Her feet moved and she followed them, climbing into his bunk before her brain had a chance to object. His face was barely visible in the dark, but it didn't matter. She didn't need to see his features to know what he was thinking. This connection had unsettled her before, had kept her away, but not anymore—not now that it was her last chance to be near him. He moved over and she lay down next to him. She could smell him: the musk of sleep, Old Spice deodorant over stale sweat, antibacterial soap, tomato plant sap, and another scent, one she couldn't name or describe, but that she recognized as his.

"Hi," she whispered.

"Hi." He put his hand on the curve of her waist and she laid her head beside his. They looked at each other in the dark, unseeing. She understood: everything, even the failure, even the loneliness, had led her here—it had prepared her and taught her and guided her to this. She felt a warmth rising, beginning in her toes and flooding up through her body, like a thousand doors swinging open all at once. She thought fleetingly of the house in Montana she had imagined for them, with his dog, Bess, waiting on the porch, and then she let it go, along with everything else. There was only the warmth, the opening in her chest, the unfurling of a quiet intuition, a reservoir of love that had never been touched. She moved closer until her mouth was against his prickly throat and she felt the throb of his pulse on her lips, the ridge of his jugular. They didn't speak or sleep or move, they just melted into the combined warmth of their bodies, the sum of their life force.

IN THE MORNING, just before the artificial sunrise, Sully slipped back to her bunk and slept. She heard the murmurs of activity as she drifted in and out of her dreams, but she kept her eyes closed and didn't get up until Thebes pulled back her curtain and laid his hand on her shoulder.

"There is something we must discuss," he said. "About the lottery."

Sully rubbed her hand across her eyes. "What's there to discuss?"

"Much," he replied. "Will you come?"

"Let me get dressed."

When she climbed out of her bunk she was surprised to find the other four already assembled, waiting silently at the table. She was confused.

"I don't understand," she said, and sat down with them. "What's this all about?"

Thebes clasped his fingers together and rested his chin on his entwined knuckles. "I'm staying here," he said. "On *Aether*. On the space station."

She looked around the table and saw the others watching her. They already knew. She looked at Harper. He nodded.

"So you want me to go instead?" she asked. "But, Ivanov?"

Ivanov shrugged. "I will stay also," he said. "I have decided."

"But why?" she said. "Your family—you want to go back more than any of us."

He shook his head. "I want things as they were. This is not our choice. We know only one thing about what lies below: it is not what we left behind. Everything has changed. My family is not waiting for me—this is no time for half-truths. Thebes and I, we are the oldest. We are tired. We are—how do you say? Old dogs."

Sully opened her mouth to speak and nothing came out. Thebes put his arm around her.

"We have a lot to do today," Harper said. "Thebes, if you

could check the *Soyuz* pod's seal. Tal, I know you have your hands full with plotting our course, so Ivanov, perhaps you could help? Let's run a landing simulation before the end of the day, then another in the morning before we launch. I'm going to check out the survival gear in the *Soyuz,* and Sully—could you give the comm.s one last try? Am I forgetting anything?"

"I don't think so," Tal said. "Let's get to it."

Sully remained at the table after they had gone, letting her thoughts, which whirled through her head like a dust storm, settle. She knew she should eat but couldn't manage it. She put a protein bar in her pocket for later and left the empty centrifuge. When she floated through the node into the greenhouse corridor she found Harper there, pretending to inspect the plants while he waited for her.

"Are you all right?" he asked.

"Fine," she said. "Just surprised. A little . . . scared, I think."

"Of what?"

"Of what's down there, I guess. I was all set to power down, you know, just eat and sleep and watch fifteen sunrises a day, but now—now it's all going to change."

He touched her arm, cupping her elbow in his hand. Again, the warmth: a thousand doors opening a little wider. He turned his wrist up to glance at his watch, and that simple gesture almost undid her. She eyed the thick blue veins in his arm, just beneath the skin, and imagined that she could feel his pulse again.

"I should go," he said. "Lots to do."

She nodded, her head whirling. "Of course," she said, and he moved off down the corridor. She stayed in front of the tomato plants for a while, thinking. She picked one of the yellow ones and it tasted like sunshine.

In the comm. pod, she set the receivers to scan. As she listened to the rise and fall of the static, the whistling of atmospheric disturbances, she thought about how by this time tomorrow she would either be en route to Earth or already on its surface—*if all went well,* she reminded herself. The levity she'd felt yesterday, the liberation of releasing everything that had come before, the choices she'd made, people she'd loved—that was gone, and heaviness crept back into her limbs like the return of gravity. The future, which just hours ago had seemed so beautifully empty, became crowded with unknown possibility. Her monotonous spacebound destiny disappeared like a fluid, shadowy creature. She thought of Harper, and the way the bittersweet finality of the previous night had suddenly cracked open into a beginning—an unknowable, untenable dynamic.

She kept scanning, hoping the man in the Arctic would hear her, but their frequency had been empty for days now. There had been something about talking to him—something that thawed her, just a little, a softening of the part of her that had been icebound since the launch. Or maybe even before: since she realized she'd lost her family, that they'd never been hers to begin with. That tenuous connection with the man in the Arctic, across such an incredible distance, had reminded her that even the fleeting things were worth their weight in sadness. Even a few words could mean something. The receivers caught nothing but atmospheric disturbances and white noise. Eventually she shut it all down and floated back to Little Earth one last time.

The crew ate a subdued dinner together. No one was in the mood for talking. Sully went to bed early while Harper and Thebes went back to the ISS to run a landing simulation sequence. Tal and Ivanov played videogames together one last time. She turned out the light in her bunk and lay awake for a long time, thinking. On the other side of the curtain she heard her crewmates getting ready for bed: the opening and closing of the lavatory door, the whisper of curtains being drawn, the rustle of bedclothes. Thebes cleared his throat; Tal coughed; Ivanov wept quietly; Harper scribbled in his journal. It was easy to tell which sounds belonged to whom, and where they were in the centrifuge. She knew her crewmates and their home through and through—but not for much longer, she reminded herself.

In her dreams that night, she was floating above Earth, no spacesuit, no propulsion pack, just wearing her navy blue jumpsuit, the arms tied around the waist, her gray T-shirt tucked in. She looked over her shoulder at the space station and saw a crowd of faces watching her from the cupola, waving to her. Saying goodbye. She saw Devi there, smiling, her brown palm flat against the glass. She saw Lucy, sitting on Jack's shoulders. She saw her mother, Jean. Everyone was happy for her, everyone wishing her well. Sully turned and dived toward Earth, speeding through the vacuum, her arms above her head, her toes pointed, ready to plow through the atmosphere like a diver piercing the water's surface. Her body became warm, then hot, then suddenly she realized she was on fire, hurtling through the atmosphere like a comet streaming across the sky. She woke up before she hit the ground. Her mouth was dry, her neck ached. She looked at her clock. It was time.

⌁⌁⌁

THE FIVE CREWMEMBERS of *Aether* crowded around the entrance to the remaining *Soyuz* pod. They all hugged one another and lingered in the doorway a few minutes longer than necessary. Finally Tal announced they had better get going with the undocking sequence if they wanted to make their reentry window. He dropped down into the pod and began strapping himself in. Harper gave Thebes and Ivanov one last handshake and whispered something into each of their ears. Sully hesitated. She gave Ivanov a hug, the third one in the last five minutes, and he kissed her on both cheeks. Droplets of water floated between them—tears, she wasn't sure whose. She turned to Thebes.

"Are you sure?" she whispered in his ear as he embraced her again.

"Positive," he whispered back, and then gave her a gentle push into the pod.

"Safe travels, my friends," Thebes said. Ivanov waved, and together they pulled the door shut.

Sully strapped herself into the remaining seat, on Harper's left. They heard the seal being winched shut on the other side of the door, then nothing. Just the sounds of their own bodies: anxious breath and restless limbs. Tal began clicking on the pod's systems. He took out the reentry sequence manual and tucked it between his legs while he adjusted the instruments. He took his time, until finally he decided everything was ready. Tal slid down his visor.

"Here we go," Tal said. He pushed a button and Sully felt the *Soyuz* slip away from the docking port, a gentle release, ending one journey and beginning another. Tal fired up the engine for a short burn, to move them away from the space station and set them on a parallel orbit. Then he initiated a longer burn, to take them around the planet and distance themselves farther from the station, sinking lower and lower until finally they hit the atmosphere at a sloping angle. It all took place more slowly than Sully remembered, and she kept looking out the small window to make sure they were in fact moving. Finally Tal shed the orbital module and instrument panel components of the *Soyuz*. From within the descent pod they could feel the bolts exploding above and below them, sending the other pieces of the *Soyuz* spinning away. A few minutes later they began to pass through the denser layers of the atmosphere. Outside the window a molten stream of plasma covered the glass, and the heat darkened the window. Gravity took hold of them, slowly at first, then exerting a greater and greater force as they plummeted through the atmosphere. Sully began to worry that they wouldn't make it—that the *Soyuz* had sat unused for too long, that the heat shield was faulty, that the parachute wouldn't open. She wanted to make it so badly, wanted to see what came next. Without thinking she reached out and grabbed Harper's arm. Tal was concentrating on keeping the descent pod on target, but Harper was watching her. He flipped open his visor and put his gloved hand over hers.

"Are you all right?" he asked. The first parachute opened and the violence of it jerked the little pod back and forth. After the silence of space, the sound of the wind shrieking around them was deafening. By then the pull of gravity had grown so strong she could barely nod. After a moment the turbulence evened out and the second parachute opened, a gentler tug and a smoother descent. She felt held, nestled in the cup of an immense cosmic palm as they plummeted toward the surface of the earth. The sound of the wind abated as they descended through the layers of the atmosphere, and the terror finally seeped from her muscles. She was ready to survive—to hit the ground and open the pod—and even though she had no idea what kind of world they were arriving in, she was ready to find out. The pod kept falling, and through the mostly blackened window she glimpsed a piece of sky, clear and blue. Even if this was the end, even if they had come all this way only to die now, that piece of sky made everything worth it. They were home. She looked over at Harper, who was still watching her, and in that second she loved him more than she would have thought was possible. A thousand doors, wide open now.

"Iris," he said. No one had called her that in a long time, but she liked the way it sounded when he said it. "I'm glad you came."

She closed her eyes and prepared for impact, hoping there would be time to hear him say it again. But even if there wasn't—

"Me too."

ACKNOWLEDGMENTS

I'M GRATEFUL FOR my agent, Jen Gates, who listened to an outlandish, unformed idea and was excited by it, who was patient and supportive, and who did so much incredible work ensuring this book found the right home.

I'm grateful for Anna Pitoniak, who is that home, and who shaped this story with her intuition for what it could be, her understanding of what it was, and her meticulous attention to detail.

I'm grateful for each and every person at Random House

and Zachary Shuster Harmsworth whose hands have touched this novel.

I'm grateful for my foreign publishers, in particular my UK editor, Kirsty Dunseath at Orion Books.

I'm grateful for Lisa Brooks, always my first reader.

I'm grateful for Michael Belt, my skywatching companion.

I'm grateful for Chuck Dube, who entertained my curiosity about radio engineering, which is where the idea for all this began.

And I'm grateful for all the friends and family who inspire me, support me, and keep me sane.

Thank you all.

blog and newsletter

For literary discussion, author insight,
book news, exclusive content,
recipes and giveaways, visit the
Weidenfeld & Nicolson blog and
sign up for the newsletter at:

www.wnblog.co.uk

For breaking news, reviews and exclusive competitions
Follow us 🐦 @wnbooks
Find us ⬛f facebook.com/WNfiction